The Bishop's Secret

By
T.C. Fairley

For Stephanie
Enjoy
T.C. Fairley

AMERICAN LEGACY™ Books • Washington, DC

**AMERICAN
LEGACY™
Books**

ISBN 1-886766-43-6

Copyright © 2005

Published in the U.S.A. 2005
Publisher:
American Legacy Books
Washington, DC

Back cover photo of author by Dennis Lemay
Page 255 photo of author and wife by Loraine Carbone

Contents

The
Bishop's
Secret

Dedication

This book is dedicated to Jean and Fred Beasley for their willingness to fulfill the dream of their daughter, Karen. When Karen died at a young age, Fred and Jean received an insurance benefit that they used to establish The Karen Beasley Sea Turtle Rescue and Rehabilitation Center. It is not currently a national treasure, but it deserves to be. Someday the hard work of its volunteers will assure its election into that august body.

Dedication

In addition, I dedicate this book to Jean Beasley and to Grace Murray in honor of their friendship and their tireless work at and for the Turtle Hospital, located on Topsail Island, North Carolina. Grace died of cancer in 2000. I conducted her funeral and Jean delivered the eulogy – a eulogy like no other I've ever read or heard or delivered myself. I stopped breathing as she spoke. I wept openly, as did the entire congregation, without any thought of propriety or dignity. As I write these words, tears once again fill my eyes as I remember Grace and relive Jean's remarkable words. With the permission of Grace's family, Jean also has given me permission to retool her eulogy and to use it in this book for the funeral of the Bishop's wife. Once again, I am in Jean's debt for her generosity.

This book also is dedicated to the many hundreds of volunteers associated with the Turtle Hospital. Some of them work daily by draining and cleaning the large round, plastic tanks that our patients use during their rehabilitation and recovery. Those same volunteers heat water in the winter months before it can be introduced into the tanks. They feed and medicate injured turtles, some of which have been bitten by sharks, poisoned by pollution, cut with boat motor blades, or caught in fishing nets. Doctors from the School of Veterinary Medicine at North Carolina State operate on our injured turtles and have worked miracles that were unimaginable just a few short years ago. Other volunteers raise funds, walk along our 26 miles of beaches to mark turtle egg nests, fence them, and watch over them when they are about to hatch. Furthermore, they attend turtle releases on those happy days when we return some of the ocean's own to their proper homes in better condition than when those patients arrived. I know that other communities have dedicated volunteers. Here on Topsail Island, ours are the turtle people. Go to www.seaturtlehospital.org if you want to know more. Better still, the next time that you are in North Carolina, come see us. We are located in Topsail Beach, right behind the water tower.

From the Author

Writing this book has been one of my happiest experiences. It has given me the platform where I can comment on my years of experience as a Presbyterian minister, crow just a little, and strut my stuff. In 1965, I was ordained by the Presbyterian Church and served that denomination until I retired in 1996. As far as ministers go, I'd rate my performance as a D+. That's probably generous. The Vietnam War and the Civil Rights Movement were huge when I first entered the church. I thought that the strength of my preaching could change the hearts and minds of my parishioners and together we could affect the course of both great social events for the positive. I was wrong. I lasted all of eleven months in my first parish and only thirteen months in my second. "Get him out of here" was the cry to Ministerial Relations. So I moved around a lot during those first few years. In the beginning, the only good thing that happened to me was that I ran out of material quickly. It took me only six weeks in my first church to tell them everything that I knew. With no material, I was forced to study. The choice of what to study was simple. I loved Biblical Hebrew in seminary. For whatever reason, it was a subject that came easily to me. So I picked up my Hebrew Bible and never looked back. The only problem for me was that many people objected to my orientation. They thought that I was more Jewish than Presbyterian, which I considered high praise, indeed. And, given my quirky way of twisting the tiger's tail, I became an expert in the language during the next 30 years, which only served to antagonize the more traditional members of my parishes. That love affair with the language left me isolated from many more of my traditional colleagues. The ones who recognized my talents were most appreciative of them, especially when I would translate passages that they planned to use in a sermon or in a study.

Over the years, I became known as something of a scholar and a natural teacher. With a piece of chalk in one hand and a blackboard behind me, students were treated to a magical hour that was over before they knew it. Much of this book fictionalizes my experiences in the ministry during a 30-year period. But, more importantly, writing this book gave me the opportunity to reflect on my heritage. Grandfather and Grandmother Fairley were both adopted. They were born in 1886 and 1893, respectively. The families who took them in were wonderful people, I'm told. James and Nellie Fairley were a sawed-off, little Cockney couple who stood no taller than four feet and eleven inches. My grandfather towered over them at six feet and one inch. I cannot go back any further than those relatives. Reynolds Carter Baxter, a central character in this book, resembles Grandfather Fairley in many ways, with one very large exception, which should give everyone a good laugh. Reynolds Carter Baxter, IV, resembles me in some ways. Finding distant relatives has been a fantasy of mine for years and years. In this book, I've finally found them, if only in my playful mind.

Appreciation

I have a large number of people to thank in the writing of this book. My wife, Kate Fairley, is the first in that long line. She has listened to passages, criticized them, made them real, corrected my grammar and spelling, and encouraged me in every way imaginable. At our house, we rise early so that we can spend precious time together. We listen to Mozart and Bach, Beethoven and Vivaldi, Verdi and Puccini, and countless others. We drink good coffee made from freshly ground beans and we talk to each other. Years ago, an older man told me that he was a better lover as an old man than he ever was as a young man. I was a young man when he said it to me. I scoffed at him as though he were off his rocker. Today, I'm the old

Appreciation

man and I know what he meant. Kate and I are able to make love with our eyes – or with a word spoken in just the right way – or when sharing a project like this book.

My editor and publisher, Donna Howell, "adopted" my child, blemishes and all, and raised it up as though it were her own. She is to me and to my book what the Fairley family was to my grandfather and what the Craig family was to my grandmother. Her courage to face me down over serious flaws and character anomalies has made it possible to bring "our baby" to maturity. Staff members at American Legacy Books also have improved the work through consultations with Donna. The graphics department created the magnificent cover that displays the most prominent key to the Bishop's secrets.

Without the financial backing of Dr. Richard Mynatt and my friend, Lenny DeNittis, this work would have suffered from a stillbirth; namely, it would have died as soon as it was published for lack of promotional funds. Also included on my debt list are this book's early readers who became my encouragers. They are Lisa Thompson, Todd Crawford, Karen Clouse, Sandy Minnich, Wendy Mobley, Frances Dyer, Eric Dattler, Jeff Loving, Rev. Jim Wright, Rev. Susan Shira Nilsen, and Wendy Miraya. Additional readers include Joan Dorazio, Don Fairley (my uncle), Fr. Steven Teague, Rev. Angus Watkins, Rev. James Camp, Dr. P. Aarne Vesilind, and Hugh Wilson. My thanks go to Harvey Byrd and Rob Clouse for their efforts to keep my ignorance of the computer from confounding my efforts. I extend my deepest appreciation to all of you.

The Bishop's Secret

CHAPTER ONE:
The Train Robbery

Reynolds Carter Baxter lived an amazing life in San Francisco – but he never was born.

His remarkable story began in 1844 when one set of his great-grandparents, Liam and Bridget Collins, emigrated from Dublin to escape Ireland's great potato famine. They arrived in Boston with enough money to build a flourmill because Liam had inherited 300 pounds sterling from the estate of his uncle. The Collins family prospered as a result of that move and their willingness to work long and hard. Of that union was born a daughter, Kathleen Collins, and a son, Kenneth.

The year after the Collins moved to Boston, the Nobles arrived there, too. Patrick and Mary Noble were newly married and penniless unfortunates who fled County Sligo, Ireland. They came to Boston as the indentured servants of the owner of Mullen's Wheelwright Shop. Brian Mullen was sickly and often unable to work. Mary and Patrick lived in three cramped rooms attached to the back of the shop, while Mullen, still a bachelor at age 46, lived with his aged mother above the shop in six lovely rooms.

Mullen's greatest asset was his ability to turn Patrick Noble, an unskilled unknown, into a highly regarded wheelwright. His business prospered as a direct result. Patrick's greatest asset was his keen mind for numbers and his ability to follow directions well. He did the numbers in his head before others could write them down on paper.

At the height of six feet and two inches, Patrick Noble was taller than most men and was quite a handsome red-haired lad, even with his hawk-like nose. It took Patrick six long years, three more than usual, to work off his passage to America. He agreed to work twice the normal time in order for his wife, Mary, to be released from her indentured status as soon as they arrived in America. Mary Noble, a skilled nurse, midwife, and maker of medicines, was the kind of woman that inspired legends. She was very tall, her face was cherubic, and her hair was golden red. Her kindness to everyone was well known and much appreciated. Because she was not indentured, she managed to save the incredibly large sum of $200 during those six long years. She and Patrick used it as a down payment to buy Brian Mullen's business.

In 1847, Mary gave birth to their first born, whom they named John. Timothy followed thirteen months later. The beautiful girls, Molly and Megan, were not far behind Tim. Then tragedy struck. At the age of 38, Patrick Noble contracted pneumonia and died during the harsh winter of 1860.

At the time of his father's death, John Noble, the oldest son, was thirteen. He told his mother that he and Timothy could do the shop work if she and the girls would handle the business end of things. Their father had taught them well and they were possessed by his good work ethics. The boys also inherited their father's physical features and mathematical skills. So alike were they mentally and physically that many mistook them for twins.

Business did not suffer as a result of Patrick's death. Megan and Molly worked just as hard as John, Tim, and Mary to keep the prosperous business prosperous. Both of them stacked wood and learned how to bend it. As the sisters aged and gained strength, John and Tim taught them how to sharpen the smaller hand tools. The girls' new skills saved many precious hours so that the boys could perform other duties. Many were the days that found all of the youngsters working fourteen to sixteen hours. Except for the time spent during Sunday Mass they didn't know what it meant to stop and rest.

That all changed suddenly in 1868 when John Noble met Kathleen Collins at Harry Sarver's funeral Mass. John repaired all of Harry's wagons and wheels, and Harry sharpened all of the Noble's large saws. Harry was delivering newly sharpened ones to a local sawyer when a poorly stacked load of timber fell on top of him and killed him instantly.

When John sat down in St. Michael's, an unfamiliar church to him, the most beautiful woman in the world, he thought, passed his pew and sat right in front of him. Kathleen's reddish hair gleamed with golden highlights. His eyes burned holes in the back of her neck and head. He never heard a word that the priest said.

His intention was to go right back to the shop as soon as Harry was buried. Instead he was pulled to the wake by the sight of Kathleen Collins. It didn't take either one of them very long to realize that they were just right for each other. Six months later, they were married at St. Michael's, Kathleen's parish church.

On March 6, 1869, ten months after the wedding, their son was born. Kathleen and John Noble's red-haired baby was given the first name of Patrick, in memory of John's father. Patrick received the middle name of John, in honor of his own father. Patrick John Noble! What a wonderful name, they thought, not knowing what lay ahead.

The day after Patrick's birth, the local paper carried the announcement. John paid his penny for a copy and took it upstairs, above the shop, for his wife and mother to read. The story at the bottom left of the front page caught John Noble's eye. Newly established wineries in California needed barrel makers who could bend wood and use metal straps to hold the kegs together. It didn't sound all that different from what he had done all of his life as a wheelwright. He was 22 years old and he had never been outside of Boston. All of a sudden, California was calling mightily to him.

He talked of nothing else for three months. His mother, Mary, didn't want him to go because of the business and her grandson, Patrick, her pride and joy. What would the family do without them? John assured her that Timothy was able to run the shop very well by himself, and Molly and Megan already were doing a great job of handling the business end. She had nothing to worry about. Kathleen was ready to walk out of the door as soon as John could get it open.

After months of discussions between the Collins family and the Noble family, all agreed, reluctantly, that California was worth the effort. Neither family was rich, but they had enough money between them to send the young couple on their way. Kathleen's family purchased their train tickets to San Francisco on the recently completed transcontinental railroad. Mary Noble sewed $300 cash into John's suit coat and promised to send another $500 after they arrived in San Francisco. She also handed him a magnificent silver eagle money clip with an additional $200 to use as traveling money. He tucked the clip and the traveling money into the inside pocket of his coat.

On June 9, 1869, John, Kathleen, and little Patrick boarded their train in Boston and headed south to New York and Philadelphia and then west to San Francisco. Both families hugged and kissed until the moment that the conductor called "All aboard." According to the Boston ticket agent, the trip would take sixteen to eighteen days, depending on the weather, breakdowns, track and trestle repairs, and possible emergencies.

The trip from Boston to New York to Philadelphia was uneventful. The Noble family watched the countryside fly by, as did so many of the other passengers. It was the first time that most of them had ever been on a train. The excitement of it all sustained their interest for hours and hours.

In Philadelphia, the train added six passenger cars and as many porters. One of the additional porters was named Abraham Walters. He had been a soldier in the Civil War with the Pennsylvania regulars. Out of habit and training, his eyes searched constantly for people or situations that called out for his help. He noticed a young family taking advantage of the scheduled stop by going into the station. The pretty redheaded mother nursed her baby while her husband, he assumed, used the men's room. Remembering the days when his only son, Isaac, nursed, he smiled to himself. When the husband reappeared, he took the baby from his mother, who then used the public restroom. On her return, she whispered something into her husband's ear. Judging from the look on their faces, Mr. Walters thought that he knew what she said.

After three and a half days of constant travel, the Nobles' train pulled into Pittsburgh, Pennsylvania. Kathleen began to have doubts about the trip and said so. She was dirty and constipated. Her period had started. The baby slept so little. She was very tired and wanted to sleep in a real bed. John's confidence and enthusiasm were boundless and he encouraged her to keep going. He promised her that, once they reached San Francisco, they would stay in a fine hotel for a few days before moving north to the wine country. She could bathe for hours if she liked.

In Chicago, there was another crew change before the locomotive left for St. Louis. Many passengers departed the train, some in Chicago and others in St. Louis. More travelers replaced them in both cities. In St. Louis, a couple named Lester and Annabelle Baxter, carrying their ten-day-old daughter, Alice, boarded the train. Mrs. Baxter was quite friendly and outgoing, but Mr. Baxter was quiet and reserved. They were also on their way to San Francisco where Mr. Baxter was going to work in his uncle's dray and livery service.

Eighty-five miles north of Reno, the train had started its descent through an extremely isolated section of the Humboldt Range when robbers attacked. They had removed three sections of rails and ties from both sides of the track. The slight downhill curve lay just before a blind spot that concealed the robbers' dirty work and made it impossible for the engineer to avert disaster. When the engine and coal tender rolled off the track at 35 miles an hour, the engine's steel wheels dug into the roadbed's dirt and stopped the train dead. The jolt was enormous. Everyone and everything inside the train were thrown forward and crashed into anyone or anything in his or her or its way. The first two cars behind the coal car overturned with the help of the curve and from the force of being shoved by the cars in back of them. They had nowhere to go. As the others broke free from their couplers, the force flipped them on their sides, too.

Just as Kathleen Noble had put Patrick back into his cradle on the floor of the train, their car derailed. She was thrown forward like a rag doll. Spear-like, her head went through the glass of the compartment door, which cut her jugular vein. She was knocked unconscious by the blow to her head and drowned in her own blood as it filled her lungs. John Noble, in the car behind Kathleen and Patrick, had been visiting with passengers who had boarded the train in Denver. The bench that he had been sitting on was propelled forward and his head crashed into a sharp corner of a table bolted to the floor. He died on impact. Baby Patrick slid in his cradle and slammed into several crumpled people who broke his momentum. He was left physically unhurt by the deadly forward movement. He also was left an orphan.

Moments after the train stopped, sixteen armed men, whose faces were covered with bandanas, moved through the cars. They threw everything of value into sacks. From the conscious, unconscious, dying, and dead, they pulled rings and took jewelry. They searched purses, pockets, and wallets for cash. One of the robbers was a large man who, instead of throwing John Noble's silver eagle money clip and cash holding $154 into his sack, quickly stuffed it into his pocket. So taken was he with the eagle – and his need to hide it from the other train robbers – that he missed the $300 which John's mother had sewn into his coat for safe keeping. In the mail car, they took everything and shot the postal clerks who had not died in the wreck. They were out of the doors and gone in less than ten minutes.

The injured began to stir as soon as they realized that they were not dead and the robbers were gone. Several porters had escaped injury because they had been leaning against the forward wall of a train car when the derailment happened. The engineer had struck his head on his instrument panel and was bleeding profusely from the six-inch cut that he had suffered. His right arm and collarbone had been broken, as well as both of his legs. When the engine dug down into the earth, flaming coal was sent flying from the train's great furnace. The coal stokers were burned horribly. One died only hours after the robbery. The other man lived for two days before he succumbed to his burns.

Lester Baxter had been urinating when the wreck occurred and, fortunately, had escaped both injury and robbery. The robbers failed to check inside the small space set aside for that purpose. Annabelle Baxter suffered minor cuts and abrasions. The large cushion that she was cross-stitching had saved her. However, their baby daughter, Alice, was crushed to death under the weight of debris and bodies.

Eight hours later, help arrived. A train from Reno brought medical aid to the wounded and transported the survivors to their destinations. The dead, numbering 63, were buried in a mass grave that the uninjured men dug a little more than two hundred feet from the railroad tracks. Annabelle Baxter was inconsolable when her precious baby was found among the dead. She did not want to leave Alice in that God-forsaken place. Nor would she board the train sent from Reno. As insanity almost descended upon her, she was approached by one of the porters who asked, "Is this your baby, ma'am?" In his arms was Patrick John Noble, who was hungry and letting everyone know.

Without hesitation, Annabelle Baxter seized him from the porter and exclaimed, "My baby! My baby! Thank you for finding my baby!" At that moment, Patrick John Noble from Boston became Reynolds Carter Baxter, who was not born that way.

Lester Baxter was dead set against keeping the baby, so his wife took him aside. She whispered that, if he would let her keep the baby, she would have sex with him every night, if he wanted it, and twice in the afternoons. "You mean it, Belle?" he asked.

"I'd do it right now, Lester, if we could," she replied, hoping to convince him of her good faith effort in the bargain. She kept the orphaned baby and loved him as though she had given birth to him. Lester resented him and blamed him for living. He should have died and Alice should have lived. Annabelle mourned Alice quietly and never mentioned her name ever again. She wondered what she and Lester would say if someone asked questions about this baby. It really didn't matter because her baby lived and someone else's baby did not. And that was that!

News of the train robbery slowly made its way back to Boston. Mary Noble wondered why she hadn't heard anything from her son and daughter-in-law. She dreaded that they might have been among those who died in the train wreck. The railroad was unable to name the dead, but it did confirm that 63 individuals were killed, either from the wreck or shot to death by the robbers. On the list were 50 adults, ten juveniles, and three babies, but no names were included. She waited six agonizing months to hear from her family, but word never came, so she knew that her precious son, daughter-in-law, and grandson had been killed. The Collins family also waited and, like the Noble family, was forced to accept the reality of Kathleen's death.

The railroad placed a wooden cross and a wooden marker over the mass grave that was dug that day, but time and weather destroyed the spot. The location where they were buried quickly became covered with new growth. The 63 nameless victims simply vanished and Mother Earth welcomed them into her bosom. The train robbers were never caught. They split their loot and rode off in different directions. John Noble's silver eagle money clip and cash stayed in his looter's pocket and not one of the other robbers ever knew of their existence.

When the Baxter family reached San Francisco and moved into their new home, Annabelle thought that Lester would not hold her to her promise of nightly sex that she made at the train wreck. But it was not to be. She had to fuck him every night. The more he got, the more he wanted. Sometimes he wanted it twice in the afternoon, too.

At first, Patrick didn't want to nurse. Annabelle's milk didn't taste like "mother's" milk. But hunger forced him and soon he was back at it. The Baxters changed Patrick's name to Rennie, short for Reynolds, the name of Lester Baxter's uncle and employer. They also gave him Annabelle's maiden name, Carter, for a middle name. She kept nursing the boy until his emerging teeth made it impossible for her to do so. She thought that breastfeeding was her magic weapon against becoming pregnant again. She was wrong. She bore Lester Baxter ten more children over the next sixteen years. And, true to her word, she fucked Lester any time and every time he wanted, which was almost every night.

At The Baxter Livery and Dray Company, it was quickly evident that Lester was an excellent teamster. He had a way with horses and mules. Although he was not very big, he was very strong. He was smart, too. But he could be meaner than cat dirt when he drank, and Lester began to drink a lot. Starting around the age of four, Rennie was singled out for a beating every time Lester got drunk. He never laid a hand on Annabelle, except for sex, and he never once struck his own blood children. Just Rennie. For years, it puzzled the boy. What had he ever done to deserve his father's wrath? Why was he the only kid in the family who got the hell beat out of him? Was it because he was the only kid with fire engine red hair? When he asked his mother, she just turned her head away and mumbled something about everyone having to pay a price some way or another.

Ren was an outstanding student at the neighborhood school. He learned to read instantly, but it was in numbers that he excelled. He understood the relationship between the figures. He could add, subtract, multiply, and divide the problems in his head faster than the other children could do the problems with paper and pencil. But, after the fourth grade, Lester pulled him out of school and made him work with him, loading and unloading the wagons at the train yard. Ren was a big kid and his father took advantage of his size.

By the time that Reynolds Carter Baxter was sixteen years old, he towered over his father by a whole head and a half. He had big hands like his real namesake from Ireland via Boston. And, having loaded and unloaded wagons for a long time with his father in San Francisco's train yards, he was almost as strong as any man. Late one night, Lester came home roaring drunk and shouted for Rennie to come down. He was going to give him the beating of his life. Expecting the worst, the boy pulled on his clothes, tied his shoes, and went down the stairs. Lester began berating his son by calling him a lazy worthless ingrate. That confused Rennie because he always had worked hard, and he didn't know what the word ingrate meant. With the preliminaries out of the way, Lester grabbed Rennie's shirt in order to hold onto him while hitting him in the face. Without thinking, Rennie struck first, hard and squarely on the nose, knocking his father backwards until he tripped and fell. Enraged, Lester jumped up bellowing like a wounded bull. He started swinging wildly at Rennie, hitting him with a glancing blow to the shoulder and another to the side of his face. Rennie ran for the door and made it through before his father could catch him.

And he kept on running. He deserved better and, by God, he was going to get it, even if it meant being on his own at sixteen years of age. But where could he go? He had no money of his own and had only the clothing on his back. Since he had no place to stay, he walked all night.

Daybreak found Rennie on the docks at the end of Market Street. Men and big boys like him were standing around waiting to be hired for the day to unload the waiting cargo ships. He saw a boy standing in a line who looked like he was nearly his own age and size. Rennie asked him what he had to do to get hired. "Just wait here with me and, when it's my turn, I'll let you go ahead of me. Tell the man your name and that you're sixteen years old, whether you are or not. We get paid at the end of the day right here at this same place. Got it?" he asked.

Chapter One: The Train Robbery

"Yeah," Rennie answered. "My name's Rennie Baxter. What's yours?"

"Tommy Moran," Tommy answered.

Tommy Moran was seventeen and his smile was just the beginning of his many charms. He knew things. Ren could tell that instantly. Tommy just knew things. He had something else that Ren would learn about very soon. He had an entire family who loved him. Working on the docks full-time at that age wasn't anything out of the ordinary in those days. Tommy's father, Tommy, Sr., had worked on the docks until he died last year of a heart attack when he was 48 years old.

The two young men were assigned to help unload an old tub called The China Star. She was carrying huge crates full of vases and statuary. Their job was to match the crate numbers with the warehouse stations so that owners would be able to retrieve their merchandise in a timely fashion. At first, the work was not difficult. But after several hours, it became impossible to place all of the crates on their marks because there were too many of them for the allotted space. The big steam-operated cranes began to stack the remaining crates on top of the ones that the boys had hand-dollied to their assigned spots. Very dangerous. On their section of the docks, only one pile of crates toppled over and smashed open during their twelve-hour shift. It became the job of Tommy Moran and Rennie Baxter to pick all of it up and to salvage what they could. Salvaged items were taken to a small office where they were logged in and set aside for special handling at a later time.

Tommy was an old pro at this. His father had taught him how to hide some of the unbroken goods in with most of the badly broken throwaways. They were to be retrieved later when their shift ended. Rennie was fascinated. When their shift was completed, the two young men returned to the paymaster for their wages. Each received seventy-five cents. They pocketed their money and started off in separate directions. Tommy called back, "Hey, Ren, how about coming home with me for some supper?"

Ren was very hungry. He hadn't eaten since the night before and he could use a good meal. But, first, he told Ren, they needed to pick up their booty from the day's work. They waited until the super left the docks before walking back to the dross pile of broken items. Several other men and boys who had worked in other sections of the docks had waited for the same purpose. They began pulling and tossing broken pieces of this and that before they uncovered the desired objects. Once they had them in hand, they ran like hell out of the front gate to their separate homes.

Tommy Moran had a good eye for what was expensive and valuable. He managed to slide two small vases of exquisite color and design under the pile of broken pieces that he and Rennie had cleaned up that day. They were deep maroon in color and had a white crane painted on the side. They were a pair because, when they stood, the cranes faced each other indicating that the artist intended for them to go together. He handed Rennie one and kept the other. "What do you want me to do with this?" he asked Tommy.

"Piss in it for all I care," he laughed. "It's your share. Sell it if you can and pocket the money. Give it away if you like. If you don't want it, I'll take it."

"Where can I sell it – and for how much?" Ren asked.

"Tell you what, Ren. Tomorrow we'll go into Chinatown instead of coming back to the docks. There's more money in selling our God-given liberated booty than there is in breaking our backs here. You'll see. But, for now, let's go to my house and eat."

"You sure it'll be okay with your mother?" Ren asked.

"She'll never know there's an extra mouth at the table. There are twelve of us Moran kids. I'm the oldest. Besides, she'll like you." Tommy said.

"And just why would she like me?" Ren asked.

"Because I do. You know how to work and you don't complain. You're a little slow on the opportunity side, but stick with me and you'll be a pro real soon." Tommy offered.

The boys walked the half-mile to the Moran home and, as

Tommy had predicted, Mrs. Moran liked Ren immediately. His red hair, she said, reminded her of her cousins from Ireland. "You wouldn't be Irish, now, would you, Ren?" she asked.

"I don't know. I never thought about what I am. Is Baxter an Irish name?" he asked.

Mrs. Moran didn't answer, but she smiled at Ren kindly and asked where he lived. When Ren told her his story of running away the night before, it broke her heart. How could anyone be so unkind to this nice-looking boy? She asked where he planned to spend the night. He didn't know. "That won't do," she said. "Tommy, you'll have to find Ren a spot here. We'll figure out what to do with him tomorrow."

Dinner was Irish stew. Ren had never eaten Irish stew, but it tasted delicious to him. He especially liked the large chunks of meat. He wiped out the light brown gravy in the bottom of his bowl with crusts of bread. Tommy's brothers and sisters thought Ren was someone special because their oldest brother never had brought anyone home before. "What did you get on the docks today, Tommy?" they wanted to know. It had become a family show-and-tell thing for the younger children and Tommy played it for all it was worth.

"Well, I didn't get as much as I usually get," he began. "I had this lummox, here, who'd never worked on the docks a day in his life. I had to teach him everything from signin' up to gettin' paid. But I did manage to salvage this lovely vase and, tomorrow, Ren and I plan to go into Chinatown to turn it into something we can use." Cheers all around. "Ren picked up my vase's twin. I figure we'll partner up and get twice the price for the two of them than I'd get for just one of them. What do you say to that, Ren?" he asked.

In truth, Ren didn't know what to say. His life had whirled out of control. Nothing was familiar to him except all the kids around the dinner table. That, he knew about.

Mrs. Moran realized Ren's difficulty and rescued him by saying that she had baked three pies for desert, and asked if he would like some. "What's pie?" he asked. No one breathed at the table. How could anyone be nearly as old as Tommy and not know what pie is?

"I'll cut you a slice and maybe you'll like it," Mrs. Moran offered. She set a large slice of apple pie in front of Ren. It smelled good, he thought, but it tasted better than it smelled. The family seemed to get a great deal of pleasure by watching Ren eat his pie, but he didn't notice. He wanted a second piece, but there was nothing left after all of the kids ate theirs.

When it was time to go to bed, Mrs. Moran suggested that Ren sleep on the floor in the room that Tommy shared with three of his brothers. Nobody objected, especially Ren, and that was that. The boys found an old pillow and a blanket. Ren was so tired that he fell asleep the instant that his head hit the pillow.

At first light, the Moran home was a beehive of activity. Food was prepared. The table was set. Everyone scrubbed, dressed, and ate. By eight-thirty in the morning, Tommy Moran and Ren Baxter were in Chinatown. They carefully carried their booty in the muslin wrapping that Mrs. Moran had given to them. She was a weaver and her loom stood at the far end of her bedroom where she made everything from rugs to sheets. Before his father died, Tommy had walked these streets with him and that's why he knew them intimately. He knew exactly where to go. Ren was amazed at Tommy's ability to negotiate the twisting alleyways and crooked lanes. Ren was lost after the first left and right turns. He had never been in Chinatown before. To Ren, everything looked so similar that nothing really stood out from anything else.

They entered an unidentified shop that was full of beautiful objects. Silk-screens that were five and six feet high and painted with the delicate strokes of master craftsmen caught Ren's eye first. He'd never seen anything like them. They were beautiful, he thought. But what were they for and who would ever buy them, he wondered. Vases, far more beautiful and much larger than the two that he and Tommy carried, were in abundance. Figurines, inlaid wooden boxes, jade jewelry, and furniture overflowed their stands and formed a clutter, giving the room a charm that overwhelmed Ren's senses. Tommy had seen it all before and was unaffected. He just wanted to see the owner, Mr. Wang, collect his money, and go home.

Mr. Wang appeared and bowed to both Tommy and Ren. He was dressed all in black and wore the traditional black hat that covered his entire head. His long braid hung down to the middle of his back. Tommy returned Mr. Wang's bow, but Ren just stood there not knowing what to do. "Forgive my friend, Rennie, Mr. Wang. It's the first time he's ever been here," Tommy apologized. "He doesn't know anything, yet."

"But you plan to teach him?" Mr. Wang asked.

"Yes, sir, I do," Tommy said respectfully.

"What have you got for me today, young Mr. Moran?" Mr. Wang asked.

"We found two small vases in yesterday's breakage," Tommy began, "and I thought they were worthy of your appraisal."

"Thank you for your confidence. Let me see them, please," Mr. Wang began.

The boys unwrapped their treasures that were liberated from the docks the day before and set them in front of him. After several minutes of concentration, Mr. Wang said that they were common and of little value to him, but, because a new supplier had appeared and because the two vases were a pair, he would pay $1.50 for them. Ren could not believe his ears. In less than fifteen minutes, Tommy had made as much money for them as they had made the day before by working very hard for twelve hours. But when Tommy said no to the offer, Ren nearly exploded inwardly.

"I couldn't let them go for less than $2.00," Tommy countered. Ren wondered what Tommy was doing. "Take the damn money," he urged silently.

"Impossible," Mr. Wang replied. "I'd never be able to sell them for more than you ask me to pay. $1.75. My final offer."

"We'll take it," Tommy said.

From inside his black shirt, Mr. Wang pulled out exactly $1.75 in coins and set them on the small counter for Tommy to retrieve. He bowed to Mr. Wang who bowed back. The two boys left the shop and started back to the Moran house.

Ren was so excited! He blurted out, "I damn near died when you turned down the $1.50, Tommy."

"Never take the first offer, Ren. It's a rule. Everyone knows how to play the game. If I had taken the $1.50, Mr. Wang would never have let me back into his shop. It would have been an insult to him. He knew he undervalued our merchandise and he wanted to see if we knew what it was worth. Get it?" he asked.

Ren didn't get it and he said so. "What was that bowing thing that you and Mr. Wang did?" Ren asked.

"Respect," Tommy replied. "It's real big in Chinatown. I forgot to say anything to you before we got here, but you must always bow when bowed to. You don't have to like it, but you do have to do it. Otherwise, you will be thought of as an idiot and no one will ever deal with you."

Mrs. Moran was waiting for the boys to return. When Tommy laid out the $1.75 on the table, Ren said nothing. He wanted to see what would happen next. Mrs. Moran gave 25 cents to Tommy and she gave the same amount to Ren. She slid the remaining $1.25 into a small money purse and tucked it inside her blouse. She was the house banker and collected all of the wages from every child. Her other children earned money by cleaning houses, delivering groceries, running errands, or selling old rags and loom sweepings to the ragman. She was also the dispenser of sums and gave every child a percentage that was appropriate to the age and amount that each contributed. Everyone got something back for his or her efforts. Ren had never seen anything like it – and like it, he did. His father never handed him so much as a penny for his work. Nor did he ever express any gratitude. He just beat Ren and called him a lazy worthless ingrate.

In his pocket, Ren now had $1.00 in cash. He had not given Mrs. Moran a cent of his pay from the day before and he felt guilty.

"Mrs. Moran, I didn't give you anything from my pay yesterday," he began. But she cut him off and explained that he was a guest yesterday. If he stayed on, he would be expected to do as all of her other children did, which was to turn over everything that he made on the day that he made it.

"You mean I can stay here, Mrs. Moran?" he asked in astonishment.

"You've a better plan, Rennie?" she asked compassionately.

"No, ma'am, I don't," he answered.

"Well, then, it's settled. We'll have to find you a bed, won't we?" she mused. "Perhaps one will fall off a ship?" she laughed.

Rennie was having a difficult time in dealing with all of this kindness. It confused him. The Chinatown experience made him dizzy. The money in his pocket made him crazy. Perhaps he should go back to his home and see if he somehow could get his father to stop beating him. But he knew that was just wishful thinking. Lester's parting words to Ren as he ran out of the house were, "And don't you ever come back here, you worthless ingrate!"

Tommy suggested that they go for a long walk and talk about an idea that he had. Ren had nothing better to do, so he agreed. The boys set off again and found themselves back in Chinatown. "I think we should become partners, Ren," he began.

"What do you mean by 'partners'?" Ren asked.

"Business partners," he replied. "The docks are just a start. Right now, we carry items to Mr. Wang and he pays only a fraction of what they're worth. He probably sells the stuff for at least ten times what he pays us for it."

"No," was all that Ren could get out.

"Yes," was Tommy's emphatic reply. "Let's go back to his shop and see if the stuff we sold to him has a price tag on it. You'll see." Sure enough, Mr. Wang had priced the two vases at $6.00 each or $11.00 for the pair. "See," was all that Tommy said in triumph. "If I had enough money, say $200, I'd find a shop to rent in Chinatown and begin buying and selling stuff the guys bring off the docks. We'd tell them we'd pay more for everything they brought to us than any Chinaman in Chinatown would pay."

"But where would two guys like us ever get $200?" Ren asked in earnest.

"Well, you already got one in your pocket, don't you?" Tommy asked. "And I've got fifty cents. All we need now is," he paused.

"$198.50," Ren finished the sentence. From the time that he was able to go with his father on jobs, Ren listened to the men count money and calculate shipping weights. They multiplied distances when figuring bills. Soon, Ren was able to do the numbers in his head. It became a game with him. Could he figure out the bills by factoring in all of the parts of the equation before his dad and the customer did? By the time that he was twelve years old, he beat them every time. When he turned thirteen, everyone just asked, "How much do we owe today, Ren?" And he would tell them to the penny!

"If we made a dollar a day between us after we pay your mother, it would take us only another 198 days before we could go into business for ourselves," Ren continued excitedly. "But you know what, Tommy?" he asked. "I want to be our banker instead of your mother."

"Why?" Tommy asked. "She's great with money. Don't you trust her?"

"Of course, I trust her, Tommy, but what are we to do after she's gone? We've got to learn how to handle our own money – and the sooner, the better, as far as I'm concerned," Ren answered. "Is there someplace in your house where we could hide our money from the others?" Ren asked.

"I don't think so, Ren," Tommy replied. "Every inch of the house is accounted for. We sort of live on top of each other, you know? We need a better idea. What about a bank?" Tommy inquired.

"What about a bank?" Ren responded. "I've never been in

one and I don't know how they work."

"Neither do I," said Tommy. "There's no time like the present to find out. Let's see if there are any banks close to Chinatown."

With that settled, Tommy Moran and Rennie Baxter set off on their quest to find a bank in the vicinity. After walking westward for only three blocks, they saw the First Bank and Trust Company of San Francisco at the corner of Sacramento Street and Jones. It was an imposing building with a white marble façade and shiny brass doors. The boys were terrified that they might be swallowed alive once inside, thus, their entrance was less than confident. A uniformed guard stationed inside the door sized up their clothing and told them that the bank was not a place to play. He asked them to leave. Tommy was intimidated, but Ren stepped right up and asked if that was any way to treat customers. Rennie reasoned that this old guy couldn't hit harder than his old man and he was not about to take any more abuse, physical or verbal.

"Customers?" the guard mocked. "You have a million dollars to deposit, do you?" he said a little too loudly for good manners. He laughed even louder, attracting the attention of the bank's president who happened to be passing by. The boys turned to leave, thinking that they would have to find another safe place to keep their hard-earned money. But, before they reached the door, an elegantly dressed gentleman begged their pardon and introduced himself as Mr. Forsythe, the president of the bank. Then he surprised them by asking if he could be of any help. There was something about the two of them that seemed different from other young boys who were their age. He was curious to know what it was.

The boys brightened considerably and both replied together, "Yes, sir."

"Then, come with me, gentlemen, and we'll see if the First Bank and Trust Company of San Francisco is what you're looking for," Mr. Forsythe directed.

He led the boys down a long corridor and into his office on

the left. He gave them a moment to gawk at everything before he asked them what the nature of their business was. His office desk was larger than three beds. The stuffed chairs that they sat in were like nothing they had ever experienced. The mahogany walls were covered with paintings of old men. Finally, Ren spoke. "Mr. Forsythe, my name is Rennie Baxter and my partner, here, is Tommy Moran."

"Partners," Mr. Forsythe smiled. He liked that. His round face, atop his ample body, was the essence of conviviality and he exuded an aura of trust. "Continue," he said.

It took Ren just five minutes to recount the last two days of his life and how they saw – for themselves – merchandise marked up from $1.75 to $11.00 or $12.00 in a matter of seconds. He told the kind man that he didn't believe the Moran family banking system would serve the partners very well in the long run. Mr. Forsythe agreed wholeheartedly. At the rate of a dollar a day, they figured, in two hundred days, they would have enough saved to open a business of their own.

Finally, Mr. Forsythe spoke. "Boys, you are ambitious. I'll give you that. But what you are doing is stealing from the importers and using the proceeds to start your own careers. Don't you see anything wrong with that?" he asked.

In chorus, they answered, "No." Tommy continued, "We all do it, Mr. Forsythe. It's kind of accepted on the docks that some breakage and some removals are to be expected."

This wasn't news to Gilbert Forsythe, of course. He had been a banker for too long not to know that all of the money in his bank was not as pure as the newly driven snow. Smiling inwardly at their naiveté, he could not find it in himself to dislike the boys or their idea. "So, you want to open a business account today, I assume?" he asked.

Again, in chorus, "Yes, sir," they replied.

"Good, good," he said. "What is the name of your business or do you have a name for it yet?"

Ren spoke right up and said that they were calling their business Moran and Baxter Import Export Company. Tommy beamed at Ren's generosity and nodded his head in agreement.

"Excellent," Mr. Forsythe responded. "I need you to fill out this simple card with your names and addresses at the top. Put the name of your business right under them. Also, put in the amount of today's deposit in the lower right-hand corner. When that's finished, we'll go to a teller and you can make the deposit yourselves. He'll give you a deposit book that shows each deposit and the date it's made. Is it clear, boys, how this works?" he asked.

"When we need it, how do we get our money out, Mr. Forsythe?" Ren questioned.

"Just as easily as you put it in, only backwards. There's a table in front of the tellers' cages that has withdrawal slips on it. You'll put your names and the name of your company on one of those slips along with the amount that you wish to withdraw. The teller will stamp that amount in your book and subtract it from the total in your account. He'll then enter the balance. There's one more thing you need to know before you make your deposit. The bank pays you interest on all of your deposited money. Your interest is paid on the first day of each quarter of the year."

Realizing that neither boy knew what interest was, Mr. Forsythe explained it to them. In response, Ren said, "You mean you loan our money to people we don't know without our permission? And, at the end of every three months, you pay us half of one percent for each dollar in our account?" Ren inquired.

"That's about it," Mr. Forsythe answered. "Your money actually earns money. Come with me, gentlemen, and I'll take you to our head teller, Mr. McLeod. He'll get you started."

In a single file, the boys followed Mr. Forsythe back down the long corridor and into the public section of the bank where the tellers were stationed. He whispered something into the ear of Mr. McLeod, who received their money most ceremoniously. "Thank you, Mr. Moran, and thank you, Mr. Baxter, for choosing the First Bank and Trust Company of San Francisco to be your bank. Mr. Forsythe told me that he's expecting great things from you. He believes that someday you'll have over a million dollars in this bank. This first deposit is a good start." With that, he handed their stamped passbook to them. It indicated that they had $1.50 on deposit in "their" bank. "Anytime you have a deposit, I'd be only too happy to help you. Good day, gentlemen," he said.

Mr. Forsythe walked with them to the front door and promptly fired the guard who had turned them away half an hour before.

Back on the street, they felt like the two richest young men in San Francisco, even though they did not have two pennies to rub together. Returning to the Moran home, both boys were worried about how Tommy's mother would receive the news. But they had nothing to worry about. She was one hundred percent supportive of their initiative. All that she asked them to do was to turn over everything that they made to her. They could bank only what she gave back to them. She had too many mouths to feed and needed every penny that she could put her hands on. The boys promised to give an honest accounting of their finances – and they lived up to their word.

Every other day found the boys back on the docks hoping for something to break so that they could scoop it up after work. When several days went by without an accident, the boys realized that it was going to take them longer than 200 days to save $200. Out of their 75 cents, Mrs. Moran continued to give them 25. It took them two days to earn one dollar for their deposit. By the end of their first month as partners, their bank account showed $17.50. By chance, Mr. Forsythe was in the bank's lobby when the boys entered to make another deposit. He greeted them warmly and told them how proud he was of them. He assured the young lads that the bank was lucky to have them as customers. Mr. McLeod agreed.

After a hot day on the docks, Tommy and Ren had only 75 cents to show for all of their hard work. That evening, Mrs. Moran suggested that the boys go to the local tavern, drink one beer each, and bring one to her on their way back. She counted out nine pennies and handed them to Tommy. He had done this a few times when his father was alive, but this was the first time that he was going to the tavern without his dad. Ren, on the other hand, didn't want to go because he had seen, first-hand, what booze had done to his father. He didn't want any part of it.

"One beer, lad," Mrs. Moran assured Ren, "won't make you mean or a drunk like your dad." Still, he would rather keep the three cents and put it in the bank. "You need to let your hair down, Ren. You work like a dog and you never complain. Life is more than just work, believe you me," she instructed.

Tommy cuffed Ren on top of his head and said, "Come on. You just might like it."

"That's what I'm afraid of," he replied.

Most of the tavern was crowded with beer-drinking men who were either morose or loud, depending on how the booze affected them. The loud ones could be quite funny sometimes. Two Germans, sitting together in a booth, stood up all of a sudden and began to sing love songs. One was singing in German and the other in English. They thought the crowd would enjoy the translation as well as the original. But they were wrong. Patrons found it a hoot, at first, but after awhile, told them to sit down and be quiet. When a spot opened at the end of the bar, the boys quickly stepped into it and asked for two beers. Tommy paid for the beers with six pennies, sipped his, and licked his lips while enjoying every drop. Ren looked at his for the longest time before he dared taste it. It was bitter, he thought. He couldn't see why anyone in his right mind would drink the stuff. But, after a dozen sips, Ren had consumed half the glass and his head started doing funny things to him. Tommy finished his beer and ordered one for his mother. The bartender handed him a bottle and Tommy paid for it. He told Ren to stay behind and finish his beer. He would see him back at the house. Ren wanted to leave with Tommy, but he was enjoying the feeling that he was getting from drinking the beer, even though he didn't enjoy the taste.

Tommy was no more out of the door when Frankie Wilson barged through it. He had come directly from McGuire's Tavern, one block away, and he arrived with a snoot full. He headed right for the spot at the bar where Tommy Moran had stood moments before. The barkeep knew what to pour for Frankie. He drank only boilermakers and his were always doubles – two shots of whiskey in a glass of beer. He picked up his drink and drained it straight down as though it were plain water. Rennie started to leave because he knew that anyone who drank that much booze had to be mean. He was right. Frankie bellowed, "And just where the hell do you think you're going, leaving half a glass of beer on the bar?" Rennie didn't answer. He just kept walking past the big man.

Frankie grabbed Rennie by his arm and spun him around. "I'm talking to you, boy. When you finish your beer and drink one of mine, you can go." Then he roared with laughter.

"I can't drink that much, sir," Ren replied.

"A chicken-shit-lily-livered-little-son-of-a-bitch, are you?" Frankie yelled back. And, without warning, he smacked Ren with an open hand that knocked him so hard that he stumbled backwards for about four feet. Before Ren knew what was happening, the big guy was all over him. He picked Ren up and held him over his head as though Ren were weightless. Then he threw him nine feet through the air until he crashed down on a table full of patrons. A beer bottle hit Ren's eye, broke under his cheekbone, and cut a small section of his nose and lip. Then the kicking began. Frankie landed several hard ones in Ren's stomach and on his left arm that he used to protect himself. Finally, the barman decked Frankie from behind with a big wooden club. Frankie crashed on top of Ren, who was bleeding and nearly unconscious. Several patrons who hadn't fled the scene pulled Ren out from under the bully and tried to help him out of the bar. But Ren was too angry to accept their help. His left collarbone was broken and he hurt all over. His face was covered with his own blood and it burned his eyes, but his head was very clear. Extreme pain has a way of focusing one's attention, even when an alcoholic haze clouds the vision. Ren had become very focused.

Chapter One: The Train Robbery

The beatings that he had taken from his father were not as bad as the one that he just received. But this was the last beating that he would take from anyone ever again! Not knowing exactly what he was going to do to retaliate, Ren stumbled around the block while looking for something that he could use to get even. On his second go-round, Ren spotted a two-by-four plank leaning beside an unfinished porch. It had a five-inch spike sticking out of the end. He picked up the three-and-a-half-foot-long board with his one good arm and hid inside a small shed that had a large board missing in its door. The shed was only a few yards away from the saloon door. This hiding spot gave Ren a clear view of anyone who was leaving the bar. He waited there for two more hours before Frankie Wilson staggered out.

When Frankie walked close enough to the shed where Ren was concealed, Ren stepped right in front of him so that Frankie could see his attacker. Frankie was so drunk that he had lost all of his reflexes. He just stood there like the stoop he was. Ren raised the board over his head with his one good arm and, with all of his might, he crashed it, nail side down, straight into Frankie's thick skull, killing him instantly. Ren did not wait for Frankie to topple and fall. He jerked the nail free from his skull and plunged the nail a second time into another spot on the top of his already-bloody head. Frankie fell dead away. But Ren wasn't finished. He was still too angry to quit. A dozen times more, he drove the bloody spike into Frankie's head and face. By then, his anger was spent. After trampling the spike with his shoe and embedding it in the eardrum of the late Frankie Wilson, he simply walked away.

An idea popped into Ren's mind after he had walked only a few steps from the body. Maybe Frankie had some money in his pocket. Ren hurried back and started going through the dead man's pockets. He pulled out many carelessly folded bills that were secured by a silver money clip. He also found a large carved jade stone of a panda bear inside a purple silk bag. Pain be damned! With what he had in his hand, he ran as fast as he could to get away from there.

By the time that he got to the Moran home, everyone was asleep. He tiptoed up the stairs and woke Tommy with a shoulder shake. "Tommy, I need some help. Can you come downstairs with me?"

Tommy rose quickly and followed Ren down the steps to the kitchen. He wanted to light a lamp but Ren told him not to. "Where have you been and what happened to you?" Tommy asked.

"When I tell you, you might not want to be my partner anymore," Ren answered. "And that's okay. I'll understand. But, for now, I need to get fixed up. That big guy who came into the bar as you were leaving did it. Do you know who he was?" Ren asked.

"Frankie Wilson," Tommy answered. "Everyone knows he's bad news."

Mrs. Moran's bedroom adjoined the kitchen and she heard the boys talking. Refusing to be stopped, she lit a lamp upon entering the dark kitchen. She nearly fainted when she saw how bad Ren looked. "Oh, Rennie," she began. "I'm so sorry for you. I should never have sent you to that bar. You didn't want to go and it's all my fault that you're as busted up as you are. What happened? Who did this to you?"

"Frankie Wilson, Ma," Tommy answered.

"Not so, Mrs. Moran," he replied. "What happened to me happened. Had Tommy been standing where I was, it would have happened to him. Just the luck of the draw, I guess." He tried to comfort her.

Then he reached into his pocket and pulled out the money clip and the jade. "I killed the son of a bitch, Mrs. Moran, and I took everything he had out of his pockets. Our deal is you get whatever we bring into the house and you give us what you can. Well, count it. It's all there."

They did. Frankie Wilson had been a bad person all the way around. He would steal anything that wasn't nailed down. He would extort everyone that he could and he wasn't averse to killing someone when he was paid enough. Frankie had $238 in the clip. A small fortune! They counted it a second time. $238!

"How did you kill him?" Tommy wanted to know.

"I hit him in the head with a two-by-four that had a big nail stickin' out the end of it," he blurted out with his tongue tripping over his words. "I found it sittin' next to that house where they're puttin' on a new front porch."

"No, you didn't," Mrs. Moran replied. "You came straight home from the bar last night after Frankie Wilson beat you. I ought to know 'cause I'm the one who cleaned you up."

"That cleaning up part is only partly true, Mrs. Moran. But it's all true that I killed that man, over and over, again and again. His own mother won't be able to recognize him when they find him," Ren confessed.

"Be that as it may," she replied, "the only part that will ever go out of this house is the part about how you came straight home and how I cleaned you up. Is that clear, boys?" she wanted to know.

"Clear," they said.

With that, Mrs. Moran told Ren to take off all of his clothes so that she could wash the blood out of them. It was impossible to know which was his and which was Frankie's, but one thing was for sure – there was a lot of it. They wrapped him in a blanket while Tommy cleaned up the spots of blood leading up to his room.

Ren was embarrassed to take off his clothing, but Mrs. Moran insisted that he didn't have anything that she hadn't seen before. But was she ever wrong. Ren hung more than two- thirds of the way to his knees. The sight of it took her breath away. "Holy Mother of God," she muttered, as she turned away to her tasks.

First light cranked the house back into its frenetic state. The younger children knew something terrible had happened while they slept. Rennie had black and blue marks everywhere that his clothes didn't cover him and his left eye was swollen nearly shut. His small facial cuts were treated with an astringent and left uncovered. His left arm had to be supported with a sling that Mrs. Moran fashioned for him. He couldn't possibly go to work that day and Tommy would not leave him. Mrs. Moran agreed that neither boy should leave the house.

Near noon, a policeman knocked on the Morans' front door. Mrs. Moran invited the officer into her kitchen where Rennie sat. She said that she was glad to see him because she was about to walk down to the station to file a complaint against a man named Frankie Wilson who beat her son the night before.

"That's interesting, Mrs. Moran, because I'm here to investigate that man's death," he replied.

"Well, how can we help you, officer," Mrs. Moran inquired.

"We think your boy did it," he started.

But Mrs. Moran interrupted him and said, "Impossible! Rennie returned home right after that madman trounced him. I ended up spending most of the night cleaning him up. Take off your shirt, Rennie, and show the officer your bruises," she ordered. Ren tried to comply, but was unable to use his left arm. "He can't even raise his arm to defend himself, let alone kill anyone. Surely, you can see that for yourself, officer," she said. The fine policeman had to agree that, although Ren might have had the motive to kill Frankie Wilson, he certainly didn't have the ability to do so. No, he thought, the boy couldn't have overpowered anyone, definitely not after the unprovoked beating that he took. Besides, many in the bar already had testified that Wilson had beaten him savagely. His written report cleared Ren of any involvement in the murder.

"Thank you, Mrs. Moran. Sorry to have bothered you," he said as he walked out of the house. "I'll have to look elsewhere for his killer," he assured her. None was ever found and the Frankie Wilson murder case aged until it ended up in the unsolved files.

Ren wanted something to eat. He felt hungry. Did she have a steak in the house? No, she did not, but she sent Tommy to the butcher and told him to come home with the best steak he could buy. From Frankie's money clip, she handed him three one-dollar bills. With three dollars, Tommy was able to buy three huge steaks, one for each of them. After all, they had been up all night and they deserved such a treat. Rennie asked Mrs. Moran to sear his on both sides and serve it to him almost raw. He didn't know why he liked rare meat, but he couldn't eat it if it was overcooked. She fixed all three steaks like Ren wanted and agreed that they never had tasted better. Ren even chewed the bones, which disgusted the two Morans.

After a week had passed, Ren decided to talk to Mrs. Moran and Tommy about Frankie Wilson's money and the beautifully carved jade stone of a panda. Ren began, "Mrs. Moran, I put every dollar from you-know-who's money clip into your hand. I'm wanting to know how much of that money Tommy and I can put into our bank account?" he asked.

"I thought we'd split it three ways. You and Tommy would each get one third and I'd keep one third," she replied.

"$79.00 each," Ren answered.

"I'll need a paper and pencil to do the division, Ren, but that sounds about right," she said.

"Yes, ma'am, almost exactly. I can do numbers in my head. Tommy and I will get $78.33 each and you'll get $78.34 because we spent three dollars on great steaks, remember?" he joked. "But I'm thinking that's not quite right, Mrs. Moran," he continued.

It was Tommy's turn to gasp inwardly. No one had ever negotiated or argued with his mother over finances. "Really?" she said. "What figures would make you happy, Ren?" she asked.

"I was thinking you should get $50 and Tommy and I should get $185. That way, we'll have just a little more than our $200 and we can start our own business right now," he reasoned. "We'll set you up on a much larger salary out of our profits than we can ever give you working on the docks. What do you say?" he smiled.

Her heart melted. "You drive a hard bargain, Rennie Baxter. Are you sure you're not an Irishman?" she smiled as she counted out $185 and handed it to "her boys." Tommy and Rennie hugged her and kissed her on opposite cheeks at the same time. But she wasn't done with them. "What about the money clip?" she asked.

"It's got to be worth something, wouldn't you say?" Indeed, they would say and decided that there had to be some way to sell it. "I'll expect a full third out of its sale and I won't take a penny less. You hear me, Rennie Baxter?" she bantered.

"Deal," was all he replied. They would have to dispose of the jade later. He and Tommy had work to do. They headed straight to Chinatown and quickly learned why it bore that name. The few shops that were available for rent were not available to them. Tommy said that they should talk to Mr. Wang.

As they entered his shop, Mr. Wang appeared and bowed deeply from his waist. This time, both young men returned his bow. "Mr. Wang, we don't have any merchandise for you today, but we are willing to pay you for some advice," Tommy said.

"Advice free," Mr. Wang smiled. "Only lawyers charge for advice." Only Mr. Wang laughed at his joke. The boys didn't understand what was so funny.

Ren continued. "Mr. Wang, Tommy and I want to open our own import export shop here in Chinatown, but nobody will rent to us. Is it just because we are not Chinese that we are shut out," he asked, "or is it something else?"

"No other reason needed, Rennie," he answered. "That one good enough," he continued.

"Is there any way around our problem?" Ren wondered out loud.

"Become Chinese and your problem will be solved," Mr. Wang said and he laughed a great belly laugh.

"What if you rented the shop for us, Mr. Wang," Ren asked, "and we pay you a percentage out of our profits? All you would have to do is accept our money every month," he explained.

"I think about that. Come back Friday. I have answer for you," he smiled.

"Thank you, Mr. Wang. Thank you very much," Tommy said. "Thank you, Mr. Wang. See you on Friday," Ren added. All bowed. The boys left feeling as though they had a slim-to-no chance of getting what they had set their hearts on.

"We need to get this money into the bank," Tommy told Ren.

"I don't think so," Ren replied. "If anyone ever asks how we got our hands on so much money, it wouldn't take very long for them to figure it out."

"What about Mr. Forsythe, Ren? Maybe he could help us figure it out. He's been so good to us. I think we should at least talk to him about it," Tommy countered.

"Okay, but you've got to let me do all the talking. If I think he won't cooperate, I want to cut it off before he figures it out and goes to the coppers. Agreed?" Ren asked.

"Agreed," Tommy answered.

Mr. Forsythe was in a meeting when the boys arrived, but he sent word out to them that he could see them at 2:30 that afternoon. True to his word, Mr. Forsythe met them and greeted them as though they were the bank's biggest depositors. "Now, what can I do for you young gentlemen? I can't call you boys anymore, can I?" he asked rhetorically. He noticed Ren's bruises and the way that he favored his left arm.

"We have a problem, Mr. Forsythe, and we need your advice. But first, I got to ask. The stuff you hear from people …"

Interrupting Rennie in mid-sentence, Mr. Forsythe said, "Doesn't leave this room. It's called 'keeping a confidence.' Believe me, the bank would collapse in no time if I didn't keep the information that I know confidential," he lied. "Does that answer your question?"

"Okay. Then, here goes," Ren, began. "Tommy and I found some money about the time we opened our account here," he lied, "but we've been too scared to do anything with it because we don't want anyone to think we did anything wrong to get it. Get it?" he asked.

"Perfectly," Mr. Forsythe responded. "You need a new bank book that says your deposits were larger than what shows now. I think we can manage that. Follow me," he commanded. And, like ducklings following a mother duck, the three marched single file to Mr. McLeod's window where Mr. Forsythe whispered something to him.

"I see," he replied. "We require a $25.00 fee to adjust your account, gentlemen. Can you handle that sum?" he inquired.

"That's robbery," Ren nearly shouted, but bit off the words so no one except Mr. McLeod and Mr. Forsythe could hear.

"Yes, it is," Mr. McLeod agreed, with a slight smile visible at the corners of his mouth, "but it takes a thief to know a thief, now, doesn't it?" he added. And, with that, all the wind came out of Rennie's sails. They knew! And they knew that he knew that they knew.

It took Mr. McLeod only a few minutes to create a new account book and to destroy the old one. After subtracting the bank's "fee," their new balance was $177.50. They were still short of their goal.

When their business was finished, Mr. Forsythe asked them if he could have another moment of their time back in his office. He could see their hesitation and quickly assured them that they were in no kind of trouble. He had a business proposition for them to consider. The boys looked blankly at each other, but agreed to hear him out.

As soon as the door to Mr. Forsythe's office had closed, he began by complimenting them on the splendid financial record that they had established with his bank. "I recognize real talent when I see it and, believe me, I'm looking straight at it right now." He paused to let that sink in. Then he continued. "From time to time, I ... that is to say, the bank needs some help finding certain clients who have disappeared and left us with an unpaid debt. I'm wondering if you would consider trying to find those delinquents and collecting what is owed to the bank any way you can? We pay a handsome fee for such work."

"How much of a fee, Mr. Forsythe?" Ren asked.

"One third," he answered.

"One third!" the boys exclaimed. "What's the catch, Mr. Forsythe?" Tommy wanted to know.

"Sometimes it can be downright dangerous," he replied without hesitation. "For example, we used to use a big guy named Frankie Wilson to do some of our collection work, but he was murdered recently."

Tommy froze, and it was not missed by Mr. Forsythe or by Ren. "Yeah, we heard about it. It happened in our neighborhood," Ren offered. "We didn't know the guy or anything," Ren continued. And, with each word, Mr. Forsythe paid more and more attention to the still-detectable bruises and the black and blue spots on Ren. "If he was a big guy like you say he was and he got murdered, why would you want a couple of skinny kids like us to replace him?" Ren facetiously asked.

"Let's just say I know brains often win out over brawn," he replied.

"Why are you really doing this, Mr. Forsythe?" Ren wanted to know.

"Because I think the two of you are going to make a huge amount of money in the next few years and I want it all to come into this bank," he said unabashedly.

Then, as if inspiration had hit him, Ren was on his feet. From his pocket, he produced Frankie Wilson's silver eagle money clip and slammed it down on Mr. Forsythe's desk blotter. He wanted Mr. Forsythe to know. Without ever admitting to anything, Ren told Mr. Forsythe everything. "We also found this clip. It was holding the money we just deposited," he said in triumph. "How much do you think it's worth?"

Mr. Forsythe recognized the clip since he had seen it many times after he paid Frankie Wilson. The week before, it also had been reported as missing in the newspaper article. He inwardly smiled and patted himself on the back for judging correctly when he intercepted the boys that first day. Ren did not miss Forsythe's momentary look of self-satisfaction.

"I'd be willing to buy it for the $25.00 fee we charged you to recreate your account," he answered casually.

"Nonsense," Ren blurted back. "I can easily get three times

that amount in Chinatown."

"I doubt that, Mr. Baxter," he countered, with an edge in his voice. "I doubt that very much. You see, I know the value of silver and silver objects. I dare say you would be lucky to get $35.00 – and, even then, only if you are really lucky."

Ren knew that Mr. Forsythe recognized the money clip. He had shown it to him on purpose. He wanted Mr. Forsythe to know that he was capable of more than making one-dollar deposits, but Mr. Forsythe already knew that. What Mr. Forsythe didn't know was just how smart the young man was. Ren surprised him when he picked up the money clip and put it back into his pocket. "Thanks, but no thanks, Mr. Forsythe. I think we'll pass on both of your offers," he answered for himself and for Tommy.

"If you change your mind, you know where to find me," he said good-naturedly.

When they were out of the bank, Tommy exploded. "What were you thinking, Ren, showing Mr. Forsythe that money clip?"

"He knows, Tommy, he knows," Ren answered. "I just wanted to make him understand that Frankie Wilson wasn't so tough. Then, maybe, he'll give us a better deal than one third. We'll go back to see him on Friday after we see Mr. Wang, okay?" he reassured.

"What are you going to do with that damn clip?" Tommy inquired.

"Let's try our luck in Chinatown," he answered.

The young men walked three blocks back to Chinatown and went directly to see Mr. Wang for more advice. After the bowing and preliminary niceties were out of the way, Ren asked, "Mr. Wang, who buys silver objects in Chinatown?"

"I've been known to buy a few, young Mr. Baxter," he replied. "May I see what you have?"

Ren reached into his pocket and produced the money clip. Mr. Wang picked it up and reverentially turned it over and over. "$15.00," he offered.

"Meaning no disrespect, Mr. Wang, but I just turned down $35.00 for it from the president of the First Bank and Trust Company of San Francisco. Would you look at it again, please?" he prompted.

Tommy froze. Time seemed to stand still until Mr. Wang made the next move. From the inside of his black shirt where he kept his money pouch, he removed a tiny pair of glasses. Tommy never had seen them in all of the years that he had visited Mr. Wang. "Perhaps I need a better look, Mr. Baxter," he offered.

With great ceremony, Mr. Wang cleaned the glasses one lens at a time while never taking his eyes off of Ren. Finally, he looped the earpieces in place and began his inspection anew. It was Ren's turn to stare directly into the eyes of Mr. Wang. The exercise did not go without reward. In a flash of recognition, Mr. Wang recalled this particular money clip. Years ago, he had bought it from the largest cowboy that he had ever seen. The cowboy said that it was his lucky piece, but hard times had fallen on him and he had to let it go. Mr. Wang paid the man $15.00 for it after twenty minutes of bargaining. Shortly after that, he sold it to Frankie Wilson for $50.00.

"$25.00," he offered.

"$40.00," Ren countered.

"Done," Mr. Wang agreed with a tiny smile of victory, knowing that the clip's recent history had increased its value by two hundred percent. Wang's uncle, Chow, had links to dealers whose clients would pay any price to own Frankie Wilson's now infamous and, more importantly, missing silver eagle money clip.

Ren pocketed the money, bowed to Mr. Wang, and walked out of the door. Tommy was amazed at how quickly Ren had learned his craft. Neither spoke until they were out of Chinatown. They hardly breathed. Then Tommy Moran burst his silence by slapping Ren on the back and telling him what a great job he did in negotiating with both Mr. Forsythe and Mr. Wang. Ren accepted Tommy's approvals, but, inwardly, he was worried. "Why did Mr. Wang agree to my price, Tommy?" he asked.

"Maybe he saw it better when he put on his glasses. I've never seen him wear them, you know? In fact, I didn't know he had glasses," Tommy responded.

"That's not it, Tommy, I'm sure. I think he knew the piece and he knew who owned it, just like Mr. Forsythe knew. I think I just gave it away," he offered.

"You call $40.00 a giveaway, Ren?" Tommy asked incredulously.

"I do, Tommy. I think I was right with Mr. Forsythe. I should have gotten $75.00 or more. Now, when we put our $13.33 each into the account, Mr. Forsythe will know we got nothing for our efforts in Chinatown. $26.66 is just a buck and pennies more than he offered. He'll think we're real assholes. We'll be lucky to get the third he offered for collection work," he said angrily.

As the partners walked back to the Moran home, Mr. Wang and Mr. Forsythe walked from their respective places of business and met with colleagues.

Wang went straight to Uncle Chow's and quietly placed the money clip in front of him. He whispered as much of its history as he knew into the old man's ear. With each new word, the smile on Uncle Chow's face widened. Chow paid his nephew $60.00 and immediately marked it up to $95.00. With such good merchandise, perhaps an exception to the Chinatown policy of no foreigners might be broached this one time, Wang thought.

Forsythe headed to his club, The Bay Bankers and Brokers Haven. Seated at one of the poker tables was Griffin Hewes, the legendary baron of real estate, construction, shipping, insurance, banking, timber, and all things legal and otherwise in San Francisco. Having married twin sisters, Gilbert Forsythe and Griffin Hewes were brothers-in-law. They liked each other. Although it was unethical and probably illegal, they eagerly shared confidential information that readily benefited both. By hand-signaling Griffin, Gilbert indicated that he wanted to talk. Hewes excused himself from the game and joined his brother-in-law in the reading room, where no reading, as such, was ever done, but where business deals were made daily. "What have you got for me today, Gilbert?" Griffin asked.

"Nothing that will line our pockets right now, but I do have a story I think you'll find as interesting as I do. About a month and a half ago, two ill-dressed unsophisticated youngsters walked into the bank and wanted to open a business account with $1.50." Griffin's eyes had started to glaze at the precise moment that he heard no money today.

Forsythe continued, "They made small deposits sporadically and, in a month's time, they had $17.50 on deposit. Then the most amazing thing happened. Today, nearly ten days after Frankie Wilson was murdered, my two guys show up with $187 to deposit. Those rascals claimed they found the money. Then they asked if we could make 'an adjustment' in their account so all the money wouldn't appear in one deposit."

The words "murder" and "Frankie Wilson" snapped Griffin Hewes' mind back to attention. "It gets better, Grif," Forsythe added. "I asked them if they would step back into my office when they finished. When they came inside, I asked them if they would like to replace our debt collector, the late Frankie Wilson. One young man turned white and froze stiff as a board. The other one asked, as casually as possible, how much I'd pay for such work. While they were considering my offer, I was stunned when the second youngster slammed down Frankie Wilson's silver eagle money clip on my desk and wanted me to buy it for $75.00."

Griffin Hewes howled with laughter. He never liked Frankie Wilson. But he did like this story and wanted to know the names of the two young men. "The older boy is Tommy Moran, but he's not the brains. The younger one is a bright redhead named Ren Baxter. The two of them are big kids and Ren appears to be the real thinker. They want to save $200 so they can open their own import export place in Chinatown," Forsythe added. "They work twelve hours on the docks unloading ships for 75 cents a day. They give it all to Moran's mother who gives each boy 25 cents. Every two days, they come in and deposit $1.00 or so. When they are able to steal unbroken goods from broken crates, they sell them in Chinatown and take all the money back to Mrs. Moran. She doles out their share, which they dutifully deposit into their account," he ended.

Hewes was beside himself with laughter. He hadn't heard such a good story in years. Truth was, it was his own story and he really liked the Baxter kid. "Sixteen years old, you say, Gil, and he's already killed a man. Gotta love it," Hewes responded.

Seated at the kitchen table, Rennie put all of the $40.00 in front of Mrs. Moran. "How much do we each get, Ren?" she asked.

"Tommy and I get $13.33 each and you get $13.34," he smiled at her.

"A darlin' young man, you are, Rennie Baxter," she said. "Just darlin'," and she reached over and gave his hair a tussle. "Now, here's a little surprise for you. I'm taking just $10.00 and I'm ordering the two of you to take the same amount. Put your $20.00 in the bank. With the other $5.00 each, buy yourselves some decent clothes. If it's businessmen you are, then you had better start to look like businessmen. And spend another dollar at the barbershop for a real haircut. Tell him not to spare any of the good-smelling stuff after he's done."

Tommy didn't know what to say, so he decided to follow Ren's lead. "You're absolutely right, Mrs. Moran."

"Patricia, Ren. My name is Patricia," she interrupted. "Mrs. Moran makes me sound so old. I'm only 38, you know."

Tommy Moran laughed so hard that he fell off his chair. "38, my ass. Try 46, Ren."

Ren didn't know if he could call Mrs. Moran by her first name, but he agreed to try. "Okay, Patricia."

Interrupting again, "Patty is even better, Ren. Please, call me Patty," Mrs. Moran encouraged.

"It'll probably take me some time to get used to not calling you Mrs. Moran, Mrs. Moran – I mean Patty – but I'll give it my best," he stumbled. "You're right, M… Patty. We need to dress the part, but it'll take more than five dollars each. How about letting us use whatever we get for the jade to buy clothes and we split the $40.00 three ways just as planned?" he asked with the biggest shit-eating grin running all over his handsome face.

Patty Moran cuffed Ren Baxter playfully. She told him that he made bad bargains sound good to her, even though she knew the jade was probably worth far more than the money clip. "All right," she said. "Tomorrow, take the jade and don't come home until you look like the successful businessmen I know you'll be very soon."

Tommy excused himself, saying that he was very tired from the day's events and needed to sleep. Ren's mind was racing too fast for him to sleep. He said that he wanted to think about a few things for a bit longer and that he would come to bed soon. Saying she also needed to sleep, Mrs. Moran retired to her bedroom.

For the next hour, Ren replayed the day's events. What had he done right? What had he done wrong? Where could he improve his negotiating skills? If he and Tommy performed collections for Mr. Forsythe, would they turn into just another version of Frankie Wilson? That thought made Ren shudder. In his mind, he vowed that was not going to happen if he had anything to say about it.

Still deep in thought, he didn't see Mrs. Moran as she stepped from her dark bedroom into the dimly lit kitchen. At first, Ren thought that she just needed a drink of water. But that wasn't what she needed. "Ren, have you ever been with a woman?" she asked.

"No, Mrs. Moran, I haven't," he answered.

"My husband has been dead for more than a year and I haven't been with a man in all that time. Rennie, I really need a man tonight. I want you to come with me into my bedroom right now. Would you like to do that, Rennie?" she asked.

"Mrs. Moran, I don't know what to do. What if Tommy or one of the other kids hears us? I remember I could hear my parents almost every night," he protested.

"They are all sound sleepers and they are one floor above

us. Come with me, Rennie, please," she begged.

Although Ren didn't quite know what to do, he figured that Mrs. Moran would help him, so he consented and followed her into the bedroom. The only light in the room was from a single candle that she had lit before she entered the kitchen. After a few seconds, Ren's eyes adjusted so that he could see her in the faint light. Mrs. Moran was a plump middle-aged woman who had given birth to twelve children, but she retained a charm that, in the dim glow, Ren found exciting. She removed her sleeper shirt and displayed herself for him while she encouraged him to get out of his clothes. From the time that she saw Ren naked after Frankie Wilson had beaten him, she had not been able to think of anything else.

She reached over, took his very long cock, and pushed back its foreskin. He liked it and started to get hard immediately. Patty stroked it several times until it stretched out to its full length and girth. Ren just stood there with his eyes closed while emitting a low moaning sound. It had been a long time since Patty Moran had been in bed with a man, but never had she ever been with a man whose cock was so big and so long. She wondered if she could take it all in, but take it she did, and gasped with pleasure in the process. Ren could not believe how good it felt. It was even better than when he pleasured himself. He wanted it to go on and on, but it was not to be. He buried his face in the pillow and muffled his own pleasure groans when his time arrived. "My God, Rennie, that was the most wonderful fuck I've ever enjoyed in my entire life," she whispered.

Ren didn't know what to say or do next, so he waited until Patty Moran told him. He dressed and went upstairs to his own bed, where he slept the sleep of the spent. In the morning, he and Tommy were gone before any of the others were up and about. They stopped for tea and some breakfast on their way to Chinatown. "How late did you stay up last night, Ren?" Tommy asked.

"A couple of hours, I think," he answered. "I was trying to

figure out how Mr. Forsythe knew we were depositing Frankie Wilson's money."

"Did you figure it out?" he asked.

"Almost, but some things are not clear to me just yet. In a couple of days, I think I'll be able to say with certainty. But, right now, it's still a mystery to me," Ren replied. "How much do you think we'll get for the jade?"

Tommy didn't know and said so. But, first, he wanted to have the gem appraised before they went to Chinatown. That made sense to Ren, but neither young man knew an appraiser other than Mr. Wang. "How about Mr. Forsythe?" Tommy asked. "If he can't do it himself, I'll bet he knows someone who can. Let's ask him, Ren," he directed.

"Okay," was Ren's reply.

When the bank's doors opened at 9:00 a.m. sharp, the boys headed straight to Mr. McLeod's window and deposited their $24.66, giving them a balance of $202.16. Each boy kept a dollar for his first haircut in a barbershop. They were in business! Then they headed to Mr. Forsythe's office where, again, he greeted them as though they were the most important clients in the bank's history. "Gentlemen, what a pleasure to see you. I think I'm going to start to charge you for my time," he joked. When the partners didn't see it as a joke, Mr. Forsythe burst out laughing until they did. "What can I do for you today, free of charge, that is?" he asked.

As before, it was Ren who did all of the talking. "Mr. Forsythe, can you appraise gems?"

"Only superficially," he answered. "I can give you a number that's close to the value, but you'll need a gemologist to give you its true worth. What have you got that needs to be turned into cash, gentlemen?" he asked.

At first, Ren hesitated, but then showed the panda jade to Gilbert Forsythe. In spite of himself and his best effort, Forsythe chuckled at Ren's stupidity or bravery; he did not know which. "Mr. Baxter, although I don't know a great deal about jade carvings, I do recognize this particular jade just as I recognized your silver money clip. But you knew that I recognized the clip, didn't you?" he began. "You wanted me to know, didn't you?" he said accusingly. Ren just looked him straight in the eye and gave away nothing. "Very well, Mr. Baxter. This gem was the centerpiece in a collection of animals carved from jade owned by the second Emperor of China's Ming Dynasty, Cheng Zu. How it reached San Francisco remains a mystery. Since it surfaced here, its three known owners have been murdered. The fourth was Frankie Wilson. He acquired it in a poker game the day before he was murdered. The fool didn't know what he had or he wouldn't have been carrying it around in his pocket. It's practically priceless. The minute you show it in Chinatown, your life will be over. I've heard some people say they would pay as much as $25,000 for it."

The silence in Mr. Forsythe's office was palpable. "What should we do, Mr. Forsythe?" Ren began.

"Put it in a safe deposit box in our bank and let me make discrete inquiries for you. Go home. Work on the docks for the next few weeks and don't come back here until I send for you. Your panda carving will be perfectly safe. The reason we call it a 'safe deposit box' is self-evident. The locked box is located in our locked safe. It takes two different keys in two separate locks to open the box. You will have one of them in your possession. I'll have the other. I won't be able to open the box without your key and you won't be able to open it without mine. Agreed?" he asked.

"Agreed," they answered in unison.

"Follow me, gentlemen, and we'll place this magnificent piece in a safe place out of sight," Forsythe directed.

The boys signed the necessary signature cards to gain access to the box. They opened it with Mr. Forsythe, who placed the gem inside for safekeeping. After the box was locked with two keys, they left the bank and started the walk back to Tommy's home. On the way, they stopped at Migliori's Barbershop, where Vincent Migliori, himself, cut their hair and doused them with lots and lots of cologne. They fairly reeked as they walked out of his door.

Mrs. Moran had been unable to get up that morning. She claimed stomach cramps, but, in truth, she had been bleeding off and on since she and Ren had been together. It took her several days to recover and, when she did, she acted as though nothing had ever happened between her and Ren. That was fine with Ren since he did not want to ruin his business relationship with his partner. Tommy had made everything happen for him and he would be grateful to him forever.

Without ever saying a word, Patty Moran and Ren Baxter shared a secret that they both would treasure, but would never speak of again. "What happened?" she began. "I like your haircuts and both of you smell real good, but where are your new clothes?"

Ren deferred to Tommy. "Well, Ma, we ran into some problems. I thought, and Ren agreed, that we should not go into Chinatown with the jade before knowing what it was worth. We might have given it away for only a few dollars after Ren had paid such a terrible price. So I thought we should show it to Mr. Forsythe at the bank. Ren agreed. Mr. Forsythe knew the stone. He said it belonged to some Chinese emperor and that the last four men who owned it in San Francisco had been murdered."

Sensing her son needed a breather, she asked Ren what happened to the stone. Did they have it? He picked up the story: "Mr. Forsythe told us that he knew some people who would give $25,000 for it. He warned us that we'd be killed for it if we took it into Chinatown."

"Holy Mother of God!" she exclaimed. "So, where is it now?" she wanted to know.

Tommy picked up, "It's in something called a 'safe deposit box.' That box is locked with two keys. Ren and I each have copies of our key. Mr. Forsythe has the one belonging to the bank. It takes his key and one of ours to unlock the box inside the safe."

"So, you just left it there?" she asked incredulously.

"What else could we do with it, Mrs. Moran?" he pleaded.

It was back to "Mrs. Moran" as it always should have been, and Mrs. Moran never again tried to correct Ren's use of her proper title and name.

"I truly don't know, but it seems you did the best you could. What happens when you want to do something with the jade?" she asked.

"Mr. Forsythe is looking into it for us. He told us to go home and work on the docks for the next two weeks. He said he'd send for us when he had something to tell us," Ren answered.

The following morning, Tommy and Ren returned to the docks to sign on for the day. Ren's arm was usable and was out of its sling. The cuts on his face also had healed and he sported two scars that, instead of detracting from his already handsome face, actually complimented it. Tommy asked Ren to hold onto his key to their safe deposit box. The pocket in his pants had a hole and he didn't want to lose it. Ren took Tommy's key and wired it together with his own before he slipped both keys into his pocket.

As luck would have it, the boys were assigned together to unload one of the newly arrived ships from New York via Cape Horn. It was full of clothing for men and women, such as shoes, winter coats, and hats. There were containers full of fur coats worth hundreds of dollars each. Of course, the boys were hoping one of them would break so that they could get a fur coat for Mrs. Moran. No such luck!

At 11:30 in the morning, four burly men grabbed Tommy and Ren as they were working on the docks and identified themselves as relatives of Frankie Wilson. "So what," Ren smart-mouthed them. "We didn't know the guy."

"Oh, you knew him, all right," Frankie's brother, Billie, asserted, "and we know that it took the two of you to kill him."

"That's a damn lie," Tommy yelled. "Frankie brushed past me as I was on my way home with a beer for my mother. Ask anyone in the bar. They'll tell you the same thing."

Ren knew that they were in deep trouble, so he decided

to strike first. He hit Billie Wilson so hard in the nose with his strong right fist that everyone could hear the bone crack from the blow. Then he turned his wrath on the guy beside him. Tommy didn't fare so well. Frankie's cousin, Jimmy, pulled a large knife and stabbed Tommy in the heart. He was killed instantly. When the attackers saw what had happened, they fled as fast as their feet would carry them. Ren ran over to Tommy, but he could see that he was already dead. The big knife was buried in his chest and Ren was afraid to touch it. A feeble call for help was all that he could do. His whole life seemed to end that morning when Tommy died.

It was his fault, he reasoned. Tommy would be alive if he hadn't lost his temper and killed Frankie Wilson. When he told Mrs. Moran what happened, she screamed so loudly that neighbors who lived two houses away heard her. "What is it about first-born sons that makes the gods kill them so often?" she asked no one in particular. Ren tried to comfort her by telling her that it was his fault. His killing Frankie Wilson was the reason that Tommy was dead.

But Mrs. Moran wouldn't accept that reasoning. It was her fault for sending the two boys to the bar to get her a beer. It was her fault because it was Divine payback for her lust. Catholic guilt fueled her life's furnace from that day forward and she fed its flames with her self-blame.

The Wilson gang was arrested, tried, sentenced, and hanged for the murder of Tommy Moran. From arrest to hanging, it took just three weeks.

Ren moved out of the Moran home immediately and took a room with the O'Connors who lived two blocks away. A week after the funeral, Ren went to see Mrs. Moran. He offered her half of the money in the account that he and Tommy had saved, but she refused it. Instead, since he and her late son were partners, she asked that she receive a weekly maintenance stipend that would take care of the family's needs. Mrs. Moran said that she could get by on $7.00 a week. That sum approximated the combined weekly incomes that her son and Ren had been earning on the docks. Ren agreed. He also said that he would increase that amount as his ability to earn increased. He assured Mrs. Moran that she and her family would always be cared for. She touched his cheek and smiled at him. "You are a good son, Rennie Baxter," she said. Tears streamed down both of their faces.

That same day, Rennie went to see Mr. Forsythe at the bank. He had several things that he needed to discuss with him. "Ren, I'm so sorry for you. Tommy was your partner and friend. I know it must be difficult for you. How can I help?"

"Thank you, Mr. Forsythe," Ren began. "There are several things I want you to do for me. First, I need to change the name of our business."

"Certainly, we can remove the name Moran."

Interrupting, Ren said, "No, no. I want my name removed. I want Tommy's name to be with me always to remind me that, without him, I still would be nothing. Don't you see, Mr. Forsythe?" he almost pleaded.

"Indeed, I do see," Forsythe responded. "Your stock just rose another 100 points in my book, Rennie Baxter."

"His mother needs to see that he is still a part of the business, and I won't disappoint her. How could I, Mr. Forsythe? They took me in when I had nowhere to go. It was Tommy's idea that we become business partners. I'll always be in their debt," Ren explained.

"What else may I do for you?" Forsythe asked.

"I have to get off the docks. I'm a target there, but I can't do the kind of work you offered. Can you think of anything I might do until I get my business up and running?" he asked.

"Yes," he answered. "Get your business up and running. Work at it full time. You have enough money in the account to support yourself for several months – plus you have a secret source of money at your disposal."

That confused Ren. He didn't have any secrets. Mr. Forsythe knew them all. Sensing Ren's lack of understanding, Forsythe said, "The jade."

Ren nearly had forgotten the jade. Quizzically, he mouthed, "The jade?"

"Exactly, the jade," Forsythe chimed in. "I've found someone who will pay $25,000 for it right now, if you wanted to sell it. But, if you don't want to sell it, I can set you up with a line of credit for as much as $10,000 to start – as long as the jade stays inside the bank as collateral. Should you walk away with the bank's money, we'd drill holes in your safe deposit box and sell its contents to recover our loss. Either way, we all win," he smiled triumphantly.

"Mr. Forsythe, are you crazy? I'll be seventeen years old on Thursday of next week. I can't possibly have that much money at my disposal," Ren protested. "What about paying back the $10,000?" he asked, revealing that his protest had been thought through and cancelled immediately.

"We'll not worry about that today, Ren," he said. "But, believe me, I'll make it as painless as possible for you to pay back the money over time. We will charge you interest at the rate of two percent per year. You see that's how the bank makes money. I loan you money and you pay it all back plus interest."

"As for your having so much money at your tender age, get used to it. As of this moment, Ren, you really have $25,000 on deposit in this bank plus whatever you have in your savings account. I know you can do numbers in your head faster than anyone I've ever known. I know you are one very bright young man who isn't afraid of anybody or anything. You've proven that. You just happen to have walked into a bank that recognizes those virtues and is willing to nurture them," he emphasized.

"Thank you, Mr. Forsythe, for saying so. It means a lot to me to hear that from you," Ren answered. After an appropriate pause in the conversation, Ren started anew. "Mr. Forsythe, I need a better place to live that's closer to the bank and I need clothes. I don't have the faintest idea how to get either. Can you help me with these non-banking problems, too?" Ren asked.

"It would be my pleasure," Forsythe beamed. "But first," he continued, "you have papers to sign and lines of credit to establish. I assure you that the contracts you sign all favor the bank. But, unless you sign them, you have no liquid cash. Understand?" he asked.

"Yes, sir, I do understand," he answered.

CHAPTER TWO:
Worthless Ingrate Transformed

True to his word, Mr. Forsythe helped Ren find adequate quarters not far from the bank. A matronly woman named Lennox had a furnished duplex two blocks further up on Sacramento Street. It was small by family standards, but huge for one young man. He had two bedrooms, a tub and sink, a kitchen, and a small combination living and dining room. Rent was $8.00 per month, which included cleaning and, for an extra fifty cents, Mrs. Lennox would do his laundry.

Two short months ago, $8.50 was an astronomical sum that Ren would never have thought himself capable of earning in half a year. Now, he had to come up with that much each month plus $7.00 each week for Mrs. Moran and her family. But that was then. After paying Mrs. Lennox his first month's rent and laundry fee, he met Mr. Forsythe at Andrew's Clothing for Gentlemen.

Ren was noticeably nervous. He had never been in such a store. His mother either sewed something for him or she bought it at the dry goods store that was three blocks from their home. Looking like he did, Ren would not have gained entry into that elegant establishment if Mr. Forsythe had not been with him.

Mr. Forsythe bought all of his clothing at Andy's, as it affectionately was known. He asked for his favorite salesman and owner, Andy Kurdale. Andy was an affable man who knew clothing and how to put an outfit together. He greeted Mr. Forsythe warmly, but totally ignored Ren. "How may I serve you today, Mr. Forsythe?" he asked.

"Oh, I'm not the customer today, Andy. I want to introduce you to a colleague of mine, Mr. Rennie Baxter," he answered.

Andy Kurdale couldn't believe his ears or his eyes. Perhaps Mr. Forsythe was playing a joke on him. "Are you sure, sir, that this 'gentleman' belongs in here?" he asked curtly.

"Quite sure, Andy," he laughed. "I want you to make him look like the successful young businessman he already is."

"You will be paying the bill, I presume, Mr. Forsythe?" Andy asked.

"On the contrary, Andy. It will behoove you to begin all over again with Mr. Baxter. He'll be spending a lot of his money in this store – and I don't mean just today. Why, I predict he'll probably buy more clothes from you than I do," he answered.

Still unable to get beyond his eyes, Andy responded by softening his sarcasm to "How nice."

Ren put out his hand and said, "Glad to meet you, Andy," completely missing the just completed supercilious charade. Mr. Forsythe stayed for the full three hours that it took Ren to make selections and to be fitted. Half a dozen suits, shirts, matching ties, handkerchiefs, shoes, hosiery, and underwear began to collect for Ren to carry home. His total was $97.12! Ren was totally unprepared for the reckoning and looked to Mr. Forsythe for help. From inside his suit coat pocket, Mr. Forsythe produced a leather case that he opened. He removed a small rectangular paper and handed it to Ren. Ren had never seen a bank check before and, therefore, didn't know what it was that Mr. Forsythe had handed to him. "It's called a bank check, Ren. This particular check is tied directly to your new account at "First Frisco." It works like cash. Date it on the top line," he said as he handed a pen to Ren. "That's right. Now, write the name of the store, Andrew's Clothing for Gentlemen, on the next line. Good, good," he encouraged. "Now write the number $97.12 after the word Gentlemen," he instructed. Then he showed Ren how to write the same dollar and cents amount in wording on the next line. "Sign your full name on the last line at the bottom, hand it to Mr. Kurdale, and we're through here. Andy, please have these purchases delivered to Mr. Baxter's home. 1125 Sacramento Street. Thank you."

Mr. Forsythe insisted that one of the new suits was to be altered to fit Ren before they left the store that morning. When the fine wool, dark blue, double-breasted suit draped Ren's fine six-foot-one-inch frame, he left Andy's not as the lower-class youth who had entered, but as the most handsome, upwardly mobile young man in San Francisco. He was stunned by his own appearance in the big mirrors stationed around the store for just such a purpose. Even Andy Kurdale couldn't believe the transformation. The white shirt and gray tie made Ren's shock of red hair stand out as never before. He turned heads as he walked down the street with Mr. Forsythe. "Hungry?" was all that Mr. Forsythe asked.

"Starved," Ren responded.

"Good, we'll have lunch at my club. I want to introduce you to someone," Forsythe said.

"Your club?" Ren asked.

"Yes, Ren, my club and, hopefully, soon to be your club, too. It's a private place where gentlemen gather to play cards, smoke good cigars, drink great liquor, eat the best food in San Francisco, and conduct real business," he replied. "Think of this as your coming out luncheon," he continued.

After all that had happened so far, what was one more surprise? Ren couldn't get over how the new clothes felt. He had never worn anything that felt that good or was that soft against his skin. The shoes were unbelievably comfortable, so unlike his big clodhoppers. They were black and very shiny. He was so excited and taken with his new image that the three blocks from the haberdashery to the club seemed to fly by. In less than four months, how could he go from a worthless ingrate to an elegantly dressed, young gentleman who was worth thousands of dollars and who was about to eat in one of San Francisco's finest places with the president of "First Frisco?" Truly, it was beyond him.

Suddenly, for no apparent reason, Ren heard that nettlesome word again, "ingrate." He froze in his tracks, as if paralyzed by the thought of it. Mr. Forsythe thought that it was just fright at the imposing structure that was his club, but it wasn't. "Mr. Forsythe, do you know the meaning of the word 'ingrate'?" he asked.

"I do, Ren, but what makes you ask that question at this precise moment?" he answered.

"My dad used to call me 'a worthless ingrate' and I need to know what it means. I need to know right now before I can go in there," he responded.

"Ingrate, Rennie, means ungrateful. An ingrate is someone who, for whatever reason, is ungrateful, for whatever reason," he said. "That term could not possibly apply to you. Now, can we go inside? We have important work to do," he chided.

Ren would think about that later. Right now, he was hungry and excited.

Inside the club, Childs, the club's manager, greeted Gilbert Forsythe. "Good afternoon, Mr. Forsythe," he said. "And who might your handsome young guest be?" he asked.

"Childs, I want you to meet the brightest and, clearly, the most handsome young businessman to hit San Francisco in many years. This is Rennie Baxter. Rennie, this is Childs." Leaning toward Rennie's ear, Forsythe whispered loudly enough for all to hear, "Childs knows everything worth knowing. If you ever need to know anything, just ask him," Forsythe suggested.

"You're too kind, Mr. Forsythe," he responded. Then it was Childs' turn. He leaned into Ren's ear and used his own conspiratorial tone to add, "In case you ever need something, Mr. Baxter, I'd be only too happy to assist you."

"Thank you, Childs," Ren said, as though he had said the line all of his life. He was a natural. He was born for this role,

Forsythe thought. He warmed to its tasks easily and with a grace that far exceeded his years and background.

They left Childs and walked straight ahead into the club's main dining room. It was full of well-dressed men seated around tables dripping with food and drink. Not only were women excluded as members of the club, they were excluded entirely. All waiters. No waitresses.

Midway into the room, an alcove containing a table for four, but set for three, had one rather small-sized gentleman already seated there. His full head of hair was coal black, as were his eyes. His facial features were tiny, as were his hands. He appeared to be very breakable if handled roughly, but his demeanor quickly signaled that his strength lay elsewhere. Forsythe headed straight for that table. "Hello, Griffin," he began, "Please greet Rennie Baxter, the young man I've been telling you about. Rennie, please say hello to Mr. Griffin Hewes – about whom I've told you nothing."

Handshakes and greetings all around.

"Your description, Gilbert, left much to be desired. The young man is much more handsome than you thought he'd be after his clothing makeover. I hope his brain power also exceeds your feeble powers of observation," he said good-naturedly.

Ren didn't know what to say or do, but he knew that the next line was his, and he had better come up with a good one. "What can you expect, Mr. Hewes, from a banker? They're all alike – only out to protect their interest."

Hewes roared at the pun. This kid had class, as well as looks and brains. Continuing, Ren said, "You should see the papers he made me sign this morning just to get a measly $10,000 of my own money." Hewes folded over from laughter.

"Stop, stop, please, or I'll never be able to eat my lunch," Hewes ordered. "And speaking of lunch, Rennie," he continued, "the steaks here are the best in the world. I'd recommend one for lunch. How do you like yours done?" he asked.

"Almost raw," Ren replied. Gilbert Forsythe wrinkled up

his nose, but Griffin Hewes went into fits of uncontrollable laughter.

"A man after my own heart, Gil," Hewes finally was able to say. "That's the way we'll have them. Two nearly raw and one cooked till it turns to shoe leather." Then he laughed some more.

Hewes ordered for them all. Ren was quite taken by the little man. He was smaller than even his father, Lester, but something told Ren that he was a giant in business and industry. Ren turned down the wine that was offered and asked for water instead. Both of his hosts approved since they were moderate drinkers themselves. This was the first meal that Ren ever had eaten in a restaurant. He liked it. It suited him. His hosts recognized Ren's reactions as both fitting and commensurate with his limited exposure. This lad was going far and, if they had anything to do with the journey, Ren Baxter would be a real somebody – and soon.

When the waiter asked if the gentlemen wanted dessert, Ren spoke up before he realized it and asked if they made apple pie there. "Indeed, we do, sir," came back the answer.

"Good, 'cause I'd like a large slice, please," Ren ordered.

"Nothing for me," Hewes said. Forsythe also passed on the pie. "Ren," Hewes continued, "would you like some coffee with that pie? It's delicious, I assure you."

"Sorry, Mr. Hewes, but I've never had coffee, so I don't know what it tastes like," Ren answered in all honesty and without the slightest hint of embarrassment.

"Well, there's no time like the present to begin your coffee education, is there, Mr. Baxter?" Hewes responded. "Bring Mr. Baxter, here, a cup of coffee with that pie and put a large slice of Colby cheese on the top of it," Hewes ordered. Then he chanted, "After all, Mr. Baxter, apple pie without the cheese is like a hug without the squeeze."

The coffee took some getting used to. As soon as he finished his first cup, the waiter refilled it. The second one started to taste delicious to him. Eating apple pie with Colby cheese became the way he would eat it for the rest of his life.

"Let's go into the reading room, Ren, so we can talk. I have a few ideas I'd like you to consider," Hewes directed. The room was completely empty of members because Hewes had booked it for his exclusive use.

The three diners walked into the reading room and took comfortable chairs in a corner around a small table. Hewes began, "Ren, I know more about you than you know about yourself. I realize that sounds preposterous, but it's true. It's my business to know all about other people's business before I ever talk to them."

Interrupting, "Who told you about me? And just what do you know?" Ren blurted out with an edge in his voice.

Hewes laughed for a full ten seconds. He loved this kid. "It really doesn't matter who or what, Rennie. Let's just say I liked what I heard and discovered on my own. For example, I know your dad is a highly respected teamster at his uncle's dray and livery service. I also know he beat you when he was drunk. And, although you've never admitted it in words, you've told Mr. Forsythe, here, that you killed and robbed Frankie Wilson."

Rennie was on his feet and as angry as he had ever been. "You son of a bitch, Mr. Forsythe! You looked me straight in the eye and told me that you would never talk about anything I told you in confidence," he yelled. Hewes' laughter was uncontrollable.

Forsythe was stunned by the outburst. He raised his arms to protect his face from the blows that he imagined were coming his way. Regaining his composure and continuing as if nothing had happened, Hewes said, "So, Mr. Baxter, are you admitting to me that you did kill Frankie Wilson, rob him, and profit enormously from the contents of his pockets?"

"I ain't admitting nothing," Rennie said in a much calmer voice, but still full of piss and vinegar. "You can think what you want, but I couldn't have killed that asshole. He beat me so badly that I couldn't use my left arm for over two weeks. How could I have killed him? Besides, the coppers cleared me of any wrongdoing," he added triumphantly.

"I killed my first man when I was sixteen, Rennie. It wasn't a fair fight either. I used an iron stake that held down the tent of a visiting circus. Some big guy wanted to rob me of my circus money. He saw me as an easy target, so I ran and he chased. I tripped on a guy wire and landed near an extra tent stake lying on the ground. As he was reaching down to pick me up, I hit him in the head with that stake. When he fell, I drove the stake through his throat. Then I robbed him and ran like hell. I used his money to buy my first pushcart, which I used to haul my instruments for sharpening knives and axes. I still have the damn thing. I keep it in a shed behind my home and, every once in a while, I look at it to remind me of where I came from and how I got here."

Rennie could not believe his ears. "Then what happened?" he asked.

"Then I went on to make my first million dollars," he answered, "just like you're going to do. And, in the process, Gilbert and I will make more millions from your efforts."

Rennie was stunned. He asked where he could go to piss. He really had to use the restroom all of a sudden. The excitement and the coffee were working on his bladder. Forsythe also had to go and he told Ren to follow him. Standing at the side-by-side urinals in the men's room, Forsythe could not believe his eyes when he saw Ren produce his cock so he could piss. The size of it was unbelievable.

When they returned, Griffin Hewes had several sheets of paper turned toward Rennie and a gold-plated pen beside them. "This is a contract, Rennie. Actually, it's a real estate lease. I own the large empty shop on Columbus Avenue directly across the street from Chinatown. I want you to start your business in it. For the first six months, until you are able to buy what you need to get started, I'm charging you the mere sum of $15.00 per month as rent. By the end of your first six months, I'm doubling your rent. It will stay at that sum for the next full year. At the end of a year and a half, this lease will expire and we will have to re-negotiate a new lease primarily favorable to me, but not too unfavorable to you."

Ren knew a great deal when he heard one, but he thought he would try to get an even better one. He started to say something, but Hewes cut him off. "In case, Ren, you think you can negotiate with me, you can't on this first deal. Maybe when you have enough experience, I'll listen to you, but, right now, pick up the pen. Sign the lease to the finest opportunity that many young men in San Francisco would kill for. Write me a check for at least $15.00, unless you want to pay two months' rent today. Take this key and go see your new place of business."

Ren picked up the pen and signed the lease without reading a word of it. Gilbert Forsythe placed another check in front of him. He filled it out for $15.00 without any coaching. "I have to pay interest on the money I use, Mr. Hewes, so, if you don't mind, I'll pay you just one month's rent today."

Hewes smiled the biggest smile he could muster, extended his small hand across the table, shook Rennie's, and picked up the check made out to him for $15.00. "Nice to do business with you, Rennie Baxter," he said. "Now, go make your first million. I expect you to join me every Friday, right here, for lunch. Gilbert will join us. I expect questions. I don't want to hear anything about not being able to do this or that. I expect you to figure out how to get a sign made and how to buy merchandise. But I do expect financial questions. Got it?" he asked.

"Yes, sir," he answered. "Now, about today's lunch," Ren started to ask.

"Unless you're a member here, Rennie," Hewes cut him off, "your money isn't any good. I sign for everything I buy. At the end of the month, I'm presented with a bill that I pay on the spot. Learn how to pay your bills on the spot, Rennie, just as you've done twice today. It will place you in good standing with everyone who wants to do business with you. Now, if you will excuse us, Mr. Forsythe and I have some other business to discuss."

Ren stood and bowed to the two men as though he were in

Chinatown. They were so taken by his manners that they said nothing to each other as they watched Ren make his exit from the room. "Gilbert, take Rennie's rent money and put it in a separate account for me. I don't want anything else in that account. Just his rent money and any other money I may direct to you, okay?" he instructed. Forsythe took the money from Hewes. Then he told him what he had just seen in the men's room. Hewes didn't believe a word of it.

At the door, Childs asked Ren if he had enjoyed his visit and invited him to come back soon. Ren thanked Childs for his hospitality and assured him that he would love to return.

Ren was extremely anxious to see his new place of business. Dressed as he was, he knew that he should not run, so he walked as briskly as he could. Fifteen minutes later, he was standing in front of an old building that had a new lock on its front door. Ren inserted his key. The door opened into a dark expanse of indeterminate dimensions. A cobweb hit him in the face and he backed away to avoid getting his beautiful new clothes filthy. He would have to buy suitable work clothes, he thought, and cleaning supplies to get this place ready to open for business. But, he thought, was that the best use of his time and money? He stepped outside and locked the door.

By the time that Ren had walked back to the bank, Mr. Forsythe was in his office. Asking to see him for a few minutes, Ren was surprised to learn that he had several other clients ahead of him and he would have to wait. Then he remembered what Mr. Hewes had said just before he left the club. Figure things out for yourself. Ren made a stop at the table where the withdrawal slips were kept. He wrote his name at the top, his company name next, and the sum of $50.00 in the lower right-hand corner. He handed it to Mr. McLeod who glanced at it, stamped it, counted out the cash, and handed it through his cage bars to Ren. His smile was approving. "You look like a young man I used to know by the name of Baxter. Are you related to him?" Mr. McLeod asked.

Somewhat embarrassed, Rennie just smiled and asked, "Mr.

McLeod, do you know who cleans the bank? Is it possible for me to speak with that person?"

"We use Sweeney's Commercial Cleaning Service, several blocks down on Geary Street," he answered.

"Thank you, Mr. McLeod." Ren folded the money in half. Just as he started to put it in his front pants pocket, he wondered if his suit coat had an inside pocket like Mr. Forsythe's did. It did and he inserted the money into the pocket. It was then that his self-pride actualized. "A lazy worthless ingrate, my ass," he whispered only to himself.

At Sweeney's, Rennie was met at the front desk by a younger-looking female version of himself. She was a little redhead named Veronica. Her father, Michael Sweeney, owned the company. She went into a back room and told him that a very handsome young man wanted to see him. When Mr. Sweeney appeared, he wasn't quite sure how to address Rennie because he was too young to be dressed so nicely and wanting to do business with him. "May I help you, Mister …?" he asked, as his voice trailed off in search of a last name.

"Baxter. Rennie Baxter," Rennie answered politely. "I need to get a large building cleaned so I can open my business in it. You do clean large buildings?" he asked.

"That, we do," Sweeney replied. "How big a building and how dirty is it?" he wanted to know.

"I'm not real sure, Mr. Sweeney, but it's one of Mr. Hewes' buildings on Columbus Avenue, a block east of Chinatown," he answered. Sweeney knew the name Hewes. He cleaned lots of buildings owned by Mr. Hewes. "When I opened the front door a few minutes ago, there were so many cobwebs inside that I couldn't tell its real size. If it's convenient, would you walk over with me and take a look? I'll pay you half your fee on the spot, if it's reasonable, and the other half the instant you finish your work," he volunteered.

Sweeney picked up his walking cane, took Rennie by the elbow, and guided him out of his front door. On the walk over,

Rennie asked Mr. Sweeney if he knew any sign makers. "Indeed, I do. My brother Seamus works out of the back of my shop. He'll paint you up a fine sign and install it, too," he added. "Just print out what you want and he'll have it for you in two days."

Ren handed Mr. Sweeney his key and Sweeney opened the front door to the Moran Import Export Company. Sweeney used his walking cane to slash through the cobwebs that blocked their entrance into the room. The room had stood empty for several years and the previous tenants had not cleaned any part of the place before they left. It was filthy with piles of garbage rotted beyond stench in several spots in the middle of the floor. Sweeney paced off 35 big steps to the rear of the room at three feet per step. Then he paced off 45 steps from one side to the other. Confessing that he would have to wait until they got back to his shop before he could figure out just how big the room was, he was impressed when Ren told him the room was 105 feet deep by 135 feet wide. "How do you determine the price, Mr. Sweeney?" he asked.

"By square feet," he answered. "I charge half a cent a square foot to clean normal dirt, but, for this place, I'll need extra supplies, rags, and help. I couldn't possibly do it for less than a full cent a square, Mr. Baxter," he lied.

Ren thought out loud for a few seconds and announced to Sweeney's amazement that the room was 14,175 square feet in total size. At one cent a square, it would cost him $147.18 to get it cleaned. "Mr. Sweeney, I know this place is filthy. However, could you see your way clear to do it for three-fourths of a cent per square foot if I include the promise of an exclusive contract to clean it weekly thereafter?" he asked and quickly added, "At three-fourths of a cent per square foot, that total would be $106.25."

Mr. Sweeney realized that he was dealing with an extraordinary young man. Even at three-fourths of a cent per square foot, he would still make $50.00 in clear profit. "If you'll pay me $50.00 right now and $56.25 when we're done in two days, you have a deal, Mr. Baxter."

Ren reached into his suit coat pocket, extracted the $50.00

that he had withdrawn from the account that he and Tommy had created for this very purpose, and started to hand it to a surprised Mr. Sweeney. But, just before Sweeney could take the money, Ren pulled it back and said, "I'll need a receipt, Mr. Sweeney, and a signed agreement from you stating what you will do and what my balance is when you do it. Let's walk back to your shop and finish our business there, okay?" Ren asked.

"Sure, sure thing, Mr. Baxter. Whatever you say," he answered while being quite surprised by Ren's business acumen.

Sweeney's cleaning staff was made up exclusively of Chinese women. He picked six of his best workers to clean the Moran Import Export Company. They worked from sunup until sundown and finished the job in one day, not two. Sweeney increased his margin of profit by $12.00 as a result. And, true to his word, Ren made arrangements to have Mr. Sweeney walk through his new shop for an inspection before he paid the $56.25 balance. Sweeney's cleaners had been perfect in their efforts. Everything was sparkling. The front windows of the store had been painted black when Ren took possession. Today, they were clear, letting in the needed sunlight.

Ren had withdrawn another $60.00 from the account established by Tommy and him. When he handed it to Mr. Sweeney, he insisted that he wanted no change. Mr. Sweeney had given him a gift and he said so. If he had tried to clean the place himself, it would have taken him two or three weeks. Even then, it would not have been as clean as Sweeney's crew had made it. Michael Sweeney was overwhelmed. In all of his years in business, no one had ever said thank you monetarily to him. What a gentleman, he thought.

On the following day, Michael Sweeney's brother installed the large sign that he had painted that read "Moran Import Export Company". He charged Rennie $8.00. Ren paid him $8.50 and asked him if he knew any good carpenters. Indeed, he did. His wife's brother, Joey Schmitt, was the best carpenter in San Francisco, he bragged. Ren asked Seamus if he would have Joey meet him at the store on the next day.

Rennie had a clean place that was clearly identified, but he had no merchandise to sell and no idea of how to display it once he had it. He walked to Mr. Wang's establishment once more. At first, Mr. Wang did not recognize Ren. It had been several weeks since he saw him and the young man in front of him was dressed too nicely to be Ren Baxter. The two bowed and Ren asked Mr. Wang if he recognized him. Mr. Wang put on his glasses and exclaimed, "Mr. Baxter. You look so different, so rich. What happened to you?"

Ren told Mr. Wang about Tommy's death, but he already knew. "So sad," he said. "He was such a good boy. His mother will miss him, I know, as will you, Mr. Baxter," he added. "How may I be of service to you today?" he asked.

"Mr. Wang," he began, "I've had some very good luck recently. I've rented a store about two or three blocks from here. It's a block across the street from Chinatown. Since I couldn't get in here, I decided to get as close to here as possible. I need to buy merchandise. I'm asking you to sell me some of yours and to direct me elsewhere to buy from other merchants. Do you still have the two vases Tommy and I brought to you months ago?" he asked.

"Just one," he said. "I sold the other one the day after you brought it to me. I think the buyers said they were visitors from Boston. They paid full price," he added gleefully. Then, as an afterthought, Mr. Wang said, "The young man bore a striking resemblance to you, Rennie." Curious, Ren thought, as he handed Mr. Wang $6.00 for the purchase of the remaining vase. Mr. Wang refused the money, but handed Ren his vase.

"Good luck, Mr. Baxter. Please accept this as a small gift. I could not take your money for this item," he said graciously. "But I do have all of these other items for you to buy at a very reasonable price."

Ren purchased $145 worth of items. Mr. Wang said that he would have them delivered at a convenient time during the next afternoon. He also told Ren to visit his Uncle Chow's establishment, which was two blocks down. He handled jewelry and weapons.

At Chow's store, Ren was introduced to items far more beautiful and far more dangerous than he had ever seen before. He bought large and small knives with inlaid pearl handles. Uncle Chow showed Ren how to keep a small dagger inside his shirtsleeve, and how to produce it to use in a flash. Ren bought the dagger and put it inside his sleeve on the spot. He carried that small dagger until the day that he died and it was buried with him. He bought boxes of finely crafted jade jewelry. His bill at Chow's climbed to $268.94. Chow would deliver it all to Ren's store on the next day.

As he was leaving Chow's establishment, a silver eagle money clip caught his eye. It was mixed in with other items in a case next to the door. Ren noted its existence, but he kept on walking. The damn thing was haunting him.

Ren had had a long day. He was tired and hungry when he passed Mr. Wang's store on his way out of Chinatown. Mr. Wang was about to close his doors when Ren again stopped in for just a short moment. "Mr. Wang, I've never eaten in Chinatown. Would you accompany me as my guest to one of its restaurants?" he offered.

"One moment, Mr. Baxter. I must tell my wife where I am going," he answered.

Ren could hear Mr. and Mrs. Wang chattering away in Chinese for what seemed like ages, but it was only two minutes in reality. Mr. Wang emerged smiling and announced that he would be only too happy to accompany Mr. Baxter to dinner. It was a first for them both. They walked several blocks and climbed a flight of stairs to the Green Dragon, which was owned by Mr. Wang's brother. At first, their conversation was brittle. In this social setting, neither man knew how to talk to the other. Mr. Wang ordered for them both. The food was delicious, – shrimp and chicken and beef and pork and so many vegetables and rice, of course. The tea was hot and replenished often. Ren was surprised at what he had missed all of his life. With every delectable bite, he emitted an um and an ah and an umm and an aah as each morsel pleased his tongue. Mr. Wang enjoyed Ren enjoying his food more than he enjoyed his own.

Ren noticed a particularly beautiful Chinese woman, at least three years his senior, who was seated two tables away from them. She kept smiling at him while he was eating his dinner. Finally he asked Mr. Wang who she was and why she smiled at him so much. Mr. Wang told him not to look at her. She was a prostitute. "A prostitute?" Ren wanted to know.

"You know, a whore," he replied. "A woman who sells herself to any man who has the money she requires. She probably uses opium. That is why she will do anything a man wants her to do to please him."

"You don't approve of her, I take it, Mr. Wang."

"Not for me, I don't. But, Mr. Baxter, I remember what it was like to be a younger man with no wife. If you would like, I can arrange for you to meet her when I leave. She will give you much pleasure," he said matter-of-factly. "Just be careful," he warned. "Sometimes the men who use prostitutes get beaten and robbed."

That was all Ren had to hear. Beaten and robbed were enough to squelch any desire he might have felt. He said he would have to learn more about such women and find ways to protect himself against those kinds of danger. Mr. Wang approved and they left the restaurant together. Ren walked the twelve blocks to his home and dreamed of the beautiful Chinese woman who would do anything he asked if he paid her.

In the morning, Ren put on yet another new suit. He matched his shirt, tie, hosiery, and shoes to it as Mr. Kurdale had instructed. Today's ensemble was a dark brown single-breasted suit, white shirt and collar, tan tie, and dark brown shoes. He was born to dress like this. He made the clothes look good, so handsome was he. The last item was the small dagger that he tucked inside his shirtsleeve, just as Uncle Chow had taught him. Out of a poppy-cock need to strut, Ren decided to visit "Andy's" where he asked to see Mr. Kurdale. This time, when Andy saw Rennie Baxter, he treated him exactly as he had treated Mr. Forsythe when the two of them had entered the store for the first time. "Mr. Baxter," he began. "What a pleasure to see you again. How may I serve you today?" he asked.

"I wanted to make sure I'm wearing the brown suit with all the right stuff, Andy. Am I?" he asked.

"Perfectly," came his admiring reply. "Mr. Forsythe was right. You are probably the most handsome young man in all of San Francisco, if you don't mind my saying so, Mr. Baxter," he cooed.

"Good," Ren replied. "Andy, I want you to find at least half a dozen other outfits you think will look good on me. Fit them with shirts, shoes, and ties. You know what I need. Have them ready for me to look at just before you close today. And tell me how I can get them all cleaned when I need to," he said as he was making his exit.

"Thank you, Mr. Baxter," he said. "I'll have everything ready for you by five o'clock."

Ren knew that Andy would be true to his word and, as a result, he walked a few inches above the pavement on his way to the bank. This morning, he wasn't made to wait to see Mr. Forsythe. Forsythe was expecting him. Ren's printed checks with his name on them had arrived from the printers. Forsythe wanted to show him how to enter each check on a record stub in order to keep an accurate balance. Ren was fascinated by the system. The few extra pen strokes made it simple for him to know how much money he had at any one time, and where he had spent each sum entered. But it surprised him when he saw just how much money he had spent out of his initial $10,000. He had drawn down his savings account to practically nothing. All of a sudden, he began to have a panic attack. All outgo and no income. Forsythe saw his look of distress and reassured him that it would get far worse before it began to turn around. If he thought that would cheer Ren, it didn't. "The trick, Ren, is to take the long view of things," he comforted.

"The long view?" he asked.

"Of course. In order to make money, you have to spend money. Never forget that or you will become timid, and timidity never carries the day," he offered. "Already you have established a fine business reputation with Mr. Sweeny and his brother. They have many contacts. I'm sure they will recommend you to people they know. It's called doing business with people who do business with you. Customers will eventually pour into your store as a result of the fine beginning you've made with them. Also, in Chinatown, you are becoming known. That takes money, time, effort, and brains, which you have in abundance. After all is said and done, you have a patron who will do all he can to encourage his associates to deal with you," he ended.

Ren wanted to ask about the word "patron" – but he didn't have to. Forsythe said, "Mr. Hewes, Ren. I've never seen him take such an interest in anyone other than himself and we've been brothers-in-law for more than twenty years," he volunteered. "Spend whatever amount you need to spend to get your business in first-class order. Customers will begin to flock to your establishment. Your biggest problem will be finding a steady supply of merchandise, believe me," he instructed. "Before you go to work, I have something for you," he said. Forsythe removed two items from his desk drawer. The first one was a gold-plated pen, just like the one he used at the club to sign his lease. The other one was a calfskin leather wallet. Ren was moved by Forsythe's generosity. "A little token," he said, "of the esteem and admiration I have for you, Ren. I hope you wear them both out in less than a year."

He had to get out of there, and fast. Great kindness and encouraging words were not items he knew how to handle with any degree of ease or comfort. He shook Mr. Forsythe's hand and mumbled something about meeting a carpenter at his store in five minutes. Before he left, he told Mr. Forsythe that he saw Frankie Wilson's silver eagle money clip at Uncle Chow's the day before and, in a triumphant tone of voice, said it had been marked up to $95.00!

Joey Schmitt, Seamus Sweeney's brother-in-law, was sitting on the curb waiting for Ren to get there. "You must be Mr. Baxter," he offered, as he stood up to greet the younger man.

"Ren, will do. You've got to be Joey, the best carpenter in San Francisco, I'm told," he responded. "I want you to make a store for me, Joey," he said, as he unlocked the door. "I don't want my merchandise to be scattered all over the place as it is in most of the Chinese stores just across the street. I want it to be divided into sections so people needing jewelry can go to the jewelry counter and people wanting vases can find them in the vase section. Understand what I mean, Joey?" he asked.

"Sure," he replied, "but you got to tell me how many and how big before I can section off each area. You want an office in this place? If you do, how big? Some guys like great big offices like they're bank presidents or something. Others want something big enough for only a desk and a few chairs. Any idea for yourself, Ren?" he asked.

"My office doesn't need to be big, Joey," he said. "You can divide this front area about here," Ren instructed as he pointed at imaginary boundaries, "and stop it about here. Make the section for the vases very large and put it next to that wall. I'd like this area, from here to there, for the display cases for the most special items. Put my office in the back, please. The rest can be split into four equal sections. Make certain that the aisles are wide. I don't want to be so crowded by merchandise that people stumble around and break things. I'd like to be able to refill the sections each day with new stuff, so nothing looks like it's been here forever. Know what I mean?" he asked. "Oh, yes," he quickly added, "and build a display area for the window. Make it easy to get into that display because I need to change the merchandise every week."

"I'm getting the idea," he replied. From his toolbox, Joey

produced a tablet of paper with small squares on it. Quickly, he sketched out the room's dimensions and began to draw walls and room separators and counter space. Ren was amazed at how quickly his store began to take shape. He made a few suggestions that enlarged several spaces that he labeled jewelry and weaponry. In half an hour, the two men had completely designed a functioning store. Ren wanted to know how much everything was going to cost him, but that was a figure that Joey couldn't give him at that time. The cost of lumber had just risen significantly and he needed to find out its new price before he could give an accurate sum. Ren wanted to know when the final charge could be determined. "A couple of days, I imagine," Joey replied.

"Not good enough, Joey. If you want my business, you'll have to do better than that," he admonished.

"What's wrong with a couple of days?" Joey wanted to know.

"I'm not willing to wait and I'm the one who's paying real money," Ren said, with an edge of irritation in his voice.

Joey realized he had made a mistake, but, fortunately, it could be fixed. "Okay, okay, I'm getting the idea, Ren. Here's my problem. I need some cash from you so that I can buy the lumber. I don't have enough money to buy everything that I need for your job. After selecting the lumber and learning its price, I can tell you the cost of the entire job. Know what I mean?" he asked.

Remembering Mr. Forsythe's words just hours before about spending money to make money, Ren offered to pay Joey whatever amount he needed in the next two hours if he just would tell him the total by then. Ren wanted Joey to get started before the day was over. "Do you have any particular lumberyard where you want me to buy the stuff, Ren?" he asked.

"I don't know any lumberyards, Joey. Name some for me," he directed.

"Well, there's Morton's, just off the plank road, and Hewes ...'"

Interrupting Joey in mid-sentence, he asked, "Hewes? Griffin

Hewes owns a lumberyard?"

"Yeah, Griffin Hewes. He owns a lot more than a lumberyard. You know him?" he asked.

"I'm having lunch with him in a few minutes," he answered. "By all means, buy everything you can from the Hewes lumberyard. I'll meet you there at 2:30. Have everything you need assembled and ready to go. I'll write them a check on the spot."

"You got it, Ren." And he was out of the door.

Childs greeted Ren as graciously as he had the first time. "Mr. Hewes is expecting you, Mr. Baxter. Mr. Forsythe has taken ill and has gone home for the day," he said. Strange, Ren thought. Forsythe didn't seem sick when he saw him earlier that morning.

"Rennie," Hewes enthused. "How nice to see you again. How are things going at the store?" he wanted to know.

"I'm pleased, Mr. Hewes," he replied. "But I'm sure you already know all about my efforts to open," he smiled. Hewes just smiled back and gave a little knowing nod of the head.

"Did you enjoy your dinner with Mr. Wang in Chinatown?" he wanted to know.

That did surprise Ren. "How did you know about my dinner in Chinatown, Mr. Hewes? You're not spying on me, are you?" he asked somewhat impertinently.

"Do you remember last Friday, Ren, when I told you it was my business to know about the people I deal with?" he asked. Continuing, "Well, the beautiful, young Chinese woman seated at the table next to you works for me. By sheer coincidence, you ate your dinner in the same place where she enjoyed her own. She told me you were the most handsome man she'd ever seen and she couldn't take her eyes off you. I was just lucky, that's all," he said.

"Mr. Wang thought she was a prostitute," Ren added.

"She is," Hewes replied.

That confused Ren. How could a prostitute work for Mr. Hewes? Hewes let it ride. "Hungry, Ren?" he asked.

"You know I am, Mr. Hewes. I've been looking forward to today all week," he added.

Hewes smiled.

"So have I, Ren, so have I," he replied. "How about trying the lamb chops today," he suggested.

"You know, I've never eaten lamb chops before, but I'm willing to try them," he replied.

Hewes ordered for both of them. Silence descended over the table for the next fifteen minutes while each man enjoyed every bite. Coffee, apple pie with cheese, and a good cigar followed the meal. Hewes handed Ren his first cigar and gave him ample instructions on how to smoke it. Ren was resistant to trying the cigar, but Hewes assured him that the experience would be both pleasant and agreeable. The youngster smoked that cigar like he had been smoking them since he was twelve. Hewes' steel-trap mind recorded every movement, every look, and every new discovery Ren Baxter made. He was an apt pupil, and Hewes was a master teacher.

"Whether you like it or not, Mr. Hewes, I'm actually paying for lunch today," he began.

"Impossible," he replied. Hewes was caught somewhat off guard by Ren's revelation.

"Not so, sir. I sent my carpenter, Joey Schmitt, over to your lumberyard to buy all the lumber I need to section off my store and to build display cases. You stand to make enough profit from that sale alone to pay for our lunch," he added triumphantly.

"Well, I'll be damned," Hewes stammered.

"Probably" was Ren's one-word answer. Hewes realized the real humor in Ren's response and laughed so hard that he began to choke. Ren moved to help him, but he waved him off and recovered quite nicely.

"You really know how to manipulate things around, don't you, Ren?" he asked.

"Mr. Hewes, I do believe you are complimenting me and I'm just not used to it," he laughed, which sent Hewes into more fits of laughter. "But I do have a number of questions for you. First, I know how to do numbers in my head to solve most mathematical questions, but I don't have any system where I can keep a list of the items I've bought. Also, how much should I charge for something I bought for, say, one dollar?"

Hewes smiled at the simple problems every beginner faces. "A set of books, Ren. You need a set of books. I'll send one of my bookkeepers over to your store tomorrow. He'll bring a new set with him. He'll help you reconstruct everything you've spent so far and he'll lay it out in categories. That way, you'll know your true costs. You'll also know whether or not you are making a profit. Do you remember the two vases you and Tommy sold to Mr. Wang your first day on the docks?" he asked.

"Yes, sir, I do. In fact, Mr. Wang gave me the remaining unsold one he had in his store," he replied. "I don't want to sell that one, Mr. Hewes. I want to keep it in memory of Tommy, so I put it in my safe deposit box."

"I heard that," Hewes tossed off. "Well, let's run the numbers and see what his mark-up was."

"He bought both vases from us for $1.75," Ren began. "He marked them up to $6.00 for one or $11.00 for two. Had he sold them separately, he'd have made $10.25 profit. That's nearly a 500% mark up. But he didn't get that. Instead he got about a 250% return on his one $6.00 sale because he gave the unsold vase to me. By making it a gift, he lost all that additional profit, but he still made money."

"Correct," Hewes responded. "So, the question becomes, how do you value your goods that are for sale in your establishment?"

"By marking them up at least 500%?" Ren answered hesitantly with a question mark in his voice.

"At least!" Hewes replied. "Some items you'll want to mark up even higher since customers will want to dicker over the price. Especially jewelry. If you mark something $12.00 for which you paid $1.75, and you sell it for $10.25 to a happy customer who thinks he got a great bargain, everyone wins. If you sold the same item for $3.50, how much money would you have made?" he asked rhetorically. "Only 100%," he answered his own question. "Is 100% a good margin to make on an item? You bet your sweet ass it is, my boy. You bet your sweet ass," Hewes said enthusiastically. "What else you got for me today?" he asked.

"How much does it cost to join this club, Mr. Hewes?" he wanted to know.

Hewes couldn't control himself. He found this kid hysterically funny. "Save your money, boy. I'll leave word with Childs that you are my guest anytime you appear. Just sign for whatever you buy. Maybe we'll settle up someday. Right now, you can't afford a membership. Maybe next year. We'll see," Hewes answered.

More generosity. "Mr. Hewes, how come you're doing this for me?" Ren wanted to know.

Without hesitation, Hewes replied, "I can't live forever, Ren. Who's going to take my place when I'm gone? I control so much of what happens in San Francisco that it's unbelievable," he revealed in an entirely uncharacteristic way. "I think you'll be able to step in when I'm gone. That's why," he answered. "Now, get out of here. You have to meet your carpenter at 2:30, if my memory serves me right."

What really was it that Griffin Hewes had said to him? Ren had to think about that one.

As soon as Ren left the room, Hewes was on his feet and out of a side door where his carriage was waiting. His driver flicked the horses' ears and they took off at a considerable trot. Hewes owned the Hewes Building several blocks away. As soon as he reached its front desk, he whispered something into the ear of one of his messengers who flew out of the door to the Hewes Lumberyard. He found the foreman and told him what Mr. Hewes wanted him to do. He nodded to signify that he understood and the messenger returned to the home office.

When Ren arrived at the lumberyard, the foreman, Dudley

Moxham, met him. Joey already had shown his sketches to him and asked Mr. Moxham to figure out a bill for the materials needed. Moxham made a few suggestions in the design and Joey realized how much they improved the work. Moxham invited the two men into his office where he began to figure out the bill. "That comes to a grand total of $43.56, Joey," Moxham said.

Joey scratched his head at the number and said, "Are you sure of your numbers, Mr. Moxham? I've bought lumber here before and you were always much higher than that."

"Well, let's see," Mr. Moxham said. He figured it out a second time. "Damned if you ain't right, Joey. I was off by 40 cents. It's only $43.16. Sorry about that. Believe me, it wasn't on purpose," he feigned. "I'll have everything sent right over so you can get started today." Ren wrote the check for $43.16 and handed it to Mr. Moxham.

Joey left the yard with Ren. He wondered why the bill wasn't twice that amount. Hewes was known for his high prices, but this was nearly a giveaway, he reasoned out loud. Then it struck Ren. His patron, Mr. Hewes, must have sent someone to the yard before he got there and had given instructions on what to charge. This was starting to get interesting.

It took four days for Joey to outfit the store. It took another three days for him to finish and paint everything. He hired two helpers, one of whom was an excellent glasscutter. Joey designed several glass cases for jewelry and weapons that were larger than any he had ever seen. He thought they displayed the merchandise better. While they were working, Ren was buying, buying, buying. He was a blur of perpetual motion. Once he saw a youngster that he thought he remembered from the docks. The boy had several pieces under his arms and was heading into Chinatown. He called to him and asked if he would show him what he had. At first, the kid thought that he had not heard right, but Ren was persistent. Finally he wandered over to Ren's store. He had two figurines of horses. They were so realistic that Ren could not believe that any person could make such lovely pieces out of stone. He looked at them for a full five minutes. The kid was getting nervous. At last, Ren said, "$1.25." The youngster just looked at him as though he were crazy. "My dad told me never to come home again if I didn't get at least $2.50 for them," he offered.

"Maybe I could give you $1.50," Ren said, "but I'll never be able to sell them for much more than that."

Back and forth, forth and back it went for a few minutes. When the kid had Ren up to $2.00, he said, "Sold." The kid smiled inwardly. He knew that he had gotten more than either he or his father thought that they would get for the horses. As Ren handed the $2.00 to the youngster, he told him that he did a good job in bargaining. "What's your name?" Ren asked.

"Bobby Green," the boy answered.

He had acquitted himself well with Ren who said to him, "Here's the fifty cents you're short. I wouldn't want you to get into any trouble with your dad. I know what that feels like."

Bobby took the money and smiled. "Thanks, Mister." he said.

"Tell your friends to send their stuff to me," Ren said. "I won't give any of them what I gave you, but you can tell them that I'm an easy guy to deal with. Tell them that they'll probably get more for their stuff from me than they will in Chinatown."

"I will," Bobby said.

As he turned to leave the store, Ren had an idea. "Bobby," he called. "On your way home, how would you like to deliver an envelope for me?" he asked. "I'll pay you an extra fifteen cents if you do," he added.

"Okay," he answered enthusiastically. Ren took paper and pen, and wrote:

Dear Mrs. Moran,

Would you please bring all of the children to the Moran Import Export Company on Columbus Avenue, across from Chinatown, this Sunday morning after

9:00 a.m. Mass? I'd like you and them to see what Tommy and I dreamed of doing. If he hadn't invited me home to meet you and without your generosity in taking me in, none of this would ever be. I'll be forever in debt to both of you.

Sincerely,
Ren Baxter

Ren folded the letter in half, put it inside the envelope, and wrote the address on it. Bobby knew exactly where the Morans lived. He lived in the next block over from them and played with several of the younger kids. When Bobbie left, Ren marked up the two horses to $7.50 each or two for $13.00.

Within days, the flow of goods into Ren's store began to clutter it terribly. It ruined his idea of display. He couldn't wait until Friday to see Mr. Hewes. This problem was too big to wait that long.

He went to the club that day for lunch and Mr. Hewes was very glad to see him. As usual, he was sitting in the same alcove reading what looked like a number of reports, but he hadn't ordered yet. Also, as before, Hewes ordered for the two of them. After desert and cigars, Hewes sensed Ren needed his advice about something. "Well, out with it, boy, out with it. Don't keep me in suspense a moment longer," Hewes commanded.

"I've run out of space already, Mr. Hewes," he began. "Do you have any storage space that I might rent that's close to my shop?"

Hewes loved this kid. Out of space already. What a problem to have, he thought. "Of course, I have space, Ren. And, if I didn't, I'd build it for you," he offered. "Have you been upstairs over your shop?" he asked. "No, of course not. How would you get there?" he asked and silently answered his own question. Hewes continued, "I'll send someone over tomorrow. He'll take you up the wide outside stairs at the back of the building. The room upstairs is a copy of the one downstairs, so you already know exactly how much space is there. It needs to be cleaned up, as well. Because it's just storage, I'll charge you only $5.00 a month rent for it. Fair enough?" he asked.

"Yes, sir. Fair enough," Ren answered. "Mr. Hewes, did you reduce the price I paid for lumber last Friday when I told you I was buying it at your lumberyard?" he asked.

"Me, reduce a price? You've got to be kidding!" Hewes offered. Not only had he reduced the price, he also had deposited the check into his special rent account. "How did the bookkeeper work out the other day?" he asked.

"Thank you, Mr. Hewes. I was going to mention that next. Dalton used a simple line-entry system. One side was for expenses and the other was for income. At a glance, I can see where I stand financially. In another section, he created an inventory system. I enter each item purchased along with its price. As the items sell, he instructed me to scratch a single light line through it and enter the sale price beside it. I've invited Mrs. Moran and her children to the store this Sunday morning after Mass. I'm going to ask her to do my bookkeeping for me. I'm also going to hire several of the Moran kids to clean the upstairs storage area, deliver some items, and act as messengers as I need them," he replied.

Hewes had to turn his face to the side so Ren couldn't see that his eyes had begun to collect tears. Not only was the boy handsome and bright, but he also was generous to a fault. "Would you mind if I dropped by on Sunday, Ren? I'd like to meet the Moran family," he asked.

"Would you, Mr. Hewes?" he asked. "I'd like you to meet them. You'll understand why I named the business Moran Import Export Company. I took my name off the title because I wanted Mrs. Moran to know that without Tommy and without her, the name Baxter would be a blank, just as it is on the sign."

With that, Hewes had to excuse himself from the table. By the time that he reached the stall in the men's room, he was sobbing openly.

Chapter Two: Worthless Ingrate Transformed

Sunday morning, close to 10:45, Mrs. Moran and her eleven children entered the Moran Import Export Company. On purpose, Ren had not put on a tie and coat, but he did wear a nice pair of trousers and an open shirt. He looked grand to all of the Morans. They couldn't believe the sign over the door and asked where the name Baxter was. Only Mrs. Moran understood his answer. He told them to go everywhere and see what he had to offer. He had stopped at a local bakery that morning and had purchased sweet rolls and other treats for them. Mr. Hewes arrived when nearly all of the treats had been eaten. He recorded yet another thoughtful gesture that Ren had executed. The visit from Mr. Hewes was very short. He simply greeted Mrs. Moran, told her what a fine young man Ren was, and let her know that he appreciated what the Moran family meant to the young man. After giving all of the children new nickels, he left as quickly as he appeared.

"You've done well, Ren," Mrs. Moran began. "Better than I ever imagined. You are so good at this," she offered, "and to us, as well. I appreciate the $3.00 weekly raise."

"Thank you, Mrs. Moran. I couldn't have done any of this if it hadn't been for Tommy and you," he said. "But I didn't ask you to come down here just to see the place. I want to hire all of you to work here. I want you to be my bookkeeper. You've been your family's banker forever, so I figured I could use your abilities to keep my books. I want the children to carry packages, run errands, deliver messages, and anything else I can think of," he said. "In addition to the money that I send to you every week, I'll pay good wages to you and to them. What do you say?" he asked enthusiastically.

Mrs. Moran declined his offer for herself, but she said that Peter and Nathan, her next two oldest boys, could work for him. Ren thanked her for that and soon the visit was over. Ren did ask Peter and Nathan to stay behind when the family started its walk home. He explained what he wanted and asked if they were interested. Both said yes and promised to be back in the morning.

Ren watched the boys run to catch up with the others. He

began to wonder what was going on in his own family. He realized that he missed them. He wondered if he ever would see them again. Maybe he could send a note to his mother.

Those thoughts were interrupted when the beautiful Chinese lady from the Green Dragon entered Moran's. He recognized her instantly. He had dreams about her and pleasured himself while thinking about her and what she could do for him. He bowed to her as she came closer to him. She bowed to him and smiled all the while. "Good morning, Mr. Baxter," she said in perfect English. "My name is Lian Sheng. Mr. Hewes asked me to see you today." She paused in her presentation to let that register. "He suggested that you close your shop and accompany me to my apartment nearby."

There was the name "Hewes" again. This beautiful woman worked for Mr. Hewes. He had sent her to him. Mr. Wang thought she was a prostitute who would do anything to please a man if he paid her. "I've been warned that I could be in danger of being beaten and robbed if I visit you," he began.

"Mr. Wang was correct to warn you, but, in my case, there is no need for alarm. Should anything ever happen to you while you are in my company, Mr. Hewes would avenge the incident 100 fold. He is a most powerful person. He wants me to please you today and that is what I intend to do," she said. "Can you find your way back to the Green Dragon?" she asked.

"Yes," he answered.

"Good," she replied. "It would not look good if we walked there together, so I will leave now. In ten minutes, walk to the Green Dragon, pass it, and count three buildings on the same side of the street. At the third building, go up the outside stairs. I will open the door myself when you knock. I assure you I will be the only person there."

She exited as gracefully as she had arrived. The ten minutes passed very slowly for Ren, but pass, it did. He followed her instructions to the letter. The beautiful furnishings and exotic scents inside her apartment overwhelmed Ren. She had large, wonderfully painted folding screens like the ones he had seen on the first day that he and Tommy Moran had gone to see Mr. Wang. The screens stood in front of the entrance to what appeared to be a dining room. Lian Sheng poured him a cup of tea and invited him to sit down on her luxurious couch. Although he didn't know how to proceed, he figured that he didn't have to. Lian would lead him through everything one step at a time.

"Ren, have you ever been with a woman?" she asked.

"Just once," he answered truthfully. "But it all happened so quickly and it was dark and I don't remember much about it," he lied.

"No matter," she replied. "I will guide you. Would you like to get started?" she asked.

"Yes," he said.

"Follow me, please," she requested.

They walked through a doorway that had beads hanging from lintel to floor. It was Lian's bedroom where she ruled. She asked him to sit on the edge of the bed so that she could be as tall as he. He complied. Very gently, at first, she took his head in her delicate hands and drew his mouth to hers. It was the first kiss from a woman that he had ever received. It was wonderful. She lingered. He began to have problems in his pants. When she reached down to help him liberate his cock, she could not believe what she was feeling. She let him go and asked him to undress. There it was in all its glory, sticking straight out. Lian slipped out of her garments. She wasn't certain if she could accommodate the monster, but she was willing to try. She pushed back his foreskin. To his surprise, Lian put it in her mouth and began to suck on it. It didn't take long before Ren realized that he was getting close, so he told her. She told him to enjoy it and to come in her mouth whenever he was ready. That stopped him cold, but it was feeling too good for him to care. Then it happened. He discharged his cannon while she sucked and stroked with both hands. Ren nearly lost his balance, but she steadied him with his own cock. Lian nearly choked on the load. It was more than she had ever received before. She spit out what she hadn't been forced to swallow and gently guided Ren to lie beside her on top of the great bed.

"Did you like that?" she asked.

"It was great," he replied. After several minutes, he started to soften and to reduce in size. She had never been with a man who, even at his hardest, was as large as Ren, after his reduction. She excused herself and told Ren to rest awhile. He fell asleep. When she came back to Ren, nearly an hour had passed. In her hand, she had a glass vial with some golden liquid in it. It was a slippery scented oil. As she poured some in her hands, she began to rub it all over Ren's cock and balls. He started to get hard all over again. Lian knew he would not come as quickly the second time, and she told him so. Then she told him to pour some of the liquid on his hands, rub it around her pussy, and push some of it inside of her with his fingers. She lay back and tucked a pillow under her rump. When she spread her legs and pulled herself open, Ren saw a woman's counterpart to his own for the first time. Lian's felt wonderful. So soft. He put one finger in and she gave a small moan. She encouraged him to put more liquid on his fingers, to put two or three in, and to move them in and out slowly. He did and she moaned a little more. Finally she asked him to put his big cock in her, but not all of it all at once. She didn't know if she could take it all at once. Even though he didn't understand why, Ren complied. It took him no time to get the first five inches in, but the rest took some time and effort. Both were enjoying the excitement, but Lian stopped everything and told Ren that she needed more oil. He withdrew completely and she opened herself with her fingers while he poured oil directly inside. When he mounted her again, he was surprised at how easily she took the first nine inches, and barely had to wait any longer to receive the rest. She began rubbing herself while Ren fucked her slowly at first – then like a mad man. At first, when she started to shake and scream under him, he thought that she was crying out in pain, but, as his own voice joined hers, he realized that she was in as much pleasure as he was.

When he finally withdrew from Lian, he rolled over on his side and she cuddled up next to him. "Ren, you have the largest cock I've ever seen," she began. "Was your dad's that big?" she wanted to know.

"No, it wasn't," he reflected. "None of the younger kids had anything, either. Why is that?" he wondered out loud.

"Perhaps you were adopted," she offered.

"That's it!" he jumped up like a wild man. "I had to be adopted. I didn't look anything like the other kids. I'm the only one with red hair. No wonder my dad beat only me," he said sadly.

"Are you hungry, Ren?" she asked.

"I'm always hungry, Lian," he replied.

"Give me a few minutes and I'll make something for us," she informed him.

Ren lay back and began to think about contacting his mother. She would tell him if he had been adopted or not. Maybe she was married to someone else before she married Lester he mused. But before he could formulate an answer or a plan of action, Lian was back in the bedroom carrying a tray full of egg rolls and several bowls of rice. More new treats!

He was ravenous. After he had eaten everything that Lian had prepared for him, she suggested that the two of them get into her huge tub. She had filled it with very hot water. Ren liked it immediately. When five or six minutes had passed, Lian thought Ren could be encouraged one more time. She was right. He was hoping that they could do it again before he left. She dried him off and led him back to the bedroom. This time, she oiled his big cock with both hands and slipped him inside. In no time, she had adjusted to his size. He rode her like the wind. But nothing was happening for him. It felt good and all, but not the way it felt when something really was happening. Lian sensed what the matter was and told him to fuck her like a dog. Ren withdrew. Lian turned over and rose up on her knees. She guided his dick into her and he drove it all the way in. She groaned with pleasure. So did he. This time, it started to feel like it should and Ren finally arrived after a much longer ride.

When it was over, Lian lay face down in the bed with Ren on top of her and in her at the same time. Soon he realized that he was slipping out of her by contracting and going soft. He withdrew and rolled beside her. She held him in her arms and kissed him gently on the mouth. "Did you enjoy yourself, Mr. Baxter?" she teased. But before he could answer, she added, "I know I did."

"Lian," he began. "I know I'm supposed to pay you something, but I don't know how much."

"Five dollars," she answered. "You can leave it on the table when you go out, Ren," she smiled at him. "That's five dollars a fuck, Ren, so your total is ..."

"Fifteen," he answered for her. There had to be a cheaper way, he thought to himself.

CHAPTER THREE:
The First Secret

Ren's business became wildly successful. In six months, he needed even more space. In a year, he began to look into buying other kinds of businesses. Nathan and Peter Moran had worked out wonderfully well, and it left Ren free to think about other business opportunities. At lunch one day, he told Mr. Hewes that he wanted to buy another business. Hewes surprised him when he said, "How about buying my lumberyard?"

They agreed on a selling price of $29,500 and Forsythe arranged for Ren to borrow most of that sum from the bank. When the deal was completed, Griffin Hewes handed Gilbert the check and told him to put it into his special account.

Another year passed and Hewes, now a widower, approached Ren about buying another of his successful ventures: his extensive shipping interests. Forsythe opposed lending Ren the $2.5 million to pay for it, but Griffin Hewes convinced his brother-in-law to make the loan because he was willing to cosign the note and would personally guarantee it.

Then the most extraordinary thing happened. Griffin Hewes invited Ren Baxter to his home for dinner on Sunday. Another first! He told Ren to come at 4:30 because he wanted to show him the grounds and to talk over some business ideas he had.

That week dragged for Ren. Although he was as keen as ever at his businesses, all that he could think about was Sunday dinner at the Hewes home. When he arrived, Hewes' livery people cared for his horse and carriage. Hewes' butler, Clifford, greeted him at the door and indicated that Mr. Hewes was in the study and was expecting him. "Ah, Ren," he began. "Welcome. I don't know why I never thought of doing this before," he lied. It was all that he could think about since the day that he had met Ren, four years earlier.

Griffin Hewes did nothing by happenstance. He had a lovely daughter, six months younger than Ren, whom he kept hidden away in order to avoid having all of the gold diggers of the world come a-callin'. Hewes walked Ren everywhere. He talked incessantly about how much he admired Ren and how well he had been doing in his businesses. He showed him the pushcart that he kept in a shed at the back of his property. When they returned to the front porch, Ren saw a beautiful young woman sitting and reading a book in an overstuffed rocking chair. She was Griffin Hewes' daughter, Victoria. The effect of her long coal black hair under a stark white sunbonnet was a vision of loveliness. She was a tiny person, slightly taller than her father, but her smallness only increased her beauty. Hewes watched Ren's handsome face and was rewarded by the effect Victoria had on him. "Victoria, dear, please say hello to my business associate, Ren Baxter," Hewes ordered.

Victoria rose from her seat, looked up into Ren's handsome face, extended her hand, and smiled the most glorious smile that her father had ever seen. He thought for a moment that his own heart had stopped. The two youngsters hit it off from the first word. Victoria severed whatever connection her father had with Ren and whisked him off for a tour of her own. He left Hewes in such haste that it was as though Hewes had vanished – or never existed. They like each other, he thought.

Half an hour later, Victoria returned with Ren to the house that was a 59-room mansion on 42 acres that overlooked the bay.

Dinner was served at 6:00 sharp. They served Ren's favorites. Nearly raw steak. Baked potatoes. Apple pie with Colby cheese. And coffee. "Daddy," Victoria began, "why have you never brought Mr. Baxter home before today?" she asked playfully.

"He was too rough, my dear, until recently. I've had to work on him for a very long time just to get him this far. He needs more work, though, don't you agree?" he teased.

"Definitely," she teased right back, her black eyes sparkling all the while.

Ren didn't quite catch the signals that the two of them were enjoying between themselves at his expense until Hewes asked, "Don't you agree, Ren, that you need more work before you can come back here?"

When he was so flustered that he couldn't answer, the two of them laughed out loud until Ren got the joke.

Sunday afternoons at the Hewes mansion became a regular part of Ren's life. He and Victoria were falling in love and Hewes did everything that he could to encourage it. After four months of courting steadily, Ren asked Victoria if she would marry him. She said yes, but only if her father approved. He approved. The couple was married on Christmas Day, 1890, when they were both 21 years old. The Episcopal Bishop of California performed the ceremony in the great room of the Hewes mansion. No guests other than the Forsythes were invited.

When the ceremony was over and the Bishop and the Forsythes were gone, Hewes took his son-in-law into his study. There he handed him a beautifully wrapped box that was as long as a bread knife and as wide as a man's hand. "Open it," he urged. When Ren did, he didn't know what to do or say. There was Frankie Wilson's silver eagle money clip with a check in it for three million dollars. Hewes explained: "I put every cent I ever received from you into a special account that Gilbert set up for me. Every purchase, large, or small went into it. I added a few dollars at the end, just to round it off to a tidy sum, but most of it came from your hard labor. As for the clip, I thought it added a nice touch, don't you?" he smiled. "I bought it the same day you told Gilbert that you saw it in Uncle Chow's place. I'll have it put away with the jade and the vase while you're gone, if you like. As for the money, I think it can wait until you get back from your honeymoon."

Ren reached out and down, and hugged his father-in-law for the first time in his life. It was a moment.

Hewes had recently acquired several of the best hotels in San Francisco and had made arrangements for the couple to spend their wedding night in the bridal suite of the King's Castle and Keep. Victoria was very nervous. She didn't know exactly what to expect. Her aunt, Millie, her dead mother's twin, had told her what Ren would do. She had explained that Victoria would have some pain and maybe some bleeding the first few times it happened, but after a few weeks, she would be okay. She assured her that she would probably end up liking it very much.

Pain be damned, she thought. She loved her husband and wanted to please him. She asked that they not have any lights on during the first time because she was so embarrassed to take off her clothes in front of him. Ren said that was okay with him. They undressed in the dark and got into the bed. Ren reached for Victoria and pulled her close to him so that he could feel her body for the first time. She liked everything, especially the kissing and the touching. She wanted more. And Ren was ready to give her more. In his excitement, he forgot that even Lian had to get used to him He started into Victoria with some vigor. She screamed out in great pain. "Stop, Ren. It hurts. Take it out, Ren, please, take it out," she begged.

He stopped the forward motion and withdrew a few inches. Victoria stopped screaming and said that she would try again. When he pushed it in a little further, she cried out another time to stop. Again, Ren withdrew, waited, and tried again. By this time, it really was feeling good to Ren and he wanted to come badly, so he told his young bride that he was at that point. It would all be over soon if she would let him push it in all the way and move it a couple of times. Victoria agreed even though it was the worst pain that she had ever felt in her life, and it doubled when Ren was all of the way in. She fainted from the ordeal, as Ren unloaded in her to his great satisfaction and shame, proving once again that a stiff dick has no conscience. He had hurt his beautiful bride whom he loved more than anything. He withdrew and watched in horror as blood began to run out of her. He grabbed a robe and ran out of the room and down to the front desk. "Get a doctor, please," he begged the man at the front desk. "My wife is very ill," he said. Then he ran back into the room where Victoria still was unconscious, but she was not bleeding anymore. He was afraid to touch her for fear of hurting her more.

Twenty-five minutes later, a doctor arrived. Before he allowed the doctor to see Victoria, Ren explained what happened. The doctor had seen other women torn after their wedding night, but never had he seen anything like this. At first, he thought she would need stitches, but then reasoned that he might stitch too much and prevent any intercourse later on. So he put cold compresses on Victoria's forehead and brought her around after several minutes. Ren was holding her hand and stroking her hair. "I'm sorry, Victoria, I'm so sorry I hurt you," he began.

She looked blankly at him and slowly remembered where she was and what had happened. "This is Doctor … sorry, doctor, but I didn't get your name," he said.

"Aaronson," he replied. "Mrs. Baxter, you've suffered some severe trauma. I'm ordering you not to move for at least the next two days. I'll send a nurse around just as soon as I can rouse one, but unless you want to compound what you've already suffered, I suggest you follow my instructions of complete bed rest," he instructed. "I want you to take these little pills for the pain and these for the bleeding. I'll come by tomorrow and see how you're doing." And, with that, he started to leave. At the door, he said to Ren, "It should be clear to you, Mr. Baxter, that Mrs. Baxter will be unable to resume relations with you for quite some time now, and maybe forever. Much is going to depend on what happens to her in the next 48 hours."

The doctor realized that Ren was thinking of himself as a monster. He touched Ren's arm and said, "It's unfortunate. You are not a fiend. Sometimes life takes a bend we hadn't anticipated. She needs your love and support, not your self-pity," he added encouragingly.

Ren asked the doctor if he knew Griffin Hewes. "Not personally, but I know who he is," he responded.

"Would you send word to him that Victoria and I need him? Ask him to come here as fast as he can," Ren requested.

"Certainly, Mr. Baxter," he added. And, with that, he was out of the door and gone.

Returning to their marital bed, Ren was afraid to disturb his bride of ten hours. So he sat on the floor beside her and held her hand. Several times, she squeezed his to let him know that it was okay and that she wasn't angry with him. In fact, she felt as though she had disappointed him. How ironic!

Hours went by slowly. Finally a faint knock on the door sent Ren to answer it. It was a nurse and Griffin Hewes. The doctor had informed both of them of the situation, and had instructed them not to enter in anger or in a blameful state of mind. What happened was unpredictable. But Hewes knew better. He had ignored what people told him about Ren's unusually large size because, surely, the reports must have been false. This was entirely his own fault. "Ren," he began. "I'm so sorry for the both of you. How's Victoria?" he asked.

"Frankly, I don't know," he said. "There was so much blood at first. I thought she was going to bleed to death, but it has stopped. She's been asleep most of the time."

The nurse went right to her patient. She did think Ren a brute. Neither Ren nor Hewes missed her judgmental looks, but they could deal with that. She was very caring and good with Victoria and that's all that mattered.

Dr. Aaronson returned at 7:30 a.m. and was glad to see that his patient was conscious and taking some tea. She had eaten a small piece of toast with strawberry jam and that was very encouraging news to him. He thought that she could go home in another day, but she still would be restricted to bed rest with assisted bathroom breaks only. Around-the-clock nurses were a must. Griffin Hewes made sure Victoria had two for each eight-hour shift.

In two days, Victoria returned to the mansion. She stayed in bed for three months until she felt well enough to dress and leave her room. Then she discovered that she was pregnant. At dinner that evening, she announced her condition to her father and to her husband. Each man had a smile that stretched from ear to ear. "A baby," Hewes repeated several times. He thought he would probably die without benefit of grandchildren.

"Are you sure, Victoria?" Ren asked. "Perhaps it's something else?" he questioned.

"No, I'm sure it's a baby," she replied. "I'm not sure, but I think it's kicking a little."

"We'll get a doctor for you today," Hewes announced.

"Could you get Dr. Aaronson, Daddy?" she asked. "I liked him so much and he has been so kind to me," she added.

"Of course. We'll get him," Hewes answered.

Dr. Aaronson confirmed the pregnancy and was amazed. He was surprised, first of all, that Victoria was pregnant and, secondly, at how well she was tolerating everything, given the circumstances of the conception. Hewes wanted to spend more and more time at home with his daughter. Ren wanted to spend more and more time away from her so that he could attend to his businesses and to Hewes'. He kept returning to Lian Sheng when he needed a woman. He made arrangements with her to see only him. He moved her out of Chinatown and into a house of her choosing. Hewes knew and approved wholeheartedly. He realized that Ren never would be able to have relations with Victoria. He knew that the young man needed a woman and who better, he thought, than Lian Sheng. He had enjoyed her company for years, too.

It became clear to Hewes that it was time to turn over his

extensive holdings to Ren. He had lost interest in them. All he wanted to do now was to care for Victoria and his heir. When she gave birth to Reynolds Carter Baxter, II, Ren immediately said that they would call the boy Griffin. Hewes was moved to tears by the gesture. Victoria loved the idea that her son would have the names of her father and her husband.

Griffin was a small baby. He weighed only four pounds and eight ounces at birth. His hair was coal black like his mother's and he had her black eyes. He had tiny hands and tiny feet. In fact, he was such a tiny guy that everyone wondered what Ren had contributed to him. Had he been any larger, he would have torn his mother worse than his father did at conception. Dr. Aaronson ordered Victoria confined for another three months and her father never left her side.

Ren returned home every evening and, most of the time, he had his evening meal with Hewes and Victoria. The couple still slept in the same bed, but each knew that intimacy never would be a part of their marriage. Victoria never once thought of what Ren would do or did to satisfy his needs. She was quite happy with the arrangement as it was. She and her husband and her baby all lived happily in her family home. Quite idyllic, she thought.

Griffin Hewes was a new person. He doted on his daughter and grandson. The Bishop was invited back to the Hewes' home for the christening. Religion wasn't something Ren ever had much time for or interest in. He was surprised at his father-in-law's spiritual observance, given the nature of some of his businesses and questionable practices. Victoria, he understood, loved the formality and the music and the beauty of the church, but Hewes' sudden interest confused him.

To avoid any problems after he died, Hewes took Ren aside late one evening after Victoria and Little Grif, as the baby was known, were asleep. "Ren, I'm having my lawyers prepare papers transferring all of my legitimate holdings into your name and into Victoria's name. I know you love Victoria and I think you care greatly for the baby. So, here's the deal. As long as you stay married to Victoria and care for Little Grif, denying neither of them anything, you will be in complete control of my empire. However, should you ever divorce her, all ownership of my holdings will revert directly to Victoria and Little Grif will be my heir."

"That's quite generous of you, Griffin, but I'm not surprised. You have been so generous to me from the first day I met you for lunch," he responded. "I'm sure you will still retain the rights of check writing anytime you feel like it."

"Count on it, my boy, count on it. I have accounts you have no idea exist," Griffin admitted by referring to his illicit ventures. He never exposed those to Ren in order to protect him from possible dangers from felons and the law. "I'll draw on them when I need to," he offered. "I'm putting those monies into trusts for Little Grif. I want him to be financially independent after I'm gone. You and Victoria will be the trustees. I'll have my lawyers give you copies of the instruments that detail the trusts, along with my required instructions about how both of you are to manage it."

Two weeks later, Griffin Hewes died in his sleep from a heart attack. He was 57. His funeral was private and the Bishop conducted it on the grounds of the mansion. Griffin Hewes was buried near his favorite oak tree and beside his beloved wife. Ren burned the old pushcart stored in the shed as Hewes had instructed him to do and put the ashes on the floor of the grave before the coffin was lowered into it.

Victoria was devastated by her father's death. Bishop Roland Chamberlain called on her daily. Ren began to wonder why the Bishop didn't send one of his minions to comfort his wife. Then, one day, Victoria announced that she was giving $300,000 to the Diocese of California to finish St. Martin's Cathedral in San Francisco. Ren started to object, but he remembered that Griffin told him not to deny Victoria anything, so he wrote out the check and had it ready for the Bishop's next visit.

The following week, the Dean of the Cathedral, Fr. Willard Ingersoll, began to make weekly visits. He was a kind man whose greatest attribute was his compassion. He loved Victoria and Little

Grif, now called Griffin since his grandfather of the same name had died. It was Dean Ingersoll who suggested to her that she should build her own private chapel on the side of the mansion where he and others could say Mass as often as she wanted. The idea thrilled her and she asked the Dean if he would send the same architect to see her who had designed the cathedral's main sanctuary. Indeed, he would.

Once again, Ren was not thrilled by the idea, but, true to his word to Hewes, he funded the project good-naturedly. It took three years and another $200,000 to complete the construction, but it made Victoria happy and that was all that he cared about. The completed chapel was a miniature of St. Martin's sanctuary. It seated 90 comfortably. Like the rest of the mansion, it was made of Indiana limestone. The altar was hewn out of Vermont marble that was hauled by a special train from the quarry to insure that the large slabs didn't crack or break. Ren had to admit that it was beautiful, but, for the costs involved, it should be. The organ, imported from Germany, cost an additional $50,000 and it was worth every penny. When a master played it, Ren could close his eyes and visualize Bach seated at his organ composing, composing, composing. For some unknown reason, he loved Bach. On the few occasions that he attended services on Sunday mornings in Victoria's private chapel, he asked that the organist play an all-Bach program.

His son continued to resemble his mother's side of the family. At four, he was half a head shorter than average. He was tiny-boned and had none of his father's fire. He preferred the company of the Episcopal priests parading in and out of the house. When Griffin was five years old, his mother had a schoolroom built onto the chapel. She decided that the best-educated priests of the Diocese would teach Griffin. Ren, again, had no real objection because he was so removed from the boy and his mother. His was in a world of business. Hers was a world of religion and their son.

Griffin began playing the piano at six years of age, the violin at seven, and the organ at eight. He mastered the instruments in much the same way that his father automatically mastered numbers. Ren continued to support every idea and practice that Victoria put into play, but, with each one, he felt himself being pushed aside. Victoria moved out of their bedroom because there was no use pretending anymore. She dearly loved Ren, but her life had become Griffin.

Ren, on the other hand, bought another home for Lian Sheng and spent most of his time with her. Victoria didn't know who "the other woman" was or what she was. She was just grateful that it was she, and not herself, who serviced her husband. Ren made sure he had Sunday dinner with his wife and child, but, other than that, he was free to live his life as he chose.

One day as Ren was sitting alone in his office, the idea came to him that he should buy the Baxter Dray and Livery Company where his father, Lester, worked. He had his lawyers contact old Reynolds Baxter, for whom he was named, to see how much money it would take to buy it. $18,000 was the reply. Ren wrote out the check and had the attorneys handle the closing. He also asked for them to arrange for all of the employees to assemble in the office on the next day at 8:00 a.m. He gave special instructions to have Lester Baxter seated in the first row. At the appointed hour, Ren walked into the newest business that he had bought. He wore an elegantly cut, expensive suit that he had made just for the occasion. He looked and played the part of a rich successful man who was full of himself. "Good morning," he began. "My name is Reynolds Carter Baxter. I just bought this company from my great-uncle, Reynolds Baxter. Lester Baxter, there, is my father. Dad, how are you?" he asked.

Lester Baxter looked at the giant of a man in front of him. He slowly realized that it was his son, Rennie, whom he had abused as a child and thrown out without so much as a penny about fifteen years ago. He said nothing, but he did lower his eyes and refused to look at Rennie who continued: "I bought the company for one reason and one reason only. I bought it to make sure it stays in the

Baxter family when my great-uncle is no longer with us. It is not a worthless company. That's another reason I bought it. Indeed it is a profitable one. I'm grateful to all of you for making it so. The only changes to be made around here are ones of ownership and management. I'm going to own the company, but I'm turning the management of it over to my dad, Lester Baxter. I think he's gotten too old to work the rigs and to lift the loads. I know he's a smart man who can improve this company in the long run. The only time you'll ever see me is if there's a problem too big for Lester to handle. Any questions?" he ended.

There were no questions. "Then I guess that's it. You can all go back to work doing what you do best. Dad, I want you to stay behind so we can talk about the company and catch up on family matters."

The men all shuffled out and returned to their jobs. Lester was too scared to move. He continued to look down at the floor until Ren spoke directly to him. "Dad, it's all okay. Do you hear me? It's all okay. You did me a favor by chasing me out of the house. I've had a lot of luck as a direct result. So I'm asking you not to beat yourself up. You have nothing to worry about from me," he said as kindly as he could.

"Ren, I'm sorry," he said. "I'm truly sorry. When I drank, I was a crazy man. Since the day you left, I ain't had a drop. I swear to you."

The younger Baxter touched his father's shoulder and said, "All's forgiven, Dad." He let a few moments pass before he launched into the business end of his visit. "You can run this company, I'm sure. I'll send over bookkeepers who will take care of the finances. All you have to do is find new ways to expand the business. Horses and mules are not going to be with us much longer. I want you to investigate how motorized wagons can be used." For the next twenty minutes, Ren dictated policy to Lester who was indeed a smart man and who saw the merits in his son's ideas. "Double your salary, Dad. Give all of the employees a pay hike of three cents an hour. You'll be loved instantly. For every

$1,000 you increase profits over last year, I'll give you a bonus of $25.00."

It was too much for the elder Baxter. This lazy worthless ingrate was anything but. He tried to say as much, but nothing came out. Finally Ren got to the real crux of the buyout and the family promotion. "Dad," he began, "I have a question. Was I adopted?"

After being asked that long-dreaded question, Lester seemed to have been bitten by electricity. He sprang into the air, knocked over his chair, and then crashed on the floor. Ren helped him up and waited for his answer. "No," he said. "You were not adopted." Ren sensed there was more, so he waited patiently. "You were stolen!" When he got to the word stolen, he began to sob uncontrollably for the next two minutes. "Your mother and I were very young at the time. We boarded a train in St. Louis in 1869. We were heading out here so I could work for Uncle Reynolds. We met another young couple already on the train. They came from somewhere out east, – Pittsburgh or Philadelphia or someplace else. I really don't remember. Anyway, about 100 miles out of Reno, Nevada, all of a sudden, the train jolted to a complete stop. Train robbers had removed some sections of track and ties. When the train hit that spot, the passengers inside were thrown forward. Your mother, a beautiful redhead, was thrown through the glass of the car door she was in. It cut her throat and she bled to death. I think your dad, another redhead, tall and good-looking, had his head smashed in. He also died. I was in the pisser when it happened and I wasn't hurt. My dear wife, Annabelle, was jostled around and had only cuts and bruises. We had a tiny ten-day-old daughter named Alice who was killed in the wreck. She was crushed to death. You were in a wooden cradle and unhurt. I can't remember how many people I helped to bury that day. I think it was around 50 or 60. Our little girl was one of them. Well, you can imagine how hysterical Annabelle was. Then this porter came right up to her and asked if this was her baby. I was dead set against us taking you, but your mother made me an offer I couldn't turn down. That baby was you, Ren. She grabbed you from his arms and we raised you as our own until the drink made me crazy," he ended.

"Do you remember my other parents' names?" he pleaded.

"I don't Ren. Maybe your mother did, but she died last year, I'm sorry to tell you," he answered. "We never talked about that day ever again."

"What about my name?" he asked.

"We changed it, Ren. I think your real parents called you Patrick, but I'm not sure. Sorry," he said.

"That's okay, Dad, that's okay," Ren responded. "What was it Mom said to you that made you change your mind about keeping me?" he asked.

Lester said it was embarrassing to tell, but he would if Ren insisted. "I insist," he responded.

"She took me aside and promised she'd have sex with me every night if I wanted it," he said red-faced. Then Ren put it together. That was what she meant about everybody having to pay some price for things. In order to keep him, it cost her a bout in bed every night with Lester. Resentment costs were too much, Ren thought. He certainly refused to pay as much as a nickel for the shit load of it that he had carried for too many years, so he dumped what he had harbored in that instant.

The following Sunday afternoon, Ren recounted his meeting with his father, Lester Baxter, to his wife and son, now nine. When Victoria challenged its veracity, Ren didn't know whether to storm out and never return or to listen further to her thoughts. "You didn't look anything like your father, Lester, did you, Ren?" she asked.

"Correct," he answered.

"Well, Griffin doesn't look anything like you and we both know you are his father," she replied. Ren couldn't deny that. But Lester's story had too many details for him to have made it up on the spot. Ren agreed that it was possible that Lester had lied, but why would he after all these years? Victoria suggested that he did it to salve his guilt. But Ren didn't agree. Griffin sat silently throughout the entire conversation and listened in rapt interest. When his father was about to leave for the week, he asked him, "Father, why don't I resemble you in the least? Maybe I'm someone else's son. Maybe that someone else would care about me, do you think?" he asked in all innocence.

Ren's heart broke. The boy's question held the mirror for him to have a look-see – and it was true. His businesses and his life with Lian made it appear to the boy that he really didn't care much one way or the other for him. "Griffin," he began, "our looking alike or not has nothing to do with my being your father. You resemble your grandfather, for whom you are named, and your mother. Rub black and red together and you still get black, right?" he asked. "I'd be delighted to spend more time with you, but it would have to be away from here. Your school is here and so is your music. My world of business is so far removed from yours of pure pleasure that I hope you never enter my end of the world. Saying that doesn't mean that I don't care about you. The fact that I support your choices should tell you that I do care," he ended.

"I'd like for us to have a family picture taken next Sunday when you return, Father. Would that be okay with you? That way, I'll have the sense that you are here even though you are not," Griffin asked.

"I'd really like that, my boy," Ren said. And he was out of the door. It did not occur to him then that he had been on a quest ever since Lian Sheng first suggested that he was adopted. His need for a father's approval ended when Griffin Hewes entered his life. Now his own son was begging him for his approval and love and all he could do was consent to a lousy picture.

That week, Ren bought two new businesses. The first one was a slaughterhouse and meatpacking operation. The second one was a newspaper. Ren's special gifts had been honed much finer than those of Griffin Hewes. Ren was able to buy businesses for which he had no particular knowledge and find the right people to manage them for him. He simply managed the managers. Over the next four years, he bought 32 new businesses and sold 14 of his other holdings. His wealth had tripled after Griffin Hewes died. He was nearing the $25 million mark.

In 1908, two years after the great San Francisco earthquake, Ren's only son, Reynolds Carter Baxter, II, known as Griffin, was seventeen years old. Ren was 39 and so was Victoria. It was time for their son to go to college. The good fathers from the Episcopal Diocese of California had educated him at home, but Griffin needed others to carry him further. At Sunday dinner, Griffin and Victoria announced that Griffin would be attending Bards College, three blocks away from the newly rebuilt Hewes Building where Ren maintained his central business offices. Griffin would live at home and be driven each day to and from classes in the family car. Neither he nor Victoria was ready for the cord to be cut completely. "That's wonderful, Griffin," Ren responded. "Perhaps you'll have time to have lunch with me at the club once classes begin."

"I'd like that very much, Father," he replied happily. Victoria wasn't so sure that was a good idea and said so.

"For God's sake, Victoria, the club is where I met your father. He loved the place and Griffin will, too," he remonstrated.

"I'm aware of how important the club was to Daddy," she said, "but I think Griffin should not be exposed to that kind of a life since he wants to become an Episcopal priest after college and then go into seminary."

"He what?" Ren asked, not believing what he just heard.

"A priest, Father. I want to become a priest and serve God," he said matter-of-factly.

"Well, I'll be damned," he said. Remembering his comeback when Griffin Hewes said the same line to him years ago, he continued his own sentence, "probably."

In spite of themselves, the three laughed as they had never laughed at the Sunday table. "Are you sure Bards is the best for Griffin? I mean there's Yale and Harvard back east. They're really good schools. Have you thought about them?" he asked.

"I've considered them, Father, but not for college. Bards is the place for me. But I might consider going there for seminary work after Bards," he answered.

"Good, good," was Ren's reply.

In spite of Victoria's concerns, Griffin met his father each Friday for lunch at the club. Ren now occupied the same alcove enjoyed by his late father-in-law, Griffin Hewes. The boy had a good mind, that was certain, but he had no head for business. Some of the older members treated him to stories of his namesake and he began to look forward to his weekly visits. During Griffin's college career, father and son developed an appreciation for what the other brought to the table. Each improved his view of the other. One day, Griffin asked his dad why he didn't live at home. Ren thought that, at age 21, the boy ought to know. But first, he extracted a promise from him that he would never let his mother know that he knew. After receiving it, he told him. Griffin was appalled. "But I'm not huge, Father. Why not?" he asked.

"I guess you take after your mother's side of the family in every way," he replied. "Fortunately you're taller than both your grandfather and your mother." Griffin made it all the way to five feet five inches. His father's height contributed something to Griffin's overall being, but that was the only noticeable attribute.

"So ... uh ... you and mother," Griffin hesitantly groped, "'did it' only one time in nearly 22 years of marriage?"

"Yes," Ren said sadly. "But I've loved your mother in spite of that, Griffin. Just as I have loved you in the best ways that I can. Your mother has monopolized your entire childhood. That's okay because look at how well you've turned out," he praised.

"And that's why you've lived apart, so you could ..." he stopped his thoughts abruptly.

"Yes," Ren answered without sadness or apology.

"Do I have any half-brothers or sisters?" he wanted to know.

"None, Griffin, none. My personal life has been very private. I've done the best I could under the circumstances," he answered. "If you ever want to enter my private world, I'll admit you, but only if you can promise me that you will not judge me," he said.

"I'm not anywhere near ready, Father. This is a lot for me to swallow. Any more," he said, "and I might choke."

"There are a few family secrets I think you should know about, however," he continued, "and they are neither pretty nor moral. Do you think you could handle them?" he asked.

"I suppose so," he answered tentatively.

"Good," he said. "Let's go for a walk."

Father and son walked past the Moran Import Export Company. Ren had turned over full ownership of the company to Peter and Nathan five years after he had opened it. It was the least he could do for the Moran family. Besides, it was his way of giving and receiving absolution for Tommy's death. Ren recounted that the sign above the door should have been Moran and Baxter. Then he told him the story of Tommy Moran and Frankie Wilson. "You actually killed a man when you were sixteen years old?" he asked incredulously.

"I did, Griffin," he answered, "and so did your grandfather. He also killed a man when he was sixteen." He told him the story of the circus and the pushcart, and how all of their fortunes were based on two murders and two robberies. The Biblical phrase "Righteous use of unrighteous mammon" sprang into Griffin's head, but he said nothing.

Ren walked Griffin to the First Bank and Trust Company of San Francisco where he had become its largest shareholder and depositor, as well as the chairman of the banking committee called oversight. He motioned for an officer to meet them in the safe. From inside his wallet, Ren produced two keys bound together by an old wire. He placed his in the lock and turned it and the bank officer did the same. The locked box opened and Ren removed three items. One was Frankie Wilson's silver eagle money clip. The second was the panda jade. The third was one of the two vases that he and Tommy carried from the docks on their first day together. All three items verified his father's incredible story of their immediate family's beginnings. "On the day your mother and I married, Griffin," he began, "your grandfather handed me the money clip. He'd purchased it shortly after I sold it to Mr. Wang. Mr. Wang had sold it to his uncle, Chow. It held a check for three million dollars. That's how I got it back. I intend for it to stay locked away as a family secret. If you want to do something with it after I'm gone, that will be fine by me. For now, it stays here. The same order applies to the vase and the jade. The jade is probably worth $50,000 by now, but its value to our family far exceeds any monetary consideration. I'm giving you my only partner's key to this safe deposit box. Put Tommy's key – which is now your key – away from sight. Don't let your mother know that you have it or that it even exists. She'll not understand," he cautioned.

"I'll do that," he answered truthfully.

CHAPTER FOUR:
The Kindness of Friends

The following Sunday afternoon, three guests were at the family table. Bishop and Mrs. Ronald Chamberlain and their daughter, Lucy, were waiting to meet Ren. Ren knew the Bishop, but he had never met Mrs. Chamberlain. He certainly had never met Lucy, a beauty if ever there was one. Griffin did the introductions. Dinner, delicious as always, was made more pleasant by adding a few guests. After they had enjoyed their apple pie with Colby cheese, Victoria didn't object when Ren lit his cigar at the dining room table. Ren knew that something was afoot. He was right. It was a grand surprise. Griffin announced his proposal of marriage to Lucy if she would have him and if her father approved. He did. All of it had been scripted before Ren arrived.

Ren was astonished that Griffin had it in him to be interested in a young lady, let alone have the time to find and court one. Victoria beamed her approval. The couple planned to be married in June following Griffin's graduation from Bards. Because the Bishop was a graduate of the San Francisco General Seminary, he encouraged Griffin to go there, too. So much for Harvard or Yale, Ren thought.

Victoria suggested that the young couple buy a house close to the seminary. Ren agreed completely. He had his best real estate agents begin to scour the newly rebuilt neighborhoods around the seminary for the best house, available or not. When they reported to him that the best house wasn't for sale, he said that he would pay any price within reason to purchase it. The Quinns were reasonable people, especially when the agents showed up with $27,000 in cash and politely asked them to sign the newly prepared warranty deed and bill of sale. Ren gave the keys to the home to Lucy and Griffin during the next Sunday dinner. Victoria was pleased by the gesture.

Ren didn't know what Victoria would do with herself after Griffin left home, but he was sure that she would find some way to occupy her time. For now, she had a wedding to help plan.

The Bishop was to perform the wedding ceremony in the completely rebuilt nave of St. Martin's Cathedral on June 2, 1913. Anyone who was anyone in San Francisco received an invitation. The entire Episcopal clergy from the Diocese and their wives and kids were to be in attendance. Most of Ren's business associates received invitations.

The wedding was flawless. It was the social event of the season. The reception was held in the cathedral's nearly completed Charter House. When the 1906 earthquake had leveled almost everything at St. Martin's, Ren and Victoria donated nearly 90% of the money to rebuild it. It was a thoroughly enjoyable day until the moment when the bride and groom were about to depart for their honeymoon in Los Angeles. When Lucy came over to say goodbye to Ren and Victoria, Victoria turned and fled the room. Ren told the young couple that he would take care of Victoria. They were to go ahead and not worry about anything. They left not knowing for sure if they should go, but realizing, at the same time, that Ren was a strong person and would take care of any problem that Victoria was having.

He found her getting into the back seat of her car. He got in with her. She flung herself into his arms and cried for the longest time. Finally she looked at Ren and wondered out loud if Griffin and Lucy would have a problem on their wedding night like she and Ren had so long ago. He assured her that Griffin was normal and that he and Lucy would have no problems. "Ren," she continued, "I know I've been a disappointment to you all these years."

He cut her off and said, "Not so, Victoria. Ours has been a different kind of marriage and love. I've always loved you. I'll always love you. Sometimes, life takes unexpected turns, that's all. Ours certainly did. But that should not give you cause to grieve about something that happened so long ago. Griffin has the finest mother in the world. You've overseen his education and all of the important choices throughout his life. I wouldn't doubt that you and the Bishop arranged for Lucy and Griffin to get married." Her little smile gave it away.

She brightened some and asked, "Do you mean it, Ren?"

"I do," he replied.

The two continued to talk for another twenty minutes before Victoria felt well enough to go home alone. "Thank you, Ren. You've been most kind over the years. I bear you no ill will or resentment for your life. I hope we will continue to be friends and that you will continue to come for Sunday dinner each week. Griffin and Lucy will probably be frequent guests, I'm sure," she added.

"Count on it," he replied and he kissed her lightly on the cheek, which was something that he hadn't done for many years. But he had to go and so did she.

The Bishop's Secret

Chapter Five:
A Tangle of Secrets

Griffin sailed through seminary. He had been given excellent preparation and had mastered Latin and Greek in home school and at Bards. The only language requirement that he needed to complete seminary was Biblical Hebrew. He loved the challenge and the riches that he was able to mine from those ancient texts.

What he discovered about the language was its simplicity. It had only 1,100 verbs to memorize. All other parts of speech were derived from them. Names especially. When he translated the name, it generally gave him the person's job description. English names originally told the occupation of the person's family, too. For example, Smith was used for blacksmiths, silversmiths, and other types of smiths and Miller was used for grain mill workers. He had two favorite names. Joseph and Joshua. Joseph means "he adds" and Joseph was the family's accountant who rose to be Egypt's accountant during great famines. Joshua means "he helps, saves, or delivers." Since English wasn't a language until the year 800, Mary couldn't have named her little baby Jesus. Rather, she named him Joshua.

Three Sunday afternoons each month, the young couple ate dinner with his family. On one Sunday each month, both sets of parents came to their new home near the seminary for dinner.

Lucy had a house staff, naturally, so she was free to entertain at leisure. The Bishop was aging and was laying the tracks for his son-in-law to succeed him one day in the near future.

Victoria volunteered at the Episcopal Hospital for the poor four days every week. Medicines and supplies were in short supply there, so she wrote out quarterly checks for $10,000 and for $15,000 to buy both without consulting Ren. He didn't really mind since he had set aside money for her to use for that purpose. It kept her busy and close to the work of the church, which she had always loved. Besides, he was still making so much money as a result of the 1906 earthquake that he felt proud when he donated to her causes. He let her spend it as she wanted.

Two years into Griffin's seminary education, Lucy announced that she was pregnant. Her mother and Victoria were beside themselves with joy. The Bishop was more reserved and Ren was very pleased. Reynolds Carter Baxter, III, was born in Griffin's senior year on March 6, 1915. Unknown to Ren at the time, that same date in 1869 was the real date of his own birth. Ren believed that he was 46. His Baxter parents had chosen February 28 as his birthday, so Reynolds Carter Baxter missed the real significance of the date of his grandson's entry into the world.

The couple announced that they would call him Hewes, after Griffin's late grandfather. Victoria and Ren were extremely pleased with the choice and, after awhile, the Bishop was reconciled to the name, although he would have preferred that they had named the baby after him. But he was a good sport and he realized that he couldn't write a check in the way that Reynolds Carter Baxter could and did. So he smiled a lot and groused little.

Following Griffin's graduation from seminary and his ordination as a deacon, he was assigned to the cathedral staff as a personal aide to the Bishop and the Dean. His duties were calling on the sick, teaching in the cathedral school, attending staff meetings, and raising money. He found calling on the sick quite challenging. He hated it. He told the Bishop, who quickly reassigned him to a less taxing duty. But he loved to teach and was very good at it. He also found time to play the great organ and was surprised at how quickly his skills returned.

The next year in 1918, Griffin was ordained a priest. His parents were seated in the front row of St. Martin's when Griffin knelt before his father-in-law, the Bishop of California, and took his vows. Victoria cried the entire time. She had lived her entire adult life waiting for this very moment. And here it was. Ren held her hand. He whispered how proud he was of her and what she had accomplished with their son. Lucy, Hewes, and Mrs. Chamberlain sat beside the Baxters.

Several days after the ordination, the Bishop announced that he was sending Griffin to a large parish called All Saints in Daly City. He would start there as an assistant priest under the direction of Fr. Edgar N. Charles. Fr. Charles had the finest reputation for starting newly ordained priests in the right direction. Ren purchased a much larger house for the couple so that they could be close to All Saints. As usual, he provided whatever cash they needed to refurbish and furnish it to their tastes. Victoria was delighted with his continued participation in their son's life. And, true to his word, Ren continued to have Sunday dinner with Victoria or with Griffin and his family at their new home.

Griffin's new family and church responsibilities made it impossible for him to continue seeing his father for lunch at the club each Friday. But he did have an open invitation to come any day that he could, especially if he could on Fridays. Both men missed the regularly scheduled luncheons, so Griffin made sure that he ate with his father at least once each month.

At one of those luncheons in 1919 when World War I was winding down, Griffin was not his usual self. His sense of humor had been erased or he was having a problem at home. Ren wasn't quite sure what the matter was, but he sensed that his son had something important that he wanted to discuss. He was right. Ren listened in horror as his only son indicated that he intended to volunteer for the army as a chaplain. "Why you, Griffin?" he asked. "Aren't there plenty of others who could go? You have a young baby and wife to care for. Have you thought about them?" he wanted to know.

"They are all I've thought about, Father, but I feel it is my duty to go, even at this late stage in the fighting," he replied. "Chaplains," he continued, "aren't usually killed in wars. But, if for some reason I am killed, I want you to have a hand in raising Hewes. Tell me that you will continue to have an ongoing relationship with him and with Mother," he pleaded.

"Of course I will, but this is the only idea you've ever had, Griffin, that I'm opposing," he replied.

"I don't need your opposition, Father," he responded. "I need your support and I'm asking for it. Without it, I'm not sure I can follow through with my good intention. I'm not as strong as you are and nowhere near as savvy. I think the war experience can give me the strength that I lack. My life always has been one of privilege and ease. I think it is past time for me to make a significant contribution. Please, Father?" he begged.

"It means that much to you, Griffin?" he asked.

"It does," he replied. "I'll need you to act as the trustee of my estate now that I've taken it over. I want our lawyers to draw up the papers that will make it happen. Grandfather's money hasn't really been touched, thanks to your generosity and mother's," he said.

Ren agreed to everything. His worry was replaced quickly with admiration. It was a brave thing that his son was doing. His own efforts in the War were not limited to ship building. He supplied guns and munitions and medicines, uniforms and shoes, foodstuffs and gasoline and oil. His wealth at the war's end exceeded $250 million.

Then Griffin surprised him further. "Do you remember, years ago, when you made me an offer to take me into your private world?" he asked.

"I do," he replied.

"I'd like to know a few things about you before I go away," he said.

122

"Like what?" Ren asked.

"Where you live and with whom," he answered. "Could I meet her and see your house?"

"Yes, but only under the same conditions I specified earlier. I don't want you to judge me in any way. If you'll agree to that, then let's go," Ren declared.

"I'll not judge you, Father," he said.

Ren and Griffin drove separately to Ren's home with Lian Sheng in South San Francisco on Point San Bruno overlooking the Bay. Lian was painting another beautiful watercolor in their backyard when Ren entered the house. She put down her brushes immediately when Ren called to her to come into the house. "Lian, this is my son, Griffin. Griffin, this is Lian," he said. Her beauty had not faded and, even though she was in a paint-stained smock, Griffin could see why his father loved her as he did. "Welcome," she said. "I've listened to the details of your life since you were born. I'm honored to meet you – finally."

Griffin froze. How could his father have a Chinese woman in his home for all of these years? Even one as beautiful as Lian. Without a word, he turned, ran back to his car, and sped away. Ren held Lian and apologized for his son's bad behavior. She said that it was nothing and that she was all right. Her concern was for Griffin. "Go to him, Ren, and bring him back. I know I'm a shock, at first, but you deserve better from him," she urged.

But Ren wasn't able to catch his son. Three days later, they found Griffin's body at the base of a cliff. His car had gone over the cliff at its sharpest turn. He never lived to see his 30th birthday.

Ren never told Victoria about the visit that Griffin and he had made on the day that Griffin died. Nor did he ever tell Griffin's young widow, Lucy. Just what Griffin was doing on that road was a mystery to everyone else and, as far as Ren was concerned, it would always remain one. It took years and years of Lian's tender love to help Ren let go of the terrible guilt about his role in his only son's death.

The news of Griffin's death sent Victoria into severe bouts

of hysteria. Her precious son was dead! She did not know why the Almighty could let such a thing happen. She was inconsolable until Lucy showed up unannounced at the mansion with her grandson, Hewes.

Lucy had a problem. She could no longer live in their house by herself with the baby and her father was too ill for her to move in with her parents. She asked if she could live with Victoria.

Miracle of miracles! Victoria was reborn at the age of 50. It struck her that she could begin all over again with little Hewes just as she began so long ago with little Grif. Her chapel was still active and the schoolroom could be cleaned in an instant and made ready for its next pupil. Ren saw it as the solution to numerous problems. He made all of the arrangements for the move and for the disposal of Griffin's home. He met with his attorneys and told them of the conversation he had with his son regarding the trusts. They assured him that they would appear in court with the proper papers to make it all legal. Ren, now, had control of Griffin Hewes' entire estate, including all of the ill-gotten gain that he had converted into a trust for his namesake. Even Ren was astonished when he learned its total. $183 million!

In honor of their son, Victoria and Ren established several trusts at Bards College and San Francisco General Seminary for promising students who lacked adequate funding. At St. Martin's, they set up a scholarship for musicians desiring to learn to play the great organ.

With each donation in memory of their son, Ren's guilt was assuaged a little more. By the time that Griffin's son, Hewes, was fourteen, Ren's guilt had diminished significantly. That year was 1929 and Ren was 60 years old. The stock market crash in October of that year had little effect on Reynolds Carter Baxter, who lived an amazing life in San Francisco, but never was born, as such. He saw it coming and was able to pull all of his money out of the First Bank and Trust Company of San Francisco before everything went belly up. He kept it in numerous safes that he maintained at the mansion and in several business locations. He put the remainder in a large safe that he and Lian had in their home. At the same time, he liquidated all of the trusts that he had established and moved their sums into an old iron safe that he kept in his private office in the Hewes Building.

Hewes proved to be an even better student than his father was. And, like his father, Griffin, Hewes was a small person with small features and a small guy. But he was three inches taller than his father and stood at five feet and eight inches, a full eight inches shorter than his grandfather. Some of the same priests who educated his father also educated Hewes.

Although Ren had promised Griffin that he would stay involved in the raising of his grandson, Ren found it more and more difficult to drive back to the mansion for dinner every Sunday. The two women doted over Hewes and Ren felt that they totally ignored him. When he didn't show up one Sunday, he wasn't missed. It was then that he stopped his practice of Sunday dinner with his family. He sent the obligatory gifts for holidays and birthdays. He telephoned several times a year. But, other than that, from the age of fourteen, his grandson was a stranger to him.

When Hewes was eighteen, he followed his father's path into Bards College. At 22 in 1937, he entered San Francisco General Seminary. At 25, he was ordained a deacon and, by special dispensation, he was ordained a priest in only six months. Ren was 72 years old in 1941 when he died of a brain aneurysm while signing a contract at his office. His grandson, a newly ordained priest of the Episcopal Dioceses of California, was given the honor of conducting his funeral in the completely restored St Martin's Cathedral. In part, he said:

"When I was too young to remember, my father, Griffin, was tragically killed in a motorcar accident several miles from here. He had been a priest of the church for less than a year when that happened. I have no real memories of my father. But my grandfather, Reynolds Carter Baxter, filled my father's shoes for many years until he became too old to visit back and forth. My mother, Lucy, and my grandmother, Victoria, here in the first row, were my real parents and I owe everything to them.

"Grandfather Baxter made it possible for this great cathedral to be completed and then completely rebuilt after the 1906 earthquake. He was a businessman of distinction. I'm told that my maternal grandfather, Griffin Hewes, whose last name I was given to use as my first name, was also a businessman of distinction. He and Grandfather Baxter were both friends and business associates. They were somewhat secretive and not much is known of their origins, but they were gentlemen capable of making visible many of the tenets of the church, including generosity. The number of checks they signed during the last 70 or more years significantly contributed to the stability of our city.

"Formal religion, however, wasn't something my grandfather had much time for. His interest in the church was through my father and me. He never denied either of us anything when we asked. When he liquidated all of his assets last year, he made certain that his family would be taken care of for a long time. He wanted the rest of us, the living, to direct the remainder of his estate into charities of our choosing rather than ones he might have selected. He trusted our judgments in these matters more than he trusted his own. That was his real strength. He could size up others' abilities and let them perform according to their strengths. In the future, I hope that his example will instruct and guide me in my ministry wherever it leads me."

Victoria didn't notice Lian Sheng who was seated and weeping at the rear of the balcony. Nor would she have known her if she had. Lian, like Ren, had grown old. He had seen to it that she would want for nothing for as long as she lived. He had entrusted her with his key to the safe deposit box containing the money clip, the jade, and the vase. He had asked her to see that Hewes got it after he died. He also asked her to tell Hewes about the story of Tommy Moran, Frankie Wilson, and Lester Baxter. She did not go to the interment at the mansion where Ren was being buried beside Griffin Hewes, his old friend and father-in-law.

Within Ren's casket and tucked inside his shirtsleeve was his small pearl-handled dagger, exactly where it had been every day since he bought it in Chinatown decades ago. Victoria wanted to be buried next to her husband and insisted that the two of them should lie side-by-side when her time came. Her wish was granted six weeks later. Fr. Hewes Baxter was again pressed into service.

A week later, Fr. Baxter was in his office at the cathedral, where he had been appointed to the position of dean, when his secretary asked if he had time to see an elderly Chinese woman named Lian Sheng. "She's dressed very nicely," she said.

"I wonder what she could possibly want with me?" he asked. "Please, Miss Simmons, find out and let me know."

When Miss Simmons returned moments later, she informed Fr. Baxter that it was about his grandfather. She had some information and a key for him.

"Show her in, Miss Simmons," he directed.

Lian Sheng entered his study and bowed. Hewes stood still, not knowing what to do. Lian smiled and said, "Father Baxter, my name is Lian Sheng. I was your grandfather's mistress for more than 50 years."

"Impossible," Fr. Baxter blurted out.

He was about to dismiss her when she said, "And I know why your father died. May I sit down?" she asked.

"Are you here for money, Miss Sheng? If you are, I'm afraid I don't take to blackmail," he blustered.

"Ren left me quite well off, Father. I'm here only to fill in the gaps you have in your family history. I heard you say at his funeral …"

"You were at the funeral?" he asked incredulously.

"Of course. As I said, Ren and I lived together for more than 50 years. You did not have much information about his early history and I'm prepared to enlighten you. But I need at least an hour to talk and then another hour to walk," she said.

"Walk where?" he asked.

"After I talk, we'll walk, Father," she answered. For the next hour, Lian Sheng regaled Fr. Baxter with the story of his grandfather, Reynolds Carter Baxter. She spared no details. When she told him of his grandfather's enormous penis, Hewes nearly suffered a stroke. "It is why he moved out of the mansion and in with me. Victoria almost died on their wedding night. They never ever had sex again for as long as they lived."

"But you were able to – you know?" he motioned.

"Oh, yes. I was a prostitute at the time," she said. "Your great-grandfather, Griffin Hewes, brought me over from China. I served him before he directed me to serve only your grandfather. Griffin Hewes was the most brilliant criminal and lawful businessman that I've ever known, Father Baxter. He made fortunes from the prostitute trade, as well as from opium, gambling, pirating, and many other activities that even I didn't know about. He could be ruthless in his dealings with that element, but he always turned profits from them into legitimate business ventures. That was his genius. Before he died, he liquidated all of his illegal ties and turned the money he made into trust funds. Those funds were for your father - and now for you. I just hope some of that side of the family has rubbed off on you to some extent. Someday it may serve you well." Hewes couldn't imagine that ever happening, but he didn't dismiss the thought.

Lian told Fr. Baxter that Lester Baxter thought Ren's real name was Patrick, and that his birthing parents came from the east, possibly Pittsburgh or Philadelphia – or somewhere else. She added that Boston was a possibility because of a casual remark made to his grandfather regarding someone from there who re-sembled Ren. The Tommy Moran and Frankie Wilson narratives fascinated Fr. Baxter. He felt great excitement as Lian related the details of Frankie's murder. Perhaps some of Griffin Hewes' blood was asserting itself. When Lian finished her story, she said that the two of them needed to take a walk.

"Where are we going?" he questioned.

"To see some things," she answered.

As they went out of his study, Fr. Baxter told Miss Simmons that he would be gone for another hour. Lian led him to the First

Bank and Trust Company of San Francisco. One of the young bank officers asked how he could help Fr. Baxter. The officer completely ignored Lian. When she spoke up, he didn't know quite how to react. "Please open box number 152. I have its other key. The signatory on your card will say Reynolds Carter Baxter. This is his grandson, Father Reynolds Carter Baxter, III, Dean of St. Martin's Cathedral," she said.

The box was opened and Lian handed Hewes the three items that were inside. He took each item and handled it as though it were a holy relic worthy of devotion. When he finished, he placed each item back inside the box and locked it again with the key. He handed it back to Lian, but she refused to take it. She told Hewes to put it in a safe place where he would always know where it was. Later he would be able to view the three items at his leisure. "The panda jade," she said, "is worth at least $100,000 according to Ren's last appraisal. But I know its value is far in excess of that number."

As they were leaving the bank, Fr. Baxter asked, "Do you still live in the same house that my father visited the day he was killed?"

"Yes. You are welcome to visit anytime. I have many items that belonged to your grandfather. I would be happy to give them to you. Over the years, I've painted many portraits of him. You can see him as a young man like yourself and as an old man like you will become someday," she said. "But do not delay too long. I'm several years older than Ren and have no idea how many more years I have left. Please come see me soon."

Fr. Baxter bowed this time when Lian bowed as she parted company from him. He walked back to the cathedral and into his office. He asked Miss Simmons to interrupt him only for an emergency. He had much work to do and did not want to be disturbed.

Not wanting to forget a word that Lian Sheng had told him, Hewes began to write down as much of the family history as he could remember. Again, when he recounted the Tommy Moran and

Frankie Wilson sagas, he noticed that he was getting an erection and couldn't figure out why. He paused long enough to satisfy himself at his desk and then returned to his writing.

When he returned home, his mother, Lucy, now in her tall fifties, had supper prepared for him. The two of them wanted for nothing. The trusts, re-established by Ren following the Great Depression, generously supplied all of their needs. The trustees' job was to perpetuate the earnings of the corpus and not to deny its beneficiaries a penny. He began, "Mother, did Gram ever say anything to you about Grandfather Baxter?"

"How do you mean, dear?" she asked hesitantly.

"I mean about why they lived apart for so many years and things like that," he answered.

"She did tell me one or two things over the years, but they are hardly proper dinner conversation, Hewes," she responded.

"Well, let's pretend we aren't having dinner, Mother, and, in conspiratorial whispers, act like common gossips," he shocked her.

"It's not the kind of conversation we've ever had, dear, and I'm not sure I can use the proper words with you. After all, I am your mother," she dismayed.

"Then I'll use the words and you can shake your head yes or no. Fair enough, Mother?" he asked.

She shook her head yes. By the question and headshake method for the next half hour, Hewes was able to confirm every detail of Lian Sheng's incredible story. When he finished asking his questions, Lucy wanted to know where he got his information, so he told her. That led to other revelations. Hewes hardly could wait to get back to his study the next morning to add those details to his account. He locked his script in the bottom drawer of his desk when he finished. The key was tucked inside his wallet beside the safe deposit box key that Lian Sheng had given him the day before.

He went to the restroom afterward and satisfied himself again. He thought that he was alone in the room, but another priest, four stalls down from him, was doing the same thing. They emerged slightly embarrassed by the knowledge of what the other had done. The other priest was an older gentleman there to visit the Bishop about a matter of concern in his parish. As he passed Hewes, he said, "Next time I visit the Bishop, maybe we could have lunch or something." It was the "or something" part of the sentence that Hewes thought about for some time. Several times in his life, friends from seminary had tried to "fix him up" with their cousins from out of town or with friends in for a visit, but Hewes found the women tiresome. He hardly could wait to get home where Lucy waited up for him.

Realizing for yet another time that he was sexually stimulated by stories of men, he finally allowed himself to think the unthinkable: He had no sexual interest in women, but he had great sexual interest in men. He never had acted overtly on any of his interests, but his dream life was full of having sex with other men. Often he awakened after having experienced a nocturnal emission and remembered just how it happened. It was always with another man. His secret was something that he could not share with another living soul. It was too heavy.

Heeding Lian Sheng's advice, he drove to her home and picked up twenty watercolors of his grandfather, Reynolds Carter Baxter, late of San Francisco, who never was born. And, as she had promised, they captured Ren as a young man through his journey to being an old man. In each rendering, Lian captured the goodness in him that she had experienced and made it dominate Ren's features. Hewes was astonished by the artistry of Lian and by her incredible mastery of her craft.

He made an arrangement to have all of his grandfather's portraits boxed and delivered to him at the mansion. Lian also included many of his favorite clothes and books. Hewes was impressed with the breadth of his reading. History, theology, geography, and railroading figured large in his library. One book in particular had an old marker sticking up. Hewes read a small footnote that mentioned a train robbery in 1869 outside of Reno where 63 men, women, and children had died. Hewes made a special section in the mansion's library just for his grandfather's things. He hung the portraits that Lian had painted, in the order of their creation, along the main corridor of the first floor.

When Lian Sheng died the following year, Hewes had her body delivered to the mansion and buried at the foot of his grandfather's grave. Ren had his wife on one side, his father-in-law and business associate on the other side, and his lifelong mistress at his feet. As far as Hewes was concerned, all was well in heaven and on earth.

CHAPTER SIX:
A Bride for the Bishop

Hewes developed into a powerful preacher. For years, he poured all of his thoughts and energy into sermonizing. When special events were celebrated in various parishes in the diocese, he frequently was called upon to speak. His duties also placed him in front of numerous classes in the cathedral and at the seminary where he regularly conducted seminars in Old Testament theology and Hebrew exegesis. Over the years, he developed and taught over 150 series of lectures, ranging from specific Biblical books to church government.

It was as an administrator that Hewes excelled. His abilities to size up an argument and to see its merits or its holes became legendary. Bishop Reginald Wentworth, who succeeded Hewes grandfather on his mother's side as bishop, depended more and more on Dean Baxter to be present when disputes arose within congregations. Most of those problems centered on clergy who split congregations down the middle.

One such problem cropped up shortly after Hewes became Dean at St. Martin's. He was asked to meet with several upset representatives from All Saints parish, his father's first assignment. The new priest at All Saints, Fr. Haywood Kingsley, preached that the Virgin Birth was nothing to get excited about. "Virgin births," he explained to his congregation, "were not uncommon in the history of that era. Because people didn't live as long as they do now, marriages sometimes were arranged for young girls who had not yet experienced a first period. And, when such youngsters became pregnant before they experienced their first period, it was called a virgin birth."

All Saints Church went nuts! Half of the congregation realized the wisdom of the information and the other half cried for blood, namely Fr. Kingsley's. Denying the Virgin Birth or, more dastardly, reducing it to trivia destroyed a central tenet of the Church for many. This guy had to go, according to the faction seated in front of Dean Baxter. End of story. Period.

Clearly, the Bishop had a duty to keep the congregation together, the Church whole, and the doctrine pure. But he also had an equal duty to the priest who served there as his vicar.

The enlightened group didn't want to lose their young priest, but the bloodthirsty group wanted him sent to Alaska for the next 50 years, preferably the most northern part of that state where it was cold and where he could reflect on the error of his ways. It became abundantly clear to Hewes that Fr. Kingsley certainly would never be able to return to his pulpit at All Saints. He was the bone over which the two groups scrapped incessantly and ferociously. It wasn't that Kingsley was wrong in his presentation. It was just that he was wrong in presenting the information at all.

After only four weeks with Dean Baxter, the Bishop reassigned Fr. Kingsley to work as an associate with a much older priest across the Bay in Oakland. Fr. George Morgenstern of St. Paul's on Myrtle Avenue met with Fr. Kingsley in Hewes' office. Hewes and Morgenstern laid out a course for Fr. Kingsley to follow. Fr. Morgenstern asked Kingsley to enter the office and, without any introductory small talk, began detailing his new life: "You will learn to call on the sick by observing my work with them. You will learn to conduct funerals, weddings, and baptisms by watching how I do those rites. You will submit four sermons in advance for my approval. For your entire year at St. Paul's, you will preach only the approved text."

Fr. Kingsley hardly could contain himself as he listened to the list of rigid requirements. "You self-serving, narrow-minded basta ...," he caught himself in his fury, "You can shove that deal and your Church up your asses!" He stomped out of Hewes' office and never was heard of again. Years later, a Rev. Haywood Kingsley surfaced as the minister of an independent Baptist church in San Diego. His existence as an Episcopal priest ended as soon as he challenged the Virgin Birth doctrine.

Over the years, Dean Baxter realized the pattern. "Ah, yes," he thought to himself, "Save the Church at any cost and to hell with the local priest!" He now knew that once a priest threatened the stability of the congregation that he served, he had to go. The only exception to that rather rigid rule was alcoholism. People in nearly all churches were willing to tolerate a drunk as a priest, but they were unwilling to deal with a doctrinaire.

When the Bishop of New York City died unexpectedly in 1953, Bishop Reginald Wentworth of California was tapped to fill his shoes. There was no question in anyone's mind that Bishop Wentworth would be replaced by none other than the Dean of St. Martin's, Reynolds Carter Baxter, III.

Hewes' elevation the following year was a magnificent event. He was 39 years old. Out of his personal fortune, he paid for every bishop in the church to fly into San Francisco for his investiture. He even arranged for the Bishop of Canterbury in England to attend and to be the chief celebrant. Hewes was unmarried and still living in his childhood mansion.

His first act as Bishop of California was to endow the Diocese with a trust fund of $50 million. He and all future Bishops had complete control of the money. It could be spent any way the then-Bishop decided. Only the bankers and the newly appointed Dean of the Cathedral, named McGinnis, knew of its existence and, upon the death of Hewes, his successor would be informed of its existence. During his lifetime, Hewes never touched the money. Instead, he paid for "extras" out of his personal fortune.

His mother, Lucy, had died years earlier so he lived as a virtual recluse, except for the mostly male house staff who maintained the mansion. Rumors had been whispered for years that Bishop Baxter preferred the company of men to that of women, but nothing ever surfaced with a direct charge of homosexuality. But it was true. Hewes had several lovers who doubled as members of his staff after Lucy died. All of them were completely loyal to him. Anytime guests were invited to the mansion for dinners or business meetings, the staff was completely professional. No gestures ever gave away their secrets. No language was ever used to suggest anything but aboveboard behavior. But, when the guests left and Hewes was alone, he invited certain favorites to share his bed at night.

That following year, one of Bishop Baxter's lovers left the mansion suddenly. A week later, a story of the Bishop and his love life appeared in the San Francisco Tribune. The Bishop denied the story and threatened to sue the disgruntled employee, but that was not to be. Instead, he called his family attorneys, O'Mera, Sullivan, and McConnell, and ordered them to make the problem go away. They were to employ anything and everything necessary to accomplish that directive. It seemed that Lian Sheng had been right years earlier. The ghosts of Griffin Hewes and Rennie Baxter both lived in Reynolds Carter Baxter, III. It was his first murder, but, unlike his ancestors, he had not committed it at the age of 16.

No notice ever was taken when Ronnie Jenkins, the Bishop's accuser, just disappeared. Mutts of discernment, working for the lawyers, were paid $5,000 each to snatch him from his own bed one night and to take poor Ronnie four miles out into the Pacific. They dispatched him wrapped in heavy chains and hooked to heavier lead sinkers to the bottom of the ocean. Within days, Ronnie was fish poop.

But the Bishop knew that he had been savagely attacked and that he had to respond quickly. The curious would not let go of something as juicy as this. Again, he called his family attorneys and asked them to come to the mansion. Not knowing and not wanting to know anything about Ronnie Jenkins, yet wanting them to know that he was grateful for their help, he handed each man a briefcase containing $50,000 in cash. The partners were most pleased.

"If I'm to survive this scurrilous attack," the Bishop began, "I'm going to have to marry. My problem has been one of devotion and service to the Church. I've never found time for a wife and family. But, if it's a wife the Church wants me to have and if it is a wife I need to put to rest these vicious rumors, then find one for me. Pick one. I don't care who she is. Just don't embarrass me with a dog. Each one of us knows the truth, but the public can be fooled with a woman. So find me one and get her here quickly. Make up any story you like. We've known each other for years. We wanted to marry earlier, but my career prevented it. There was never enough time, et cetera, et cetera," he said.

The three attorneys who were assigned to finding a wife for the Bishop were not part of the firm's inner circle. They were young associates who didn't think playing cupid was the reason that they became lawyers. They soon were disabused of that notion and told that, if they ever hoped to make partner in the firm, they better damn well play cupid for all the role was worth. The law, they were told, was not always about justice. Sometimes it was about serving clients regardless of the assignment and regardless of what any particular attorney thought about that duty.

Attorneys Bob Ahers, Sherman Etheridge, and Brian Sherwood retired to the conference room with yellow legal pads and pens. For the next hour, they played "Who Do You Know?" Too old. Scratch. Too young. Scratch. Too tall. Scratch. Too short or too fat or too whatever. Scratch. Clearly, this was not going to be an easy assignment.

Days went by and discrete phone calls were placed to distant relatives. No candidate surfaced. After a second week went by, the senior partners wanted to know what the problem was in finding Cinderella. Their sympathy was at an end. Their client was driving them crazy. They didn't care how they did it, but they were to find this magical person by week's end – or they were out the door.

Sherman Etheridge thought that he might have an idea that possibly could work. He asked if such a woman existed who was a member of an Episcopal parish. But the others were disinclined to call parish priests, tell them that their bishop was looking for a bride, and ask if they had one. Etheridge saw their point. They sent out for lunch and, when the local deli sent their meal to the law firm, a strawberry blonde named Frances O'Brien delivered it. Age, about 34. All three lawyers nearly frightened her to death when they said, "That's her." But they were wrong. Frances already was married and had three boys at home. Back to the drawing board.

But Frances gave them a vision of what they all agreed was the perfect wife for the Bishop. Now they just had to find her. And quickly. Again it was Etheridge who remembered that the firm's senior partner had an unmarried daughter who looked like Frances O'Brien. They asked for a meeting with Brandon O'Mera and he gave them fifteen minutes immediately. "Sir," Etheridge began, "we think we've found a bride for the Bishop."

"Wonderful," he responded. "Who is she?" he asked in anticipation.

"Your daughter, Kathleen Mary, sir," he answered.

Brandon O'Mera sunk deeply into his chair. Even though she was still a beauty at 36, O'Mera knew that he had a spinster on his hands. She didn't like the company of men. She played tennis and rode horses, raced cars and smoked cigars. And she did all of this with several of her female friends. O'Mera's heart was hurt by their suggestion, but he didn't want his younger associates to think that they had done anything wrong. "I see," he began. "Let me talk to Kathleen this evening. I'll let you know what she says in the morning."

Knowing that the meeting was over, the three matchmakers paraded out of O'Mera's office. They felt good about their choice.

Chapter Six: A Bride for the Bishop

He cried like a baby. O'Mera was a widower and his daughter, Kathleen, had taken over the house for her father. She was well educated and had studied abroad in France and Germany.

That evening at dinner, Brandon O'Mera began a conversation with his beautiful daughter. This was the conversation that he had dreaded from the time that she was six years old when he found her playing doctor with her little neighbor, Peggy. "Kathleen, three of my young associates came to see me today," he began. "I'd given them an assignment several weeks ago to find a bride for Bishop Baxter and today they handed me a single name. That name was the result of an exhaustive search to find the right wife for him. I'll spare you the details and just say that they handed me one name and one name only. It was your name, Kathleen," he ended.

"My name?" she questioned with fear instantly showing in her eyes and in her voice.

"Yes, my dear, your name," he answered. "I know that …"

"You only suspect, Father," she cut him off. And the thirty-second pause in their conversation was an eternity for each. "But you are correct," she added very quietly and very slowly. "You do know. You've always known, just as I have known that I can never love a man that way."

"What if I told you that the Bishop is interested only in men and that, once you produce a child, your embarrassing duties would end?" he asked. Kathleen sat motionless. "After all, darling, the man is rich beyond belief," he added, thinking that this was an argument of merit.

"Hell, Father, you're rich. How much more money do I need?" she fired back.

"You're right, of course, darling, but I'm inclined to think my young associates have hit on an idea that will provide both you and my client with an ideal arrangement. I'm not going to live forever, you know. Then what happens to you?" he asked. "As it is now, you are your mother's stand-in and that's all well and good. But who and what will you be when I'm dead and gone?"

"I like the idea of having a baby, Daddy, and I'd really like to have one," she confessed, "but I can't stand the idea of what I have to do to get one," she lamented.

"I know, I know, but you wouldn't have to do it forever. Maybe the first time would be the only time. We could hope, you know?" he said. "And there is another positive side to things. The Bishop would not require your attendance at every function. And you will always look lovely no matter where you go. His reputation will be saved and, quite frankly, Kathleen, so will yours."

For several minutes, Kathleen sat quite still with her eyes closed. Then, in a clear firm voice, she announced, "I'll do it, Father. Yes, I will. I'll do it. You're right for all the right reasons. The little sacrifice I'm being asked to make won't take very long. So my answer is yes. But I do have conditions and I'm unwilling to negotiate on any of them. First, I want my own space in the mansion and as much of it as I require. Second, I will not ever be told what I can and can't do. Ever! Or with whom. My friendships are none of his business. And I'll hire whatever staff I require without approval! Nor will money ever be an item for which I must apply. I will go where I want to go and I will go with whom I want to go. Nothing will change in my life as a result of this marriage. Understood?" she asserted.

Her father walked over to her chair and kissed the top of her head. "Understood, my darling. Understood," he said.

Brandon O'Mera couldn't wait for the next business day. He called the Bishop that night and asked if he could come to see him. He had some important news that he thought the Bishop would like to hear. When he reached the mansion, the Bishop was waiting for him in the library. Brandy was served and O'Mera began: "Hewes, my father served your grandfather for many years. The day your father died, I'm told, my father thought Ren Baxter was going to die as well. His heart was broken. He was very proud of you especially because you filled an empty space in your grandmother's heart and home that only you could fill. For that, he was very grateful. And I should know. I still have a copy of the will my father and he drew up before he died."

Hewes interrupted the story and asked if he could have a copy of the will. He was collecting family items and that one would add greatly to his collection. O'Mera agreed to have it sent over the next day.

"Now, about keeping your good name a good name. I put three of my young go-getters on the project to find you an appropriate wife. They've spent the last three weeks chasing down lead after lead. They found her this morning," he announced. "I want you to know that I had nothing to do with the selection. After I tell you her name, I'll tell you why I did not think of her as a logical choice for you."

Hewes was squirming. This was probably the worst day in his life. "Well, on with it, Brandon. Don't keep me in suspense another moment. Who is the unlucky girl?" he asked.

"My own daughter, Kathleen," he said with great pride. "She's 36 years old. Never married. A beauty. She wants at least one child. But she doesn't like men – or what she has to do to get that baby."

The Bishop sat still and just thought for the longest time. His mind was running at super speed. Finally he smiled and said, "I accept. Make the arrangements. I want it to be big and splashy. I want it soon. Get it in all the papers. I also want to talk with her tomorrow."

"She has a few conditions that are not negotiable. If an iota of any one is not adhered to, she will back out of the deal," O'Mera said. Then he told the Bishop about Kathleen's conditions. The Bishop roared with laughter in much the same way that Griffin Hewes did when Gilbert Forsythe first told him about a kid named Ren Baxter.

"Tell her yes to everything, Brandon," Hewes replied. He liked her already.

O'Mera left immediately and, true to her word, Kathleen went through with it. At the Bishop's request, she visited him at the mansion the next day. He greeted her warmly and invited her into the library where he had talked with her father the night before. "This has got to be as awkward for you as it is for me," he began. "Two perfect strangers, unaware of the other's existence 24 hours ago, agreeing to marry and neither one preferring the company of the opposite sex."

She laughed and so did he. "Well," he continued, "we will make a handsome couple. By the way, I'm Hewes," and they laughed some more.

"Kathleen," she replied, holding out her hand to shake his. "That's close enough for me," she said and they nearly doubled over in laughter. They liked each other, just as his wonderful Gram, Victoria, "liked" his grandfather Ren.

"By the way, your conditions are perfectly acceptable," he said. "You'll never get a smidgen of guidance, correction, or prohibition from me." Then he added, "Let's do this in a grand fashion, Kathleen. I mean, let's have the biggest wedding San Francisco has ever seen and will probably never see the likes of ever again," he proposed.

"Let's," she replied.

The wedding was held in St. Martin's on April 26, 1955. Bishop Baxter asked his old friend, Bishop Reginald Wentworth, formerly of California and now of New York, to perform the ceremony. The pomp and circumstance was elegant. Bridesmaids were long-term friends of the bride. The groomsmen were clergy with whom the Bishop had absolutely no association. In fact, they were surprised when the Bishop asked them to be in the wedding.

The reception was the biggest and most expensive ever seen in San Francisco. The Bishop insisted on paying for everything and Kathleen knew just how to spend his money. Eighteen hundred invited guests dined on squab, filet mignon, Norwegian salmon stuffed with crab, and every vegetable and side dish known to San Franciscans. The Bishop and his bride danced every dance and exhausted every guest. They made a magnificent couple. He was eyeball-to-eyeball with her when she was in low heels. Pictures in the Sunday edition took up three pages. Rumors of the Bishop's alleged homosexuality were squelched and his position in the Church once again became secure.

According to the paper, the place of the honeymoon was a closely guarded secret. Closely guarded, that is, because there would be no honeymoon, as such.

The couple returned to the mansion where they were served by their newly integrated staff. Because she was especially comfortable with several people from her former home, Kathleen brought them with her. The wedding night was planned very carefully and was scripted in detail. Kathleen drank several flutes of champagne that made her giddy and several more that made her drunk in order to ready herself for Hewes' "little visit" as they were calling it. Beside her in the bed was her long-term lover, Wilma Palmer. Wilma and Kathleen kept sipping more and more champagne until they both were very drunk. Everyone knew that, if they played their parts right, this might be the only time Kathleen and Hewes would ever have to "do it." They were all willing to make that happen.

Kathleen lay naked from the waist down and spread-eagled at the edge of the bed with her legs in the air. Hewes stood right beside her and looked down at his favorite lover, Michael who was doing everything that he could to bring the Bishop to climax. When Hewes reached that moment, he broke away from Michael and somehow managed to enter Kathleen and empty his entire load. As soon as he finished, he and Michael departed. Kathleen lay there holding her legs up in the air so that nothing would run out. She wept for hours and was grateful to Wilma for helping her through the ordeal. Finally she let her legs down and the two women slept.

When she missed her period that was due the following week, she told Hewes. He was ecstatic. They had succeeded. Kathleen was pregnant. And she was very sick. For the first three months, she retched every morning. But she soon began to feel better. When the baby started to kick, happiness overwhelmed her.

Hewes was just as excited. He was looking forward to becoming a father. The couple kept separate bedrooms and lovers, but, when guests stayed overnight, Kathleen and Hewes slept in the same bed where she became pregnant. That experience wasn't entirely unpleasant because Kathleen and Hewes truly liked each other, but neither one wanted it to last for more than the few days necessary to carry off the charade.

On January 30, 1956, nearly nine months to the day, Reynolds Carter Baxter, IV, was born. And he was a big bruiser. At nine pounds and eight ounces, R.C., as he was to be called, screamed at the top of his lungs for something to eat. Kathleen was reluctant to nurse him, but the doctor convinced her that it would be good for both of them if she did. She did, to her complete satisfaction and to R.C.'s.

R.C. looked nothing like his father. R.C. had fire-engine-red hair, big hands and feet, a big nose, and a really big "guy" for a baby. Hewes wanted to have him circumcised, but his mother objected. R. C. kept his foreskin. Had baby pictures been available back in Boston from 1869 and had those pictures been available in San Francisco 87 years later, a striking resemblance between one Patrick John Noble and Reynolds Carter Baxter, IV, would have been noticed immediately. But it was not to be.

Hewes and Kathleen were justly proud of their child. He fulfilled dreams and needs too complicated for his parents to explain. His grandfather, Brandon O'Mera, retired shortly after R.C.'s birth and asked if he could help with the child's rearing. He always had wanted a son and, although Kathleen could be quite man-like in her ways, she was still a she and he always had wanted a he. The parents thought that it would be quite fine if Pap O'Mera spent as much time as he wanted with his only grandson.

Each time that the sound of the organ in the mansion's chapel began, R.C. stopped nursing. If he was crying, he stopped crying. Something in that sound touched something deep inside the boy and everyone noticed it. Bach especially made the boy happy. Every day, R.C. was carried into the chapel where he was treated to the sounds of Bach, Mozart, Handel, and many other great composers.

The Bishop made great use of his son, R.C., and his wife, Kathleen. At the boy's baptism, the parents had photographers snap numerous pictures that appeared in the same paper that earlier had accused the Bishop of homosexuality. Kathleen loved to dance. She and the Bishop made the rounds where formal wear and ballroom dancing were expected.

They made a great couple. They just didn't sleep together. Each had a bedroom that connected to the master bedroom, but separated them enough to insure whatever privacy they required.

R.C. grew quickly. At six months, he wore clothing sized for babies who were eighteen months old. His feet were growing especially fast. And his "guy" kept pace with everything else. When R.C. was four, he pulled himself up on the organ bench beside the organist and touched several keys. They sounded and he laughed. He touched a few more and the same sequel occurred. For days, he did the same exercise. Then his grandfather put him on the organ bench and R.C. haltingly sounded out the first line of Bach's Little Fugue in G.

Although unable to read music, R.C. had an ear for it that he kept all of his life. Later, still unable to read a musical score, he could sit at any piano or organ and play anything that he had ever heard. He was a true musical savant. Kathleen wanted to send R.C. to the same private school that she had attended, but Hewes insisted that the boy would be educated where he and his father received their exceedingly fine education. On this issue, Hewes prevailed and R.C. entered the classroom constructed for his grandfather, Griffin, and used by his father, Hewes. Once again, the finest minds in the Episcopal clergy were employed to educate R.C. The boy showed no interest in learning to play other musical instruments, but he played the organ every chance that he could get. He also had a lovely singing voice. He could be heard humming the tunes that he had heard in chapel and on his radio.

His penmanship was remarkable. He had a fine touch and great control of his lines. But it was in numbers that he amazed everyone. He didn't need pencil and paper to figure out most problems. As new information was taught, R.C. ingested it and he was able to solve math problems in his head. By the time that he was sixteen, his instructors were unable to teach him another mathematical skill. He also excelled at reading. In fact, the good teachers believed that they were in the presence of genius and asked his parents for permission to withdraw. R.C. had exhausted everything that they had to teach him.

R.C. never showed any interest in the religious services that his teachers performed in the chapel. He went because he had to. He thought that they were ridiculous when they robed and pranced, preached and prayed. When he complained to his father, the Bishop said that he had better get used to it because he was to become a priest later. R.C. couldn't believe his ears. When he asked his mother about it, she said that his father had counted on his entering the clergy since the day he was born. "But don't I have a say in what I'm to become?" he asked. Her silence said, "Apparently not."

R.C.'s parents, for the first time in their lives, had a problem with their wonder kin. He was bored out of his skull and needed an educational challenge. The Bishop knew that Bards couldn't cut it with R.C., so he suggested that the boy try Stanford, about 35 miles south of their home. He could commute, at first, and, perhaps in time, could find adequate housing.

R.C. jumped at the chance. But there was a price to be paid. The Bishop extracted a promise from R.C. that if he were permitted to go to Stanford in the fall, he would go to seminary following graduation. For days, R.C. brooded, but finally said yes to his father's terms. His biggest problem was how to occupy his time during the summer break. Work was out of the question and so was idle play. Kathleen called her father's old law firm and made arrangements for R.C. to read law books and to ask questions, if he had any, of the associates.

One day, R.C. was getting ready to leave the mansion and accompany his father to town. For the first time, he noticed how much he had started to resemble the oldest portrait of Great-Grandfather Ren. In that painting, Ren was probably five or six years older than R.C. when Lian Sheng had painted it. The uncanny resemblance made the boy ask his father if he, too, thought he looked like his great-grandfather. The Bishop had noticed and asked R.C. if he had any interest in learning anything about RCB, the first. "Over the years, R.C.," he began, "I've kept an account of everything I have remembered and have learned about him. I remember the man quite vividly. Perhaps you'd like to read what I've accumulated. We can talk more about him at dinner some evening."

"I'd like that, Father," R.C. answered.

"Good. After we get home this evening, you and I will open a new chapter in our family history," the Bishop offered.

R.C. was dropped off at the law firm of Sullivan, McConnell, and Ahers where the senior partners greeted him. His pap had died years ago when R.C. was twelve. It was agreed that R.C. would be permitted to read at least half the day, lunch at the club with his father anytime the Bishop was available, and have conversations with assigned associates regarding legalities that he had read about that day or the day before.

In two weeks, R.C. was bored out of his mind. He hated the subject so he found reasons to escape. One beautifully clear day, R.C. went for a walk and wandered into Chinatown. Its many shops and restaurants fascinated him. He walked into several just to look. The place had a magical effect on R.C. and he forgot all about time. Hunger pains reminded him to go home. When he returned to the law firm, the Bishop was waiting and wanted to know where he had been for so long. "I needed to take a walk, Father," he answered straightforwardly. "I won't lie to you. Law just isn't for me. But I'm not sure what is. I know I felt something when I wandered into Chinatown," he said.

"Chinatown," his father repeated. "Chinatown was the beginning of your great-grandfather's business life, R.C. He was your age when he first set foot in Chinatown and he, like you, realized it was a world like no other. I have a busy morning tomorrow, but I'd like us to have lunch at the club. I'm going to show you a few things. I hope you are ready for them," he added.

Father and son rode home in their chauffeured Cadillac limousine. Kathleen Baxter had just left on a world cruise with her beloved companion, Wilma Palmer, so Hewes and R.C. dined alone. Hewes ordered nearly raw steaks, baked potatoes, apple pie with Colby cheese, and coffee for their dinner. "R.C., your great-grandfather probably would have eaten his stake raw, but he knew that would not have been acceptable at the table. So he consented to having it seared on both sides. I have to admit that I prefer it done that way myself, but your mother likes hers well done and Cook usually does things to suit her. But tonight, I want you to try eating it your great-grandfather's way. Are you up to it?" he asked.

"Yes, sir," he answered.

R.C. couldn't believe how good the nearly raw meat tasted to him. He felt compelled to chew on the bone and, since his mother was away, his father enjoyed watching him. "You know, R.C., I remember my grandfather, Ren, doing the exact same thing you are doing. It's uncanny how much you resemble him so closely in many ways," he said.

When desert was finished, the Bishop surprised R.C. with a cigar. It was the first one R.C. had ever been handed and the Bishop made a great ceremony out of the event. "I'm told that my grandfather, Griffin Hewes, introduced your great-grandfather to the pleasures of a cigar at the club when he was your age. I know he did the same thing for me when I was sixteen. Since then, I've enjoyed a good cigar every once in awhile. I hope the tradition will continue with you," he said.

R.C. found the experience and the taste to his liking. The Bishop did not offer R.C. a brandy in the library after the cigars were extinguished. Instead, he unlocked a drawer in his massive desk and placed nearly 35 pages of typed narrative in front of his son. "I hope you find this little family history both enlightening and helpful, R.C.," he said as he exited the room and closed the door behind him.

For the next three hours, R.C. read and re-read the 35 pages. He looked at the books that Ren Baxter had accumulated during his lifetime and was amazed at the diversity of his interests. Not one how-to-succeed book was in the collection. R.C. was drawn to the railroad books that Ren had collected and he found the page that most fascinated the Bishop. He vowed to himself that he would find out who his real ancestors were, no matter how long it took or how much money he had to spend to do so.

The next day, he and the Bishop rode to town together. "Find anything to your liking last night, R.C.?" he asked.

"Yes, sir, I did," he answered.

"Good, I was hoping you would," he responded. "I always thought the accounts about your great-grandfather's size were completely made up, R.C., until you came along. I know this isn't a subject we've ever talked about, so I want you to know that I have as little comfort discussing it as you do. But my mother, Lucy, and her mother-in-law, Victoria, who was married to Ren, were absolutely positive that nothing was exaggerated. They confirmed that my father, Griffin, was not so endowed. I assure you that I am not either. Perhaps it was the reintroduction of your mother's coloring and Irish heritage that brought out that characteristic that skipped two generations. I just don't know. But I do know that you are so much like your great-grandfather that it's scary."

R.C. listened without embarrassment. "Father, do you think I might have the same kind of trouble, you know, as my great-grandfather had?"

"You'll clearly have to have the right partner. Someone as tiny as Grandmother Victoria would produce another disaster. So you'll need to think about that before you get romantically involved with someone," he replied.

Then R.C. surprised his father. "I know about you and Mom," he said. "I don't understand it, but I know about it. I hope that eventually the two of you will tell me how it is that I came about. I've often wondered," he said.

As soon as that was out on the table, the limo pulled up to the law firm where R.C. got out. "See you for lunch at the club, R.C.," the Bishop said.

The morning was going to drag by for R.C. He just knew it. He wanted to bolt out of the door as soon as he opened another legal tome, but the caption at the top of the page caught his eye and changed his mind. The case was entitled: "Reynolds Carter Baxter vs. City Council of South San Francisco." It was dated 1892. When he and Lian Sheng decided to live together outside of Chinatown, Ren wanted to put the title of the home that he had purchased into Lian's name. A town ordinance forbade Chinese people to live in South San Francisco and, further, it forbade them to own property there. Ren had hired R.C.'s pap's father, John O'Mera, to sue the council on his behalf. John brought suit, went to court, and lost. He appealed to the superior court and lost again. Finally, he took his case to the supreme court of the state of California that overturned the two lower courts' decisions and ordered the city council of South San Francisco to amend its ordinance. Lian Sheng became a titled land and property owner. When she died, she willed the property back to R.C.'s father, Hewes.

When Hewes took possession of Lian's house, he removed Reynolds Carter Baxter's huge safe. In it, Ren kept large sums of cash from holdings that he had liquidated before the 1929 stock market crash, as well as money from other sources. When Hewes opened it at the mansion, he was astonished to find that it contained more than $190 million in cash! Hewes was unwilling to use that old safe for obvious reasons. Where could he put all of that money? How could he explain its existence? The safe was so old and so heavy that it would be impossible to hide or explain.

Hewes had a secret room constructed in the space then occupied by the great fireplace in the library. He enlarged its cavity to accommodate an enormous vault purchased from Wells Fargo. When it was installed, Hewes insisted that only out-of-state workers from New York were hired to do the work. It was the only way that he could assure himself of complete secrecy when the job was finished. After that had been done, he consolidated all of the family's money held in numerous places into this one modern safe.

One of the first things that Hewes did shortly after he and Kathleen were married was to take her into the hidden vault and make her memorize the combination to the safe. He told her that she could take as much from it as she required and that she never needed to consult him. The only thing that he asked from her was that she never let another living soul know of its existence. The money was not to be invested, just spent. After all, he reasoned, if the government ever discovered the money, most of it could be seized. Kathleen never entered that room again. She never took as much as one dollar from the safe. It remained the Bishop's secret stash. He used it mostly for nefarious pay-offs and for anonymous charitable donations that usually were made through his attorneys.

At lunch, the first thing R.C. wanted to know was what happened to the house Lian and Ren lived in. "I donated it to the school board of South San Francisco so art students could go there and paint. I also created a trust that will pay for its upkeep and art supplies for the next 100 years. Then I really ticked them off. I made the city council put up an official plaque naming it the Lian Sheng Art Center. It galled them to do it, but I sweetened their loss with a $5,000 cash award to each member of the council," he answered.

R.C. laughed out loud. "You bought them off, Father?" he asked.

"I suppose you could come to that conclusion," he answered, "but I prefer to think of it as a sound bit of charity. After all, many hundreds of children have already benefited from the gifts." And he laughed even harder.

When lunch was over, R.C. and the Bishop went for a walk to the First Bank of California, as it now was known. The old building had withstood earthquakes, fires, floods, and several expansions since Rennie Baxter and Tommy Moran first opened an account with $1.50 so long ago. So, it was to the old section in the old vault that R.C. and Hewes walked. Producing the same key that Lian Sheng gave him years before, Hewes and the bank official opened safe deposit box number 152.

The Bishop removed the vase, the silver eagle money clip, and the panda jade – all of the items from the narrative that he had read the night before. "My father died before he could give me Tommy Moran's key, R.C., and it couldn't be found at the time of his death. He had hidden it somewhere. When Lian Sheng brought me here and showed me the three items inside this box, she gave me his only key. She also instructed me to keep the key someplace safe and not to tell my mother of its existence. Lian said I could do anything I wanted with the contents of the box. I put the key in my wallet because she told me that Grandfather Ren kept it in his wallet, but I've never returned to this place since that day. Lian also told me that the jade was worth more than $100,000. I'm sure it's probably worth twice that much today. I'm passing the key to you, R.C., and telling you that you are to do whatever you want to do with the contents of the box whenever you want to do it."

When the Bishop returned the objects to the box, he handed the key to R.C. R.C. tucked it into his wallet and the two left the bank. R.C. went for a walk into Chinatown. The Bishop returned to his office for appointments and to finalize plans for the annual meeting of fellow bishops in just nine more weeks.

That meeting was to take place in San Francisco. St Martin's hosted the gathering and, when it opened, Hewes was in his glory. He spent lavishly out of his own fortune to upgrade accommodations and to make certain that only the finest foods and wines were served. He showered his fellow bishops with gifts of the most expensive robes and vestments. He and Kathleen, just back from her cruise, hosted the entire group at the club on the last evening of the event. She sparkled with wit and grace. She and Hewes were great friends. They admired each other for so many reasons. Over the years, she had volunteered at St. Martin's for nearly every charity event and had taken leadership roles on various boards. When they returned home that evening, R.C. was reading his father's collected history of their ancestor, Ren Baxter, and taking notes of his own. R.C. kept returning to the narrative, hoping he would find something new in it. When they asked if he needed anything, he said, "Just some information," but that it could wait. "You both must be exhausted," he offered.

"I know I am," the Bishop responded. "I'll see you both in the morning." And he left. But his mother said that she had a few ounces of energy left and wanted to know what she could do for her son.

"Talk to me about you and Dad, please," he said. "I told Dad, right after you left on the cruise with Wilma, that I knew about the two of you, but what I don't know is how I came about, given the circumstances."

Kathleen walked over to her son and hugged him close to her. "It's quite complicated, R.C., as you must know. Your father and I genuinely care for each other. Over the years, we've grown to love each other in a mutually respectful way. Just because we play the marriage charade for the purposes of career and family doesn't make what we have invalid. You were conceived on our wedding night much like your grandfather was conceived on the wedding night of Ren and Victoria. Your father and I were equally lucky, but have never been together that way since. We simply cannot love another person of the opposite sex that way."

R.C. thanked her for the information and said he probably would have more questions at a later time. But Kathleen wasn't finished. "R.C.," she continued, "you should know that neither your father nor I want you to feel any less of a person because you've come out of a different kind of marriage. We really did conceive you the old-fashioned way and no son could ever be loved more than we love you. Your father thinks the sun rises and sets on you. And so do I. I hope you go into the priesthood, marry, and have at least a dozen kids. But, if you don't, the world will not come to an end. Good night," she said, then climbed the stairs, and went to her own bedroom.

CHAPTER SEVEN:
The Family Curse

September arrived and R.C. drove himself to Stanford University, nearly 30 miles south of San Francisco. The family attorneys pre-registered him and his fees were paid from one of his trusts. He was enrolled in the college of general studies. His first year was academically unremarkable. In his home school, he had covered most of the material, so he used the time to read more about the transcontinental railroad, over which his great-grandfather traveled as a baby, perhaps named Patrick. He found a large section in the humanities library that was devoted to the history and running of the Southern and Central Pacific Railroad. He quickly breezed through the history of the transcontinental and the part that Leland Stanford played in its construction. He lingered, however, over the accounts of Stanford's manipulation of land grants and public monies when he was the governor of California. The records indicated that he had used his own construction companies to complete the work. Something in Stanford's take-no-prisoners practice appealed greatly to R.C.

The year was 1972 and the war in Vietnam still was going on.

R.C. made a handsome appearance wherever he went. He was six-feet-two and on his way to six-feet-four. His hair was bright red and his smile could melt an iceberg. Driving his new red Corvette made him look like many other young students at Stanford.

But he was not like them in more ways than even he knew. Student protests sometimes got out of hand. When R.C. expressed no interest in the radical causes that some students advocated, several began to accuse him of not caring about the country. At first, he sloughed them off, but eventually he had to deal with them. They sought him out because they had learned that his father was the Episcopal Bishop of California and he was, according to them, a spoiled brat.

Six of them waited for him to leave the library one evening. They had gotten their courage up with beer and weed. When he appeared, they started yelling obscenities at him. He just kept walking. When he got to his car, he saw the ugly marks and dents that the six had made hours before. He tried to get in and drive off, but that was not to be. It took four of them to hold him while two of them beat him severely. R.C. never lost consciousness. His anger went off any scale imaginable and it surprised him at how well it served him in that situation. His attackers ran off when campus security arrived. Security loaded R.C. into one of their ambulance wagons and took him to the university hospital, where he was treated for his injuries and released. He refused to identify his attackers to the authorities. He claimed that he didn't know any of them. His father blamed himself. Had R.C. been anyone else's son, the incident wouldn't have happened. R.C. disabused Hewes of that notion immediately. Kathleen just wanted to bring her baby home.

The leader of the gang of six was a beer-bellied scruffy-bearded fireplug named Onslow Weaver. He was a fifth-year first-semester junior who spent as much time raising hell as going to class. He was well known on campus and had some following in the media, as well. R.C. didn't care who or what he was. He didn't have the right to beat him like that. So R.C. began a serious campaign to stalk Weaver. For months, he followed him everywhere and wrote down everything that he discovered about

Weaver's activities. Wearing a cap to cover his give-away red hair, R.C. attended rallies where Weaver spoke. The other five who participated in R.C.'s beating were always around Weaver, thereby making it impossible for R.C. to retaliate.

But that changed when R.C. overheard Weaver tell a bartender about the big protest rally that he was to attend in San Francisco during the weekend. He was one of the main speakers. He was going to crash with friends just outside of Chinatown on Columbus Avenue. R.C. knew the area well and didn't think he would have any difficulty in finding Weaver.

R.C. stopped following Weaver and burned every scrap of paper and every note that he had ever written regarding the man. To his parents' surprise and delight, he went home for the weekend. About 2:00 in the morning, R.C. slipped out of the mansion, rolled his new car down the long driveway and through the front gate, and drove into the city. He began looking for Onslow Weaver.

The rally was a huge event. Hundreds of people were milling around when R.C. parked his car in the First Bank of California's parking lot, which was several blocks from Chinatown. His chances of finding Weaver were slim to none because the weather suddenly turned ugly. Then it started raining, which chased off most of those who were still wandering around the area. Fog soon replaced the rain, making visibility negligible. But R.C. was determined. He walked along Columbus Avenue from one end to the other where it ran parallel with Chinatown. He searched on one side of the street and then on the other as he strained all the while to see his intended victim. No luck.

The sun's arrival, just over the horizon, made it possible for R.C. to recognize Weaver's roly-poly form when he stumbled down the street. He was alone. The last man standing from a group of drinkers. From inside his long coat, R.C. brought out a two-by-four with a five-inch spike in its end. He greeted Onslow Weaver so that Weaver would know his attacker. Then he sank the spike into Weaver's skull. It killed him instantly. Weaver fell and R.C. trampled the spike through his victim's ear and into his brain. Then he drove a large metal stake through the late Onslow Weaver's throat, walked back to the bank's parking lot where he had left his car, and disappeared into the emerging light of day. R.C. drove home, pushed his car up the driveway, re-entered the mansion, and slept late that morning.

News of Weaver's death and the unusual instruments used to kill him made national news. The Bishop was horrified, but he said nothing. Other than the Bishop, R.C. was the only living person who knew that Ren Baxter and Griffin Hewes had killed men who had attacked them. Other than the Bishop, R.C. was the only living person who knew that Ren had used a two-by-four with a five-inch spike in it and that Griffin Hewes had used a circus tent stake. He felt himself getting hard again.

Surely the police would be calling at the mansion, the Bishop reasoned. After all, R.C. had been beaten severely by Weaver and a record of that beating was still on file. But since R.C. hadn't mentioned Weaver by name, the Bishop's fears were unfounded. What should he say if they came calling? Sunday came and the family attended St. Martin's. The Dean was the celebrant that morning and the Bishop sat in the pews with his family on that rare day. After dinner that evening, R.C. had to drive back to college. His father walked him to his car and asked if he had seen the news regarding Onslow Weaver. Looking his father straight in the eye, he said, "Yes. I'm glad he's dead. And yes, Father, I killed the rotten bastard, just like Ren and Griffin did when they were sixteen."

"You did no such thing! You were here with us all weekend. Unless someone saw you and can pick you out of a line up, you'll never be arrested. I'll see to that," he said. "Under no circumstances will you tell another living soul what you just told me. Do you understand, R.C.?" he hissed through clenched teeth. Apparently, piss and vinegar ran in all of their veins. R.C. understood and said so. The Bishop hugged his son and allowed him to return to college.

Less than two hours after Onslow Weaver's murder, the

police had a suspect in custody. He was one of Weaver's cronies, Howie Horne, who had threatened Weaver earlier in the bar. Weaver embarrassed him by dumping a pitcher of beer over the guy's head. Police found Howie passed out about half a block from where Weaver's body was found. He was one of the six who beat R.C. and R.C. felt like he had gotten two for one. Weeks later, he told his father about the two-for-one thought and the Bishop had to smile in spite of himself. At trial, Horne admitted killing Weaver. It was his only claim to fame and he wasn't going to screw it up. One week after sentencing, Howie Horne was found hanging dead in his cell. The Bishop had asked the family lawyers to use their mutts again in order to end any possible recantation at a later date. The senior partners enjoyed another large, tax-free cash bonus that came from Ren and Lian's old safe's contents now residing in the Bishop's new safe within the former fireplace. It was the Bishop's second murder.

R.C. needed a house of his own. He told his father that he had found one about half a mile from campus. The Bishop bought it for him and Kathleen helped him to furnish it. His parents also supplied an in-house staff consisting of a cook, butler, and cleaners. R.C. accepted them, as was his due, but he insisted that, if they were parental spies who sent home daily or weekly reports on him, he would get along just fine without any of them. They all lied, of course, and the parents were kept informed on a need-to-know basis.

During his senior year in 1976, R.C. met a young woman named Peipei Jiang. He was smitten! They were in the same Asian history class and sat two rows apart. He was a lovesick puppy for several weeks. One day after class, he screwed up his courage, introduced himself, and asked if she would have dinner with him. To her own delight, and certainly to his, she accepted. The youngsters agreed to meet that evening at 6:30 at the Shaw Restaurant that was just past the main campus and library. R.C. was there at 6:00 and made sure that they had the finest table in the house. When Peipei arrived promptly at 6:30, R.C. barely was able to contain himself with joy and anticipation.

Having attended large and small dinner parties all of his life, R.C. thought that he'd have no problems with one more. But he had never had dinner with Peipei and he was at a total loss. She was third-generation and spoke no Chinese. Her parents knew only a few Chinese words, but they never spoke them in her presence. R.C. was drawn to her beauty and to her modesty. When he asked her to tell him about her family's history and how she arrived at Stanford, R.C. was surprised to hear many similarities that he knew existed in his own story. Her grandparents on her father's side were both orphaned and later adopted by strangers. Just how they came to America is still a mystery. They think that her grandmother was bought as an infant in China and resold to a slave trader heading for America. They were told that the slave trader specialized in raising children to be prostitutes. Her grandfather was a laundry man. No one was sure how he got to America. When he met Peipei's grandmother in San Francisco, the two of them realized how impoverished they were from an ancestral perspective. Neither remembered anything about their real parents. So they married and vowed to provide a better home for their children and grandchildren. Obviously they succeeded. Here she was, a senior at Stanford, and only two generations away from the boat and grinding poverty.

R.C. ordered a steak, nearly raw, and a baked potato. He was surprised when Peipei ordered the same thing. When dinner was over, R.C. suggested that they go to the library because he needed help in researching some information about Cheng Zu, the second Emperor of the Ming Dynasty. Peipei was curious to know what it was about Cheng Zu that interested him. R.C. said that it was not the emperor himself that interested him, but rather his extensive collection of carved jade animals. Peipei couldn't resist the invitation.

For the next week, R.C. and Peipei were inseparable. They followed their usual routine of classes, dinner, library, and research. It didn't take them long to discover that historians had cataloged seventy-eight animal carvings at the time of the great palace fire which devastated the collection. Over the years, various pieces from that collection had been discovered in some of the great houses in China. Obviously, not all had been lost at the time of the fire. Speculation was that perhaps some of the treasures initially were rescued, taken to a safe place, and simply misplaced. But those pieces found in Europe and in the London Museum probably were "liberated" by servants or what served as firefighters in those days. Who knew?

What was known, however, was that in the last twenty-five years, seventy-three of the animals in that collection had been returned to China for display in the Great Hall of the People. The centerpiece of that collection, a panda jade, was still at large. No clues existed as to its whereabouts.

R.C. said nothing to Peipei about the panda jade in safe deposit box number 152 in the First Bank of California. One weekend, he took his and her research to the mansion and asked his father if he would spend Saturday evening with him in the study. The Bishop was only too glad to oblige. "What's on your mind, R.C.?" the Bishop asked.

"This is going to take me a few minutes, Dad, but bear with me. First off, I've met this terrific young woman named Peipei Jiang. She reminds me so much of Lian in the narrative of my great-grandfather. She's beautiful, Dad, and I want you and Mom to meet her one day soon. But, before then, I have some interesting information."

The Bishop smiled and thought, "How wonderful." It appeared that his son might be in love. But he said nothing and just listened.

"The panda jade that's been in the bank's safe for all of these years probably is the real thing. Banker Forsythe was correct when he identified it to Ren. Without telling her why I was interested in the Emperor's jade animal collection, I enlisted the aid of Peipei to help me do research on what happened to it. Would you believe a fire hit the palace? Most or all of the jade animal collection disappeared. Many thought the entire collection was burned, but, in the last 25 years, most of it has been discovered all over the globe. Many of the present owners have already returned their pieces."

Once more, the Bishop smiled and thought, "How wonderful." It appeared that his son had a conscience. But he said nothing and listened some more.

R.C. was now into his story. "The day you gave me the key to that box, you also told me that I could do anything I wanted with its contents. With your permission, I'd like to return the panda to its rightful owners, the people of China. What do you say, Dad?"

"I say let's get rid of it and close that dreadful chapter linking our family to the murder of Frankie Wilson. Do you have a plan? Remember, R.C., Ren was told that his life would be taken the minute that jade surfaced. I don't want that to happen to any of us, R.C. Do you have a plan or do you want my help?" the Bishop asked.

"I want your help," R.C. replied. "You're the one who has the contacts. I'm sure this can all be done cleanly and anonymously."

"Indeed, it can," the Bishop said. "I'll make a few phone calls. Perhaps the deed can be done within the next few months."

"The next few months?" R.C. remonstrated. "I thought …" but the Bishop cut him off.

"This will take some time, R.C. To keep our good name away from the press, tracks must be covered. That can't happen overnight. But I've been successful at covering many tracks in the past. Some of them might surprise you," he offered.

"Yeah, right, the good Bishop of California doing dastardly deeds," R.C. mocked.

"Tease all you want, R.C., but I'm no pussy. Never have been. You'll recall that Grandfather Hewes was as much ruthless criminal as he was legitimate businessman. I assure you, R.C., some of his blood still runs through me, just as it does through you, I'm afraid," the Bishop confided.

"An example, please, kind sir," R.C. asked.

"Two of my ancestors and my son have all killed other men," he began, with an edge to his voice. "I ordered the death of one of my first lovers because he dared to expose me in the press about a year before you were born. In fact, it was because of him that you even exist. I'd probably never have married had he not forced the institution on me. At my request, your pap hired killers to make Ronnie Jenkins disappear. I was told afterwards that they dumped him into the Pacific Ocean. So don't think I don't have blood on my hands, too," he said with great sadness. "What is it about us Baxters, R.C., that finds us killing someone in every generation with the exception of my own father?" he asked wistfully.

R.C. truly was stunned. "You, Father?" he asked.

"Me, R.C.," he replied. "I'm as guilty of murder as any of us, and I've done it more than one time, too."

R.C. didn't pursue that one, but, in that instant, he suspected that Howie Horne might not have committed suicide as reported. Maybe he'd ask about it one day. Now wasn't the time.

Before R.C. returned to school on Sunday evening after dinner, the Bishop told him that he was not to talk to anyone, not even Peipei, about the possibility of the panda find. His own sources indicated just how dangerous it was to be in possession of the great centerpiece. Even the most highly principled men with the best of intentions could be overwhelmed by the sum being offered for the panda these days. Six million, the Bishop learned, was the starting bid.

True to his word, R.C. broke off research on the jade animal collection of Emperor Cheng Zu. He also stopped seeing Peipei Jiang. He was afraid of what was happening and he didn't want to scare her off by what he had hidden in his pants. One day after class, Peipei walked right up to him and asked what she had done or said that made him dump her. That caught R.C. off guard. He stumbled around with some lame excuse, which he saw right away wasn't working. So he asked her to come to his house that night for dinner. He said that he would pick her up at her dorm at 6:30.

Peipei truly was amazed when she arrived at R.C.'s home. She suspected that R.C. came from money – but not this much money. Cook fixed nearly raw steaks, baked potatoes, apple pie with Colby cheese on top, and coffee. When R.C. offered Peipei a cigar, she was stunned. Women from her culture didn't smoke cigars, as far as she knew. She smiled her heart-melting smile, but declined. R.C. put his back in the humidor.

"R.C., you've not told me much about yourself or your family, while I've shared much with you about mine," she began.

"What would you like to know, Peipei?" he answered.

"Who are your parents and where do they live? Who were their parents? Things like that. And just how did you get all this money?" she responded, sweeping her arms through the air as if pointing to the entire house.

"A gold-digger, eh?" R.C. teased. Peipei smiled that great smile again and shook her head no.

"Well, I can go back only three generations. Adoption played a big part in my past, as it did in your own." For the next hour, R.C. spun his family history minus murders, robberies, a magnificent panda jade piece, and the size of his cock. When he finished, Peipei knew that she had gotten the greatly censored version and said so. She especially was fascinated with the Lian Sheng story and knew that there was something big missing in the narrative. How true, how true. She pressed R.C. for the information, but he was reluctant to give it.

Finally she said, "R.C., it's okay to talk about sex with me. I'm as interested in the subject as you are. I'm especially interested in having sex with you – as I think you are with me."

There it was. What was he to do? It took him another twenty minutes to retrace the narrative that he had spun and put back the parts that had been edited out about Ren, Victoria, Lian, and how tiny Victoria bore Ren a son. Then it took him another ten minutes to relate how size skipped two generations, but came back totally intact in him.

"You're kidding," she said.

"No, I'm not, Peipei. It's because of my size that I stopped seeing you when I did. My dad told me that I needed to be very careful in choosing a sex partner. As a result, I've never been with a woman," he admitted.

"I'm still a virgin, too, R.C.," she offered, "but not for the same reason, of course. I never found anyone who interested me in that way before. Now that I have, you're telling me that it's not likely that we can do it because you've got a large cock? That doesn't seem fair, does it?" she pleaded.

"Peipei, if we did it and I tore you the way my great-grandfather tore my great-grandmother, I'd never forgive myself and you'd hate me forever," he replied.

"Yes, but didn't you say Lian had a special oil that she used the first time? Maybe we can find some of it and then try. What do you think about that, R.C.?" she asked hopefully.

"I don't know," he answered. "Let's not rush into this, right now. I'll tell you what. Come home with me this weekend. I'm dying for my parents to meet you. My dad will have advice for us. He'll probably figure out just what we need. He's a terrific man and you'll adore my mother."

"You plan to discuss having sex with me with your father, R.C.?" she asked incredulously.

"Of course, I will. He knows everything and everyone. If he thinks we need extra help, he'll get it for us. I'd rather do this right or not at all. Trust me, Peipei," he pleaded, "it's for the best. I've wanted to make love with you from the first moment I saw you in our Asian history class," he confessed.

She broke his flow and said, "Me, too, but I was too shy even to meet you. When you asked me to dinner, I thought the ancient Chinese gods must truly be smiling on me."

R. C. reached over and kissed Peipei for the first time. She responded warmly and wanted the petting to continue, but R.C. said no. He knew where it would lead them and neither one was ready for that to happen. Peipei pouted a little, but agreed. R.C. drove her back to her dorm where he kissed her again. She responded warmly again.

CHAPTER EIGHT:
Young Love and Revenge

Thursday evening of that week, R.C. called home and asked if he and Peipei could visit for the weekend. "Of course" was the answer. When classes ended the next day, Peipei and R.C. drove 35 miles north to the mansion to meet the folks. He used the driving time to explain his parents' special arrangement to Peipei who thought it strange, but seemed to be okay with it.

The Bishop and Kathleen were enchanted with Peipei. Peipei was more enchanted by the watercolor portraits of Reynolds Carter Baxter painted by Lian Sheng so many years ago. It was as though his great-grandson, R.C., had sat for the first two of them.

Dinner was pizza and beer. Nothing special. Just friendly. The table conversation lasted until nearly midnight. At that time, the Bishop gave out, said so, and trotted off to bed. Kathleen did the same a few minutes later, which left the young couple to themselves. R.C. escorted Peipei to her room where he kissed her a little more passionately than he had before. She opened her bedroom door and pulled R.C. inside. "Just for a little bit, R.C. I promise I won't ravish you," she said playfully.

"Damn," he replied with the same playfulness in his voice.

Peipei lay on the bed and invited R.C. to join her. He sat down, but would not lie beside her. "What's the matter, R.C.?

Don't you like me to be suggestive?" she asked.

"That's the problem, Peipei, I do. It drives me crazy, but we aren't any way near ready to have sex," he answered.

"Speak for yourself, R.C. I've been ready for a long time." And with that, she pulled R.C. on top of her.

It didn't take long for R.C. to respond. When he took off his clothes, Peipei could not believe her eyes. He had not been kidding and, indeed, she did not think they were ready. Perhaps she would never be ready. The Bishop had better come up with something good or they were in deep trouble – especially her. How had Lian Sheng managed to have sex with R.C's ancestor? She wasn't sure, but she wanted to find out.

Realizing R.C's embarrassment, Peipei suggested that he put his clothes back on and leave. They would talk in the morning. He did, but they did not talk in the morning. Kathleen had planned a shopping trip with Peipei and whisked her away before R.C. could get two sentences in.

The Bishop had set aside the morning for R.C. When they were in the study, R.C. burst into tears. So uncharacteristic was this behavior that the Bishop truly was alarmed.

"R.C., what's the matter? I've never seen you like this. Out with it – this instant!" he demanded.

"Last night, Peipei and I were alone in her bed for the first time. I'd tried to tell her, even warn her, about my size, but some- how it didn't register with her as possible. When I took off my pants, she was astonished and agreed that we wouldn't be able to have sex till I talked to you about the problem. What can we do, Dad?" he pleaded.

"A little at a time, R.C., a little at a time," he answered. "Put it in until she says stop. And then stop. Remember, Lian was a prostitute who had been with other men before she was with Ren. I doubt Peipei has ever been with any man, so you'll have to go real slow at first. I've alerted your mother about your interest in Peipei and she's agreed to help her as best she knows how," he comforted. "Now, R.C., can we talk about the jade?"

"Sure, I guess," R.C. blinked. "That's it, 'a little at a time'?"

"What else do you want me to say, R.C.? Cut the damn thing off or trim about twelve inches away? I think I've given you good advice. Don't you?" he responded.

R.C. had to agree because he didn't like the cutting alternatives at all. "As always, you're right, Dad. Tell me about the jade," he answered.

"My ... no ... our attorneys," he began, "have visited the Chinese consulate here in San Francisco. They asked the Consulate General if he would be able to receive one of the last outstanding animals of Cheng Zu's jade collection. When he answered in the affirmative too quickly, they were very suspicious of his intentions. So they flew to Washington, D. C., and went to the Chinese Embassy. They spoke with the Chinese Ambassador to the United States and asked him the same question. He said they were right in coming to him because only he could assure them of the jade's return to China," he explained.

"So where does that leave us now?" R.C. wanted to know.

"Right where we are, R.C.," the Bishop answered. "I've made arrangements to fly the Ambassador to San Francisco next month where he will address an invited crowd of 1,000 on the subject of Chinese/American relations since Nixon. I'll host the event at St. Martin's. When his speech and the reception are over, our attorneys will present the jade to him and his entourage of nine armed guards just before they board their flight back to China. In that way, no one will ever know that the jade was in San Francisco or that it has been in our family's possession for over 70 years. His superiors in Peking also have been notified of the jade's return. They plan to reward the Ambassador handsomely when he returns to a hero's welcome," he concluded.

"You're good, Father. I have to give you that. You're damn good," R.C. said admiringly.

"Thank you," the Bishop responded. "If today were not today, R.C., but a day at the turn of the last century, I'd say this return of one precious Chinese object might begin to cover the value you now place on Peipei," he offered.

"I never thought of Peipei as an object of trade before, but I do see your point. I'm relinquishing my ownership of the jade and acquiring the love of another treasure of China. Not too shabby," he said.

Before Kathleen and Peipei were out of the driveway, Peipei's emotions got the better of her, exactly the same way that R.C.'s had overtaken him. She burst into tears and told Kathleen of her failure as a woman and about her fear of what she had seen the night before.

"It will all be okay, Peipei," she promised. "We all stretch. Otherwise, babies would never get born. Babies require more of us than R.C. requires of you. We'll make a few purchases today that will give you some confidence. Right now, R.C.'s father is telling him that everything will work out just fine. After we go shopping, you may be more ready tonight."

Peipei appreciated the encouragement, but didn't think that she ever would be ready to take on R.C. in all of his glory. But she was willing to find out whether or not it was possible.

Kathleen drove Peipei to all of the best boutiques that San Francisco had to offer. She spent several thousand dollars to outfit her. They lunched at the Bay Bankers and Brokers Club, where women finally were admitted with little prejudice, and told her about Griffin Hewes and that side of R.C's family.

"So that's where he gets his love for almost raw meat," she mused.

"Not entirely, Peipei," she corrected. "Ren came to this very table in this very alcove with a taste for nearly raw steak. Griffin Hewes simply educated that palate and gave it ample opportunity to grow."

Following lunch, Kathleen took Peipei into several sex shops along Fisherman's Wharf where birth control products, scented oils, and pleasure devices could be purchased. Peipei was intrigued by the entire variety of objects and potions. She walked out of the store with a sample of four. In the car on the way home, Kathleen gave Peipei explicit instructions on what each thing was for and how it worked. The most important item, Kathleen insisted, was the diaphragm.

When Peipei and R.C. went to her room that evening, both were ready for the inevitable. Kathleen had suggested that Peipei use the diaphragm and Peipei agreed that it would be best. She inserted it after she finished a long hot bath. R.C. was already in her bed and ready for her to join him there. For a short time, they kissed and touched before each felt ready. "R.C., I bought some oil for tonight and I'd like us both to use it," she said as she began pouring and stroking his already-erect dick. When it came time for him to enter her, she asked him to go really slow. She had a high pain tolerance, but it had never been tested in this particular area and she was not sure how she would react. He agreed and began his push into her with no rush.

She was able to take the first six inches of R.C. with little difficulty, but asked him to go no further. The girth of his cock was beginning to widen significantly and she told him that it was hurting her. That was fine by R.C. Just to be in her that little bit was pure pleasure. He began to move in and out. Peipei started to respond to the pleasure that she was feeling as well as to the discomfort accompanying the activity. She asked if they could stop and rest for a moment. R.C. withdrew completely from her and began to kiss her breasts. Peipei wanted more. She told R.C. to rub more oil on himself and to try again. He was only too willing to obey. This time, they were both surprised at the ease with which he plunged into her. She was unable to stretch any further than before, so R.C. had to content himself with that much contact.

He was unable to ride her in such a limited way for very long. He had to suspend his body in the air with his arms and feet, so it was beginning to be difficult for him to continue. He wanted to come, but he also needed a rest. Again he withdrew and dismounted. Then Peipei had an idea. What if R.C. lay on the bed and she mounted him while she stood on her feet? In that way, she could control just how much of R.C. she could accommodate and the rate at which she wanted to increase the penetration. He was certainly game. Peipei held onto the bottom bedposts and squatted down to receive R.C.'s cock. Her pleasure began to increase with each inch that she buried. In this position, she was able to take in another three inches. Every part of her pussy was stretched to the limit and, as she moved up and down on R. C., contact was just right for her. She came with all of the force of a young woman in complete ecstasy. R. C's moment was seconds behind hers. He shook the entire bed as he held on for dear life. They repeated their lovemaking several more times that night.

The next morning, the two young lovers left right after breakfast. Kathleen and the Bishop asked no questions. They sent them off with hugs and kisses all around and instructed them to hurry back anytime.

The Bishop had to get into the cathedral for services. Kathleen asked if she could be excused from them. She wasn't feeling well at all. "Of course," he replied. She retired to her room. She began to reflect on the great fortune that was hers because she consented to marrying Reynolds Carter Baxter, III, Bishop of the Episcopal Church of California. Her only son had turned out quite well and was now in love and able to make love. From her desk, she removed a single sheet of writing paper and began to write a letter to her son. "Dear R.C.," she wrote. Then her hand froze – as did her mouth and her heart. Kathleen died of a heart attack and wasn't found until late in the day when the Bishop returned from services.

The Bishop mourned Kathleen's death for the remainder of his life. Over the years, she had become his best friend and closest advisor. Following her funeral, he made a decision to be celibate. He never even thought about taking a lover again. The several staff members who had been intimate with the Bishop were all dismissed from his life. Each was given a large cash award and a yearly income from a trust that was both princely and guaranteed for the remainder of their lives. When they died, the trust reverted back to the Bishop's estate. All he required was their silence. If they uttered one word, they would be cut off in more ways than financial. They all remembered Ronnie Jenkins. They knew that he had disappeared and never was heard from again by anyone. Each man was reminded of that fact as he accepted his envelope and left. Having received the same considerations, Wilma Palmer left the mansion the day after Kathleen's burial.

R.C. returned home on the same evening that his father called him at his Stanford home. R.C. phoned Peipei and told her of his mother's death, but refused to take her back with him that night. He said that he would call her from the mansion and tell her about the funeral arrangements.

Of course, the Bishop made a grand exit for Kathleen just as he had made a grand entrance for her. He asked the Dean of the Cathedral to attend to the funeral. R.C. sat with his father in the front row of St. Martin's and was deeply moved by the beauty of the ceremony. For the first time in his life, he appreciated all the pomp and parading of the clergy. But it was the Dean's eulogy that moved everyone to tears and changed R.C.'s heart and mind about becoming an Episcopal priest. Dean McGinnis spoke lovingly and knowingly with measured tones and crisp sentences. It was evident to all in attendance that he knew Kathleen almost as well as the Bishop had known her and that McGinnis had loved her from afar.

He said:

"For almost two decades, I've known and loved Kathleen Baxter. Our friendship deepened and grew with our shared experiences and interests. I know a lot about Kathleen's life through moments we shared visiting the sick in hospitals or making sure needy families within St. Martin's shadow had enough to eat. One of her favorite things to do at St. Martin's was to host charity teas for worthy causes. Without her support and contacts, I assure you, many of our great city's finer institutions would have folded long ago.

"I heard the stories of how Kathleen and the Bishop met.

I'm here to tell you that they are all true. Kathleen was an independent woman whose keen mind and beauty were terrifying to most men. Her late father, Attorney Brandon O'Mera, introduced them and it was love at first sight. I shared Kathleen's grief when her father died. She was devastated at his loss, but his keen mind and combative nature lived on in her. Kathleen spoke her mind; let me tell you. Many were the times I came in for my share of her ... shall we say, 'temper'?

"Kathleen had three major loves in her life. The first was her family: her husband, Hewes, and son, R.C. As you know, R.C., you mother had just begun a letter to you when she died with the pen in her hand. The second was St. Martin's, especially the magnificent chapel choir. Kathleen wasn't able to sing a note on key, but she had an appreciative ear and stood in awe at the beauty of the choir's sound. It is no secret that music moved her to tears on many occasions. The last one was tennis. Kathleen was addicted to the game. She played like a woman possessed and could beat almost any challenger, woman or man. I can tell you that, in all the years I knew her, never once did I ever win a match against her. However, when she and I were partners, we won every doubles event we played.

"Kathleen was determined, obstinate, opinionated, bull-headed, willful, bossy, and some other descriptive words that I won't add – and those were just a few of her good points. Of course I, myself, know nothing about these traits because I'm not that way at all." Those in attendance laughed. "So, you ask, how could two such strong-willed people work so closely and yet remain such good friends? No question that there were times when we disagreed – LOUDLY – and the fur flew! We never hesitated to tell the other 'I told you so.' But we also never hesitated to say, 'You were right. I was wrong.' It worked because our bond was so strong and our respect for each other was so great. And it worked because our mutual love for St. Martin's proved to be the glue that helped hold it all together.

"In the last few years, Kathleen Baxter had been a huge

part of all we've been able to accomplish here at St. Martin's Cathedral. Being married to the Bishop didn't hurt, but she would have done her part, regardless. Seven years ago, when the board decided to go ahead with the building of a new surgical wing on The Episcopal Hospital for the Poor, Kathleen became our representative on the board of directors and served as our fund-raising treasurer. Her work there was demanding at times, but it was always challenging. Kathleen was greatly stimulated and rewarded by her years of service.

"Over the coming days, weeks, months, and years, we will share so many memories of Kathleen. Those memories will bring laughter as well as tears. Today, the image that is strongest to me is from this photograph that the Bishop keeps on his desk. It is of Kathleen and R.C. when R.C. was baptized. Her rare beauty, grace, and dignity are blended into a she-bear's protective warning look. So fierce was her love for you, R.C. In my opinion, it is the most beautiful picture of her that exists.

Kathleen, you left us too soon!

There was still so much fun to be had,

Plans to make and carry out,

Dreams to dream,

Love to share,

And, someday, we all hope, grandchildren to cuddle.

Kathleen, we pledge to cuddle the grandchildren for you and to make sure they know what a special person their grandmother was.

"Kathleen, you told me many times that the last few years have been your happiest. Today, Bishop, I thank you for Kathleen. It was your love, support, and understanding that gave her the freedom to do what she loved so much. She knew that you respected what she was doing. Her being happy made you happy. No one could have asked for more!

"Godspeed, Kathleen! You are already greatly missed. Goodbye, Kathleen, until we meet again!"

The Bishop wept silently through most of the Dean's remarks, but he gulped huge gulps of air and moaned when the Dean thanked him for Kathleen. R.C. also was unable to keep his emotions in check and, like his father, cried without shame or restraint. When the Bishop reached over for his son's hand, R.C. turned and hugged his small father for what seemed to be forever. The sight of it caused an outpouring of grief unlike any that had been witnessed before or since.

The burial was private. Kathleen was laid to rest on the other side of the great oak, away from Griffin Hewes, Reynolds Carter Baxter, and the others. The Bishop left instructions that, when he died, R.C. was to bury him beside his wife.

CHAPTER NINE:
Doing the Right Thing

A month passed and the Chinese Ambassador to the United States was in San Francisco to make his address at St. Martin's. Bishop Baxter looked tired and he acted distracted, but the Ambassador was gracious when he realized the Bishop recently had buried his wife. The evening went exactly as planned. At the airport, just before the Ambassador and his nine armed guards were to board the plane to China, Peipei Jiang approached him. She carried a small box containing the precious stone, which was still inside its purple silk bag. The Ambassador received it with a deep bow, but he didn't dare to open it. In fact, the box stayed closed until he handed it over to the curator of the Great Hall of the People. There, with great ceremony, the missing centerpiece of Cheng Zu's priceless collection of animals, all carved out of jade, was restored to its rightful place.

R.C. had asked the Bishop's permission for Peipei to make the presentation. At first, the Bishop didn't want to be associated with the piece, even at arm's length, but the more R.C. pressed, the less he resisted and, finally, he gave his consent. Peipei's parents were invited to the mansion for dinner on the evening of the Ambassador's speech. Quyen and Cho-mi Jiang were medical research scientists at Cal. Tech. Only with great difficulty did they warm to the idea of their only daughter dating a non-Chinese. The Bishop took them aside and explained the facts of life to them. By the time that dinner was served, they were all smiles. Bishop Baxter was a true salesman, if nothing else, and making Peipei's parents comfortable with R.C. was truly one of his finer accomplishments. That he had a million dollars delivered to their home the next morning never had anything to do with her parent's consent.

That day, the Bishop had hired a dozen armed security officers to accompany R.C. to the First Bank of California when the panda jade was removed from its resting place of 70 years. They took it directly to the mansion and stayed on duty up to and including the moment Peipei presented it to the Ambassador at the airport. The Bishop relented on another of R.C.'s requests. He allowed the panda jade to grace the Bishop's table as the only decoration.

Questions of possession were not voiced, but Peipei's parents certainly wanted to ask them. The Bishop sat on pins and needles for the entire length of time that the Ambassador's flight took to reach The Great Hall of the People. News of the panda's recovery and return made national news, but there was no mention of the jade's whereabouts since it left China so many years ago. Nor were questions permitted. As far as the world knew, the jade appeared suddenly from oblivion and, indeed, that was true to a very large degree. Safe deposit box number 152, First Bank of California, San Francisco, branch. Reynolds Carter Baxter, IV, custodian.

CHAPTER TEN:
The Secret in Plain View

R.C. and Peipei graduated in May and were married the following month. The year was 1977. R.C's decision to become an Episcopal priest, made during the delivery of his mother's eulogy, was not just an emotional one that later would be rescinded. All of his life, he had not been able to visualize himself in that role. However, knowing what his father had done and how his mother also had served the Church made him reconsider everything. That reconsideration made it possible for him to embrace the ministry wholeheartedly. He and his father had a long talk. The Bishop assured him that he did not have to become a priest just to satisfy some life-long dream of his. R.C. assured him that he was not doing it for the wrong reasons. He explained that he truly believed that it was God who was calling him to the office through everything that he had experienced in his short, but eventful life.

"What about Onslow Weaver, R.C.?" the Bishop asked. "Can you proceed knowing that you took his life in cold blood?"

"I live with what I've done, Father," R.C. answered. "You have your own ghosts and you still function. How do you do it?" he asked.

"Believe it or not, R.C., each day, I ask the Divine for just enough strength to get me through that day and that day only. There is an ancient Chinese saying that goes something like this: 'Even the Emperor cannot buy back one second of yesterday.' So

I just do the best I can today. If Almighty God plans to wreck me in the hereafter, then I know I certainly earned it. I take comfort in knowing that David in the Bible was a murderer and so was Moses. They have not been vilified as a result of their actions. Maybe I'll be as lucky. Maybe you will, too, but I'm not concerned about that end of things, R.C. Believe me, 24 hours have enough concerns needing my attention. I can't pay any attention to something I did years ago and cannot change one iota," he responded.

"Have you thought about where you want to go to seminary?" the Bishop asked.

"Not really. I'm open to your suggestions. I think I'd like to stay here and go to San Francisco General," he answered.

"Nothing would give me more pleasure, R.C. If you have problems or questions, I'm here every night. Besides, I was hoping that you and Peipei might want to stay here. If not, I can easily get you your own house nearer the seminary," he said. "Remember, our progenitor, Reynolds Carter Baxter, bought a house for my father when he went to seminary. I'd be willing to do the same thing for you and Peipei, but, frankly, I'd enjoy your company. There is enough room in this old barn for you and Peipei to have all the privacy you want. Just let me know what the two of you decide," he ended.

Peipei was thrilled with the idea of living in the mansion. The Bishop hired contractors to tear out and rebuild ten rooms to suit the young couple. He had a kitchen put in, just in case they felt like eating in their own "home" rather than joining him. A separate entrance was created so that they could entertain their own friends without dragging them through the main part of the mansion. Peipei asked for and received permission to add a Chinese chef to the staff. She enjoyed American foods, but she also wanted to eat the more traditional foods of her girlhood home. The Bishop was introduced to new and wonderful taste treats. He took to them in the same way that his grandfather had done years before.

Seminary breezed by for R.C. Like the Bishop, he loved Biblical Hebrew and soon realized that his passion for it outweighed everything else that he studied. Many times, he would ask the Bishop for help in analyzing passages and, without fail, the Bishop suggested ideas that R.C. had not imagined. He became the most promising student ever to graduate from San Francisco General. Should the Episcopal Church ever elect a Pope, everyone at SFG was sure that it would be Reynolds Carter Baxter, IV. He sang second tenor in the sixteen-member men's choir. The Bishop invited them to sing at St. Martin's as often as schedules permitted. Each concert was followed by a visit to the mansion where the Bishop entertained lavishly. In his senior year, Peipei became pregnant. R.C. and the Bishop were full of anticipation and happiness. But her pregnancy was filled with problems. Bleeding on and off terrified her. Her feet and ankles suffered from severe swelling. Her kidneys shut down several times and she became quite depressed. And, although the best medical care that money could buy was made available to her, she lost the baby at four months.

Her guilt and depression deepened. A psychiatrist was provided, but Peipei seemed to draw further and further into herself. Her parents were summoned and enlisted in attempts at recovery, but to no avail. For the first time in his life, R.C. had a problem that neither he nor his father could solve. Peipei lost all interest in sex. Food nauseated her. R.C. came home from class one afternoon and found her dead in the tub of the shower. She had slit her wrists and had bled out. The shower above her still was running. It had washed her blood down the drain as soon as it had appeared. The flowing water had kept her wounds open. Her parents arrived at the mansion with a hearse and removed her body. Neither R.C. nor the Bishop had strength to object.

Peipei's body was cremated and her parents would not tell R.C. or the Bishop what they intended to do with her ashes. In fact, they would not talk to either man and sent word through an emissary that they were not to contact them ever again. That they blamed both R.C. and the Bishop for Peipei's death was quite clear. They blamed themselves more and, for that, there was no cure. They sent the million dollars back to the Bishop on the same day. They had cut themselves and had dripped their blood over the top layer of the bills. Bishop Baxter called Attorney Ahers and asked him to come to the mansion. When he arrived, the Bishop handed the returned money to him and asked him if he served on any charity boards. Ahers said that he served on the San Francisco Orchestra and Opera Boards.

"Clean this up and donate it anonymously. Never mention it ever again" was all he said. Mr. Ahers was excused.

When his class graduated, R.C. did not attend the ceremony even though he graduated first in his class. Everyone understood and the Bishop received his diploma in his stead. He also addressed the assemblage in R.C.'s place.

Slowly, yet firmly, he began. "My son, Reynolds Carter Baxter, the fourth, and I have both lost wives to death. I had the pleasure of knowing my wife Kathleen for more than twenty years. Out of that marriage, we produced one son, R.C. I cannot begin to imagine what R.C. is feeling right now, having lost the love of his life after knowing her for only a few short years. Anger, guilt, grief, emptiness, and fault jump into my mind without effort or thought. That he mopes around should surprise no one here. His whole world has been turned upside down. I'd probably want to do something physically painful, but my office and good sense prevents me from doing either. His youth and inexperience have left him stunned and he seems incapable of movement or thought at the moment. So I'll indulge him for a while longer and hope I don't have to pull him out of his funk. But I will if I have to. He's bigger than I am, but, believe me, I'm not afraid of him or any six just like him." Ignorant of the extent of the Bishop's grit and courage, the graduating class chuckled.

"He met Peipei in their senior year at Stanford. Both of them told me that it was love at first sight. When she announced her pregnancy a few short months ago, she glowed with happiness. So did we. The thought of a grandchild thrilled me beyond words. I know my Kathleen would have been beside herself with joy. But that glow quickly disappeared when complications set in and the debilitating effects of the pregnancy began to assert themselves. No medicines, physical or psychological, helped. Peipei blamed herself for her condition when, in fact, the pregnancy was doomed from the start. Her sense of shame and guilt at losing the baby overwhelmed her. She chose death rather than what she thought to be dishonor. So, R.C. and I are left mourning twice within the space of a few years.

I'm reminded of what one father felt at the death of one of his children long ago. David of old, when told of Absalom's death, wept. As he wept, he cried, 'O Absalom, my son. Would to God I had died for thee. O Absalom, my son, my son.' Gladly would I have exchanged my life for Peipei's, but it was not to be. She did not give me that option. But you can and, if you do, I will! That being the case, I'm going to tell you where the land mines are so you can avoid them and prevent a trip to see me. Some of you will see this as pastoral advice. It is. And it's good, like gold. You are about to enter into the world of parish ministry. I hope you have the stomach for it because it is the toughest thing anyone can do. Once, when R.C. was just five years old, I was asked to conduct the funeral for a little girl, who was five, too. She lived on the military base where her father was a sergeant in the army. She was playing outside with her little friends. Her daddy's best friend got in his car and backed out of the driveway, as he had done hundreds of times before. Only this time, the sergeant's little girl was playing directly behind his best friend's car. She was crushed to death. At the graveside, the sergeant stood at attention and addressed me. He said, 'Sir, can you say the 23rd Psalm?' I swear to you that if it had not been printed out for me in my service book, I'd have been unable to say the 23rd Psalm. All I could see was R.C. behind that car and the sergeant and me trading places. It was the hardest thing I've ever been asked to do. "O Absalom, my son, my son."

But life goes on. It did for that sergeant, whom I've never seen again, and it will for R.C., just as it did for me after my wife died. If your number isn't called today – if your ticket isn't punched today – go on. What the Divine has in store for you around the next bend could be worse or better. For example, you cannot begin to imagine the number of women who will want you as a sex partner once you put that collar on. But you are about to find out. Remember, bankers have to deal with embezzlement and priests have to deal with adultery. Mostly their own.

As long as I'm your Bishop, you must know one thing. I've been there and I've weathered it. I didn't get this 64-year-old crusty appearance because I've lived in the spa. Because of my experience, you cannot bring a surprise in my door. So at the first sign of trouble or difficulty, come to see me. For you, I will step into the breach so that I may never have to cry out, as did David, "Would to God I had died for thee, O Absalom, my son, my son." For you, I'll actually do it."

The Bishop let his son mope around the house for another two weeks. R.C. had returned to his old room in the mansion and had abandoned the suite that he and Peipei had shared. He entered R.C.'s room and told him to shower, shave, and put on his best suit. They were going to the club for lunch. His father's tone of voice let R.C. know that this was neither negotiable nor worth fighting about. Besides, he could stand a change of scenery. The Bishop waited downstairs in the study. When R.C. appeared, his father asked him to lock the door behind him and to step over to one side of the room.

"Years ago," he began, "I removed the enormous fireplace that graced this wall and I installed this in its place."

He pointed to an almost undetectable button that was knee high and formed the right eye of a small stone gargoyle stationed to the right of his desk. When he pressed the eye, the entire library wall with its load of books began to open effortlessly and silently. Behind the wall stood an enormous safe. The Bishop spun the dial on its door and an electric motor opened the heavy steel door. The two men stepped inside a room full of cash.

R.C. was stunned and was not able to speak. He wanted to,

but nothing came out. The Bishop recognized his son's predicament.

"There's probably over $200 million in this safe, R.C. It's the residue of your great-grandfather, Griffin Hewes' illegal activities which, as you know, included prostitution, piracy, gambling, opium, and Lord only knows what else. It's also the residue of your great-grandfather, Reynolds Carter Baxter's legal activities. I've sort of mixed them together in hopes that the latter will bless the former. Your mother knew about this safe and she knew how to access it. I'm pretty sure when I say I don't think she ever entered this safe after I brought her here the first time. When you were born, I changed the combination to the day, month, and year of your birth. I also told her about that change, but, to my knowledge, she never came in here for anything."

Interrupting his father's narrative, R.C. asked, "Why don't you put it in a bank or in the stock market, so it can earn something?"

"Because the government would become interested in it. As long as it remains here, we are the only two people in the world who know that it exists. This money is to be spent and, I dare say, there is more here than either you or I can spend in a lifetime. When I became Bishop, I had $50 million removed from here and I created a trust fund with it. The presiding Episcopal Bishop of California has complete control over its use. Since I've never touched it, I'm told it's grown to nearly $65 million. I use what's left here to fund special projects and to see that certain people get pulled out of bad situations they've gotten into. But you, R.C., can come in here and take away whatever you need at anytime. Just don't flash it around and call attention to yourself. I know that isn't your style, but I'm mentioning it as a caution, not as a directive," he paused.

R.C. began to laugh. Just a little at first, but then loudly and uncontrollably. All of his life, he had been in a house with hundreds of millions of dollars hidden behind a wall that he had seen thousands of times, but he never knew it. The Bishop joined in as he realized the comedy involved.

"Why did you choose today to show me this safe?" he wanted to know.

"No reason. I just thought it was time and you needed a good laugh. Let's face it. Neither one of us has been good company as of late," he replied. "Are you hungry, R.C.?" he asked.

"Starved – for the first time in a long time," he answered.

As they left the safe, the Bishop showed his son how to close the safe's door and to reset the dial. When that was accomplished, he told R.C. to press the right eye in the gargoyle again. When he did, the wall closed as silently and as effortlessly as it had opened.

"Make sure the door to the study is locked when you open the wall, R.C. You don't want anyone barging in and discovering our little 'family secret'," he warned.

The chauffer was summoned and the limo was brought to the front door. After they were inside, the Bishop told R.C. that he had invited a guest to join them for lunch. He had invited the Dean of the Cathedral because he had certain business that he needed to discuss. Dean McGinnis was an old friend and R.C. was quite comfortable with the arrangement. The Bishop now owned the alcove where Griffin Hewes held court long ago. He ordered steaks for them all, apple pie with Colby cheese, coffee, and cigars. R.C. chewed on the bone to the Dean's disgust and the Bishop's delight.

Without preamble, the Bishop delivered an order that was not to be contested. He declared that R.C. was to begin his new duties in the cathedral on the following Sunday morning. He was to preach his first sermon and the Dean was to assist him as lector and celebrant. The Dean was thrilled. But R.C. rose from his seat and announced in his most menacing voice that he wasn't ready and that he wouldn't be there even if ordered. Bishop Baxter had never backed away from anyone or anything. He jumped up on the table so that he could tower over his son. Again he announced that R.C. would preach his maiden sermon at St. Martin's and that it would happen on the following Sunday morning just as he said it would. A hush fell over the great room. Such a spectacle had never been witnessed in the club – and certainly never from that alcove. R.C.'s Irish dander was up. So was the Bishop's. A pissing contest ensued. The Dean and all of the others wisely sat quietly, breathing only enough air to keep body and soul alive. Not even the maitre d' had the courage to interfere with these two titans. Finally the Bishop ended it. He slapped R.C.'s face as hard as he could and, in doing so, he broke almost all of the bones in his small hand. The sound of bones breaking could be heard all the way back to the kitchen. Immediately R.C.'s demeanor changed and he rushed to his father's aid. The Bishop was so stunned by his own outburst that it caused him more pain than his broken hand ever could or did. He began to apologize to R.C., who began to apologize to him. Had it not been so painful, a good comedian would have turned the exchange into a funny routine. The Dean suggested that they go to the hospital right away.

Doctors were able to set the hand with no complications and the Bishop was released the following morning. R.C. picked him up at a side entrance, away from the press who had heard about the incident and wanted to get the details. Rather than keeping the contest alive, the Bishop began to laugh as soon as R.C. entered his room. R.C. followed suit and each belittled the other in playful jousts.

"Did I ever tell you, Father, that you hit like a girl?" R.C. chided.

"No, but did I ever tell you your head is full of rocks? If I'd used a bat, it probably would have broken just like my hand did," he responded. "Oh – and get this, R.C. – did I tell you, you are preaching this Sunday at St. Martin's?"

"You did, but, for some unknown reason, I didn't hear you," he replied. "But, this time, I did and I accept, reluctantly," he finished.

Still playful, the Bishop continued, "Did I ever tell you the one about the farmer who got married, and when he and his bride were leaving the church, his mule sat down and refused to pull their wagon?"

"No, Father, you didn't," R.C. replied.

"Well," the Bishop continued, "the farmer told the mule, 'That's once.' The farmer pushed the mule up and urged the mule to pull. The mule sat back down. The farmer said, 'That's twice.' He pushed the mule up again and urged the mule to pull. The mule sat down for the third time. The farmer pulled out a gun and shot the mule dead. His new wife began to berate the farmer who turned, gun in hand, and said to her, 'That's once.' You see, R.C., I treated you like the mule that you are, but the gun backfired on me."

The two laughed at each other until their sides hurt.

Finally R.C. got serious and said, "I'll need your help, Father, if I'm not to make a fool of myself."

"You'll do just fine," he comforted, "but I'll do what I can to make it as painless as possible. Just don't make me hit you again," and they doubled up in laughter.

CHAPTER ELEVEN:
God's Grace Works through Human Sinfulness

R.C. agonized over his sermon. The assigned texts for the morning were from Genesis 45:1-8 and Luke 15:11-24. The Epistle was Hebrews 8:6-12. The lectionary had to have made some mistake linking these three texts together. They made no sense whatsoever to R.C. On Wednesday at breakfast, R.C. told his father what he thought about the texts – and where he thought the lector should cram them.

"Bring me my Bible, R.C., will you, please?" he requested.

R.C. retrieved the book from the library and handed it to his father. The Bishop opened to the assigned texts and smiled. "R.C., I've not lectured on these three texts before, so I'm talking off the top of my head. I've seen this linkage before and I understand it. Get your paper and pen ready 'cause here comes the freshest manna you'll ever receive."

R.C. complied and sat in complete fascination as his father spoke effortlessly and without notes for more than 45 minutes. When he finished, all he could do was to shake his hand because it hurt from writing so fast and so furiously. He also shook his head for not understanding the depth and the breadth of his father's scholarship. The Bishop told R.C. that the three texts were combined because they all told one idea. He emphasized that preaching was good when it said just one thing and said it well. Three-point sermons with a poem at the end were as useless as a tit on a boor hog. The Bishop helped his son to interpret Latin phrases. He explained, "Loosely translated, 'errore hominum providentia divinia' means 'God's grace works through human sinfulness.' That is what Joseph told his brothers twice in the Genesis passage in verse 5 and again in verses 7 and 8a. 'It was not you who sold me into slavery. It was God who sent me here to preserve life for many.' See it, R.C.?" he asked.

"I do, but why wasn't I able to see it on my own?" he asked.

"Because you are a raw green rookie and you don't know, pardon the expression, 'shit from Shinola if it were on your shoes.' That's why. You think I learned this stuff in seminary? All seminary does, R.C., is show you how to find the men's room at a church. Everything else you have to learn yourself. That takes time and nosebleeds because of mistakes all green rookies make," he laughed.

"Look at the Luke text and tell me the theology involved," he instructed.

R. C. looked and looked, but came up empty.

"It's the same theology that's in the Joseph text. The story is different, but the theology is the same. This kid returned and expected to manipulate his old man. Instead, what did he get? Unmerited grace. There's the connection. 'God's grace works through human sinfulness.' And the Epistle has the same theology, doesn't it, R.C.?" he asked. "The Book contains some history as it contains some geography and genealogy, but, in truth, it is a book of theology. A story you read in one place surfaces again somewhere else. The Sarah and Mary stories are the same. The theology is that God is a womb opener, regardless of the age or previous use or disuse. See what I mean?" he asked.

R.C.'s smile widened into a full grin, which let the Bishop know that he had transmitted his thoughts and ideas successfully.

"Go get 'em, tiger," the Bishop ended playfully. "I have real problems to solve in my office. See you tonight," he said as he walked out to his limo.

For the next three days, R.C. shut himself up in the mansion's library. He wrote draft after draft, and tossed them all away. Each effort ended up sounding like he had parroted his father's "lecture" of Wednesday morning. He was having trouble finding his own voice. When the Bishop asked to see what he had done with the texts on Saturday evening, R.C. confessed that he had been unable to write anything that was his own. Everything he had come up with so far sounded just like a poorer copy of what he had heard at Wednesday's breakfast.

Smiling, the Bishop patted R.C. on the head with his unbroken hand and said, "Don't stay up too late, R.C. Eleven o'clock in the morning will be here before you know it." Then he retired to his room to sleep.

At eight the following morning, the Bishop startled his son awake in the library where he had fallen asleep on his books and papers sometime after three a.m. "Showtime, R.C., in just three hours. Ready or not, here it comes." And he laughed heartily as he made his way to the kitchen where he ate a huge breakfast of Canadian bacon, fried eggs, muffins, coffee, and apple pie with Colby cheese.

R.C.'s hands shook from lack of sleep and the sheer terror of having to preach in St. Martin's before 1,100 of the city's faithful. He didn't have even one word down on paper. Of course, the Bishop knew it and only played up the good time that he was having at the young man's expense. "Did I tell you, R.C., that I've invited U.S. Senator Boggs, Mayor Cornfield, and Congressman Schneider to services so they could hear you?" Then he roared with laughter. R.C. could have killed him – and said so. This made the Bishop laugh even harder. He was really enjoying watching his son squirm. It was good for him, he reasoned. Besides, it will tell him that preaching isn't for pussies. It takes more than research and cleverness. It takes some grit in one's belly and some fire in one's demeanor.

The shower felt good to R.C. When he was about to step into the new suit that his father had tailor-made for him, the

Bishop appeared and helped him to fit his clerical collar into the ensemble.

"You'll do just fine, son," the Bishop cooed. "Just fine, believe me. Even if you bomb, everyone in the joint will tell you what a good job you did. I told them that's exactly what they have to say or they can begin looking for a new job Monday morning." Then he really laughed. So did R.C.

"Did I ever tell you, Bishop Baxter, that you can be one real pain in the arse?" he asked.

"In more ways than one, my boy, in more ways than one. I take each telling as a compliment." And they laughed harder still.

The limo parked at St. Martin's. The Bishop and R.C. entered through the side door leading directly to the Bishop's study. "What am I going to say, Father? I don't have word one on paper and my mind is a complete blank," R.C. remonstrated.

Again, patting his son's hand, the Bishop said, "Trust me, R.C., when the time comes, words will be given to you that will be truly inspired."

"Right," he answered in a doubting tone of voice.

"Do you think you're the only person who's been in this jam?" he asked. "Hell, there have been times when I was the visiting guest speaker and I didn't know that someone changed the text on me. Just seconds before I was to go on, someone told me, 'By the way, Bishop, we've decided we want to hear you talk about so and so, rather than the announced topic.' But the words somehow formed – and no one ever shot at me afterward. You'll do fine. You're my son. You're made of stern stuff. Smart stuff, too. If you fall on your ass, so what? If there's no blood on the floor, R.C., it's all negotiable," he advised. "Just remember what I told you at breakfast. I've told everyone to tell you what a great job you've done or, tomorrow morning, they can 'hit the road, Jack.'" And he laughed again.

The Dean stuck his head into the Bishop's study and suggested that it was time for R.C. to follow him to the vestment room. This was a first for R.C. He was given a plain white surplice to pull over his shirt. When he removed his new suit coat, he realized that he had sweated through the armpits. What had he gotten himself into, he wondered.

The Dean was the consummate liturgist. His "stained-glass voice" was perfectly pitched. It made everyone in attendance leave feeling like they had been to church. The choir in the chancel sang an all-Bach program. The music relaxed R.C. without his even knowing why. A hush fell over the house as R.C. ascended the twelve steps into the elevated hooded pulpit. He didn't know if his rubbery legs would support him. Then it hit him. Why should he be afraid? With malice of forethought, he had killed a man with his bare hands and had enjoyed a good feeling when it was done. His own father had ordered the death of a man and had paid others to do the dirty work, causing them to sin gravely, too. Here he was in the Cathedral of St. Martin's as the designated preacher of the morning. If that wasn't God's grace working through human sinfulness, he didn't know what was. By the time that he got to the top, he hardly could wait to attack his subject.

"Before I actually begin my formal remarks, I'm taking this opportunity to say a few personal things to a number of people. First, to my father, Bishop Reynolds Carter Baxter, the Third: You did this, Father. You. To you and to everyone else in this great cathedral: If I fall flat on my you-know-what, blame the Bishop."

The house fell out laughing. No one laughed harder or enjoyed the remark more than Bishop Baxter. R.C. felt a jolt go through him. He was too young to appreciate the great comedian, Red Skelton, but he acted just like him. The first laugh made R.C. laugh and he was encouraged to go on.

"Dean McGinnis and other members of the clergy who were my teachers in my youth, you did this, too. So, to you, Father, and to you, Dean McGinnis, and to you, my teachers, I'm eternally grateful for the contributions you've all made that helped me climb those twelve steps and stand here before you today."

Tears began to stream down the Bishop's cheeks, but he didn't care. Nor did any of those present who joined the Bishop in his tears of joy and pride. The Bishop thought, "The kid's good. He can take us from laughter to tears with ease and we've followed him not knowing exactly why."

"When my father announced to me on Monday that I was to preach my maiden sermon here in St. Martin's and that I was to do it today, we had words." The congregation burst into laughter. "Oh, you heard, did you?" The laughter rose, again. "All true. After I broke my father's hand while he was making his point, I realized I was in way over my head. Even though my head, according to my father, is full of rocks and made out of the same," he continued as the laughter became hysterical, "who do you think this rock head went to for help? Right. My father. For more than a half hour, he regaled me with theology, Latin, Biblical Hebrew, and Greek. Most fathers talk to their sons about baseball or ..." The thunderous laughter prevented R.C. from finishing his sentence, but he had made his point so well that he didn't have to continue. "At the end of our he-talks-and-I-listen session, he said he'd paid all of you to shake my hand when I'm done and to tell me what a great job I did, whether or not that was the case." The laughter reached its loudest peak and was sustained there for quite awhile. "I'll never know whether I really did a good job or if you just needed the money." The congregation had fits.

"I know you are all dying to know what Bishop Baxter told me. Actually, it was the secret handshake stuff that gets me into the clergy club, so I can't tell you that part. But what I can tell you is this. My father is probably the smartest and the most generous man I'll ever know and, I dare say, that you'll ever have the privilege of knowing. It wasn't what he said to me that registered, but the way he said it and the conviction and the ease with which he said it. His best advice to me was to find just one thing to say, say it, and then sit down. So here goes.

"Within the hearts and the minds of those who have been the doers or the victims of dastardly deeds, God has placed a time bomb. In the Genesis account, Joseph's brothers had sold him into slavery. When the time was right, God exploded a bomb for all of us to see. That bomb was like Fourth of July fireworks. It lit up a large foundation stone of the entire Bible so we could see it clearly. It let us see that God's grace works through human sinfulness. Joseph didn't berate his brothers for their cruelty or for the hardships they had caused in his life. Rather, Joseph was God's mouthpiece. He told them – and us – the good news that God's grace works through our sinfulness. He told his brothers not to beat themselves up for their past behaviors because, in reality, it was God who sent him before them in order to preserve life for many.

"That same message is in the parable of the 'Waiting Father'. His duty was to take his son – this prodigal, ungrateful, worthless piece of … oops," he hesitated during the burst of hearty laughter, "piece of humanity – into the public square and, according to the laws of his day, strip him naked, and beat him to death. Instead, the injured father extended mercy and grace. Fireworks again should be going off in our minds because we are seeing God's grace working miraculously in the midst of human sinfulness.

"Even the Epistle to the Hebrews, which is a direct quote from Jeremiah, says the same thing. Regardless of the past, it was all a prelude to the good news of God's willingness to pull us out of our worst messes and to clean us off and to say something meaningful through us. Look at Moses and David. Both murderers. And they've fared well over the years. God turns around some of the Bible's worst people and redeems them. They come to us as Sanctus Angelicas, Holy Angels, with encouragement that the worst of the worst can bring us messages from God.

St. Martin's has been a special place in my family's history. It is fitting and proper that I begin my ministry here. But, more significantly, it has been a special place for San Francisco. St. Martin's has become the beacon on the hill, the safe harbor, the bedrock of goodness and generosity. In brick and stone, steel and glass, music and prayers, it mirrors the very thing God did in the story of Joseph and the Waiting Father. They announced that God's grace works through human sinfulness. St. Martin's has the same message. Just coming here somehow makes life better. It is a special place where God reaches down and enables us all to become recipients of his unmerited grace, regardless of our past. It is also the place where we are converted from mere flesh and blood into His legions of holy angels. Amen."

The church exploded in applause. People were on their feet. They were clapping over their heads. Dignified Whiskypalians didn't do this, but there they were, clapping as though they had been treated to Pavarotti. The Dean was able to restore sanity to the congregation only when he asked them to receive the benediction.

R.C. was escorted to the Great East Door where his grateful congregants greeted him. Every person led off with a prelude of real thanks so that R.C. would be certain that they were sincere and not merely following the playful directions he mentioned in his sermon. It took 35 minutes for those wishing to greet and thank R.C. to file past him. When he finally got back to the vestment room, the Dean and the Bishop were there to welcome him.

Dean McGinnis gushed, but then he said something of value. Turning to the Bishop, he said, "Bishop, I'd like to suggest that you assign R.C. to the Cathedral as Preacher-in-Residence. If we put his name on the marquee tomorrow, we'll need to set up extra chairs everywhere next Sunday."

"Done," was his one word reply. So it was that Bishop Reynolds Carter Baxter, the Third, at the age of 64, assigned Reynolds Carter Baxter, the Fourth, at the age of 23, to his new post. He warmed to his task immediately. Something happened to him in that pulpit for which he had no explanation. He felt as though he were born to do just that – preach.

During the limo ride back to the mansion, the Bishop asked R.C. if he knew what Samuel F.B. Morse sent as the first telegraph message. R.C. responded that he thought that he used to know, but he had forgotten.

"'What hath God wrought?'" he reminded R.C. "'What hath God wrought?' I feel like I've created a monster." They laughed.

"I've never preached a better sermon, R.C., in all of my life and, certainly, I've never done it as memorably as you did. What happened up there? Where did you get the ability to make people laugh and cry within the space of a few sentences?" he asked.

"You were right, Father," R.C. answered, "Something came over me. The words were just given to me. I think what really happened is that my brain had some sense knocked into it when you broke your hand. It processed the many conversations we've had over the years. You had to recognize your words and thoughts about David and Moses. I mean, you had to."

"I did, R.C.," the Bishop answered, "but when they came out of your mouth, it was as though I heard them for the first time. That was the first occasion since I murdered my first man that I felt redeemed. You truly have a gift, the likes of which I've never seen. If only your mother and Peipei could have been here to hear you."

With that, silence descended and each man slid into a private world where the other was not welcome. Nor was he ever invited. Ever!

Within months, R.C.'s reputation as an electrifying speaker found its way through the church grapevine. Soon invitations to speak here and to speak there were pouring in. At first, R.C. wanted to accept every invitation, but the Bishop cautioned him against burnout. Once a month, he advised, R.C. could travel to preach because he was still learning his craft. Only his father's steady hand on prickly matters of Biblical interpretation and theology got him through numerous dry spells and incorrect doctrine. It didn't take very long before R.C. ran out of material. His father knew it and so did R.C. One evening at dinner, R.C. said he felt empty.

"Indeed, R.C., that's exactly what you're feeling because, in truth, you are empty," the Bishop replied. "You've told us all you know and now you must become what I think I still am. A student. When the dinosaurs were dead about a week, my theology professor told my class to find something that really interested us and, over the course of a lifetime, become an expert in it. It's the only thing I remember that man saying, but it has served me well. That I chose Biblical Hebrew is no surprise to you, I'm sure. You know how easy the language is to learn. But what you don't know just yet is how rich it is in helping you to understand the New Testament. I give you the same advice I was given so long ago. Pick a subject or a topic you like and, over the course of your lifetime, become an expert in it. If you want to get further education, naturally, you can do that. But I found that, for me, the thrill of learning something on my own far exceeded anything I'd ever been handed in the classroom," he ended.

"Can I have a couple of weeks off?" he asked. "I've been going at it really hard, as you well know, and I feel like I need to get away."

"Of course, you can. Where would you like to go," the Bishop asked.

"Chicago, Pittsburgh, and Philadelphia," R.C. answered.

"Why do you want to go to those three cities, of all places, R.C.? How about Hawaii or someplace in Europe, like Paris?" he asked.

"I'd like to see if I can find any of our ancestors, Father. Remember Lester Baxter's account? He couldn't remember exactly where Reynolds, the First, came from, but he thought it was either Pittsburgh or Philadelphia. I'd like a couple of weeks to go there to see if I can find any old train records from the 1880s," he answered.

"By all means, R.C.," the Bishop replied. "Go and see what you can learn. I've always wanted to travel there, but I've never had the time to go. I'll be just as interested in finding out if Reynolds, the First, as you call him, had any relatives that recorded themselves in local history.

CHAPTER TWELVE:
The $10 Tip

R.C. flew into Chicago. He went to the Amtrak offices and asked if they had any archival materials from the 1880s. Were there train lists of passengers or did they just keep a head count of arrivals and departures? What he learned was not encouraging. Chicago had no such count. Records before 1900 had been burned in a tragic fire years before. R.C. felt the ancestor links grow colder and colder. He flew to Pittsburgh. He hoped that he would discover what he was looking for in the old Pennsylvania Railroad Station. There, like Chicago, he was unable to isolate the train counts. He was directed to go to the University of Pittsburgh where old photos and some records were kept, but he learned that Philadelphia was where the "mother lode" was to be unearthed.

This time, he took the early train from Pittsburgh, which left on time and arrived in Philadelphia twelve hours later. The train was delayed twice due to troubles with the track and once for an unexplained problem. They sat in the Harrisburg station for an hour and a half. R.C. thought that the engineer must have gone into the town for a beer and stayed for three or four more.

When the train finally arrived in Philadelphia, he took a cab to the Park Hyatt, also known as The Bellevue, at Broad and Walnut Streets. He took the presidential suite. The Pennsylvania

Railroad Library was located on Broad Street Station, so R.C. thought that The Bellevue would be the best location for his stay. The hotel was top rate and he was treated like the visiting royalty that he was. He showered, changed, and went downstairs for a drink and dinner. He asked his waiter if the hotel manager would come to his table for a few moments. He had several questions for him and he quickly added that none of them was hotel-related. Several minutes went by. Then Raymond Morrow, the hotel manager, appeared. R.C. asked him if he would join him for dinner, but the invitation was declined. R.C. asked if the manager knew much about the Pennsylvania Railroad and its history. He admitted that he did not, but that one of their older bus boys, who retired just last year from the "Pennsy," as he called it, probably knew everything there was to know about the railroad. He would be happy to have him talk to R.C.

"Good," R.C. replied. "Is he on duty now?" he asked.

"As a matter of fact, he is. I'll have him in my office for you just as soon as you finish your meal, sir," Morrow replied.

"If it's possible," R.C. countered, "I'd like him to join me here. I'm pressed for time and would appreciate the courtesy."

"But, Mr. Baxter," Morrow began to back-pedal, "Old Jake is not dressed to come into the dining room."

R.C. responded without malice or attitude. He simply said, "Then dress him so he can, Mr. Morrow. What is Old Jake's last name?"

"I can't quite remember, sir," he said with growing embarrassment. "We all just call him Jake or Old Jake, depending on whether we're talking to him or about him."

"Please find out the man's name, send it in to me, dress him properly so he can join me for dinner, and send him in," R.C. instructed in a tone of voice that meant "just do it."

Morrow rose and began his exit. As he did so, he said, "Yes, sir, right away, sir."

In ten minutes, Old Jake, whose last name was Walters, appeared in an ill-fitting coat and tie. For the last 45 years, he had worked as a porter between Philadelphia and Chicago. Retirement didn't suit him and, when he appeared at The Bellevue, Mr. Morrow hired him on the spot. But he was nervous and agitated at having his routine interrupted by some rich cracker from San Francisco. Mr. Morrow escorted Jake Walters to R.C's table and made the introductions. He left as quickly as possible. He did not want to be drawn into either man's wrath, which he imagined could be considerable. R.C. asked Jake what he would like to drink. Jake didn't know what to say. He sat still and said nothing. He had never been in the main dining room to eat. As part of his job, he cleared its tables. The man was clearly out of his depth, uncomfortable, and somewhat nervous. R.C. tried again. Only this time, he asked the waiter to come to the table. He ordered a shot of bourbon and a beer for himself. Again he asked Mr. Walters what he would like.

"Just a bottle of Schmidts, please," Jake nearly whispered. R.C. learned that Schmidts Brewing Company was a local company that made an excellent beer.

R.C. didn't like beer or bourbon, but he thought it might help his quest for information if he didn't drink his usual California wine. He was right. After a second bottle of beer, Mr. Walters began to relax, but he was still on guard. The elderly man thought that he was going to be embarrassed even further by this encounter. R.C. invited him to eat with him and was pleasantly surprised when Waters said yes. When dinner was over and coffee had been served, R.C. asked Mr. Walters if he would talk to him about his years as a porter on the old Pennsylvania Railroad.

"You a writer, Mr. Baxter?" he wanted to know.

"No, Mr. Walters, I'm not. But I'm trying to find information on some relatives from the 1880s who might have come from Philadelphia?" R.C. answered.

"I'm old, Mr. Baxter," he laughed, "but even I ain't that old."

R.C. joined in the laughter and admitted that he didn't think that his guest would be able to remember back that far. He asked him if he could remember any stories that other porters who had lived in that time period might have told him. Mr. Walters thought and thought. Then he answered that he knew several stories that he had heard long ago. They came down from his father and from his grandfather who had lived and worked on the railroad right after the Civil War and beyond. But he couldn't quite remember the stories word-for-word right then. He would have to think about what they were and talk to his older brother who was in a home for retired railroaders just outside of Philly. R.C. volunteered to take him there the next day. Mr. Walters accepted if R.C. could get him cleared from his hotel duties. There was no question about that and each man knew it.

In the morning, Mr. Walters appeared at the hotel in a suit and tie that fit him and made him look ten years younger. R.C. hired a limo for the day and was pleased that Mr. Walters was willing to help him with his quest. "Where are we going, Mr. Walters?" R.C. asked.

"Paoli" was his one word answer.

The limo driver knew exactly where to go. Paoli was a quaint little town twenty-something miles west of Philadelphia on the old main line. R.C. remembered passing through it the previous day on his way to Philadelphia. The retirement home for railroad employees was in Paoli and Jake Walters' older brother, Esau, was a resident there. Esau Walters was seventy-nine, sharp as a tack, hunched over, and suffering from the early stages of "the shakes," Jake said.

"We've lived together for the last seven years after both of our wives died just months apart," Jake volunteered. "Esau's wife, Miranda, died first, and my wife, Lucy, died three months later."

"Your wife was named Lucy?" R.C. interrupted. "My grandmother's name was Lucy."

"Well, I'll be," Jake smiled. "Cancer got them both. Miranda died of uterine cancer and Lucy died of breast cancer. Terrible disease, Mr. Baxter, terrible," he offered as tears streamed down his cheeks.

R. C. let the moment pass.

"Are you a religious man, Mr. Baxter?" Jake asked.

"You might say that, Jake. Actually, I'm an ordained Episcopal priest. My father is the Bishop of the Episcopal Dioceses of California. But I never trade on my office or my father's. 'Hey, look at me! I'm an Episcopal priest' isn't my style," R.C. answered.

"I thought there was something different about you," Jake replied. "An Episcopal priest, and me a Baptist," he mused. "Wait till I tell my grandkids about this," he said to no one in particular.

"You won't hold it against me, now, will you, Jake?" R.C. teased. "I mean, so far, we've gotten along pretty good, wouldn't you say?" he teased some more. "Last night at dinner, I thought we got on famously, don't you agree?" he laughed. And the two men laughed at the awkwardness of their dinner the night before.

"I guess so, Rever ...," he started to say, but R.C. cut him off.

"Please, Jake, no Reverend stuff. R.C. is best. If you must be formal, mister is my preferred title. Reverend is a descriptive adjective and I've yet to know anyone who fits the description. People tend to treat me differently when they know I'm a priest. I don't want that from you or from your brother. So please don't mention my office to him," R.C. requested.

"Okay," Jake lied, "but I'll have a hard time calling you anything other than Reverend, now that I know. I just have so much respect for ministers, that's all. I know first-hand how much good they can do and how they can be misunderstood at times."

"I'm too new at this to come in for the 'misunderstood' part, but I know my father has had his share over the years and I know how it can get to him. But he's a tough old bird. Bishops have to be or they'll get steam-rolled real quick, know what I mean?" he asked.

"Taken advantage of," Jake replied.

The limo pulled up to the Pennsylvania Railroad Retirement Home half a mile outside of Paoli. It was a large white wooden home with a front porch that ran its entire length. Rockers and swings were everywhere. There were a few old metal ones that needed a fresh coat of paint. Some were made of wicker. Some were plastic. Esau was seated in a padded, white wicker rocker. He had a towel restraint tucked around his chest to keep him from sliding out. His exposed hands shook on and off, preventing him from holding a cup of water or a pen. But, when he saw Jacob coming toward him, he smiled. The big guy beside his brother didn't register. He blocked him out completely.

"Jacob, my brother," he cried out. R.C. remembered the Biblical story of Jacob and Esau and their meeting years after Jacob had cheated Esau out of his birthright. More of God's grace, R.C. thought.

Jake knelt down, embraced his older brother, and told him how glad he was to see him outside enjoying the bright sunshine. Then he introduced R.C. to Esau. He told Esau that R.C. was a high-falootin' Episcopal priest and that his father was the Bishop of California. R.C. cringed, but Esau brightened.

"I'm an Episcopalian, Father Baxter," Esau said. "My wife, Miranda, God rest her soul, was a staunch Episcopalian. She said she couldn't marry a Baptist under any circumstances. If we were ever to be married, I'd have to become an Episcopalian."

Then Esau became really wide-eyed and asked Jacob, "Am I going to die, Jacob? Is that why you brought Father Baxter here?" he wanted to know.

"No, Esau," his brother answered reassuringly. "Father Baxter wants to talk to us about the Pennsylvania Railroad and any old stories we can remember from our grandparents' days."

Esau exhaled as big a breath as he could and replied, "Well, he sure scared me." Then he laughed, as did his two guests.

The brothers visited back and forth for a few minutes. Then Esau asked R.C. what it was that he wanted to know. R.C. told his family history, the edited version. He said that he wanted to know if Esau or Jacob knew of any written records that named passengers leaving Philadelphia for San Francisco in 1869.

"Maybe the museum and library have some lists like that, but I wouldn't know for sure. I've never gone there," Esau said sadly. "We were porters. So were our father and grandfather before us. The railroad always treated us right. We were never hungry and the work was steady. We met a lot of nice people over the years. Some that were not so nice, too," Esau laughed and Jacob joined in knowing exactly who and what Esau was laughing about.

"Tell me any old stories you remember your father or grandfather telling you about their times," R.C. encouraged.

Esau asked, "What kind of stories, Father?"

"Just stories, anything. If my ancestors looked like I look, maybe some redheaded Irishman might have said something or done something that impressed them. I don't know what else I can tell you. I know I'm looking for the proverbial needle in the hay stack, but maybe I'll be the lucky one who actually finds it," R.C. answered.

The brothers began to name various stories that they had categorized and named over the years. "How about the suitcase that cracked open when the handle broke and it was full of ladies underwear?" Jacob asked.

"Nah," Esau replied, "that guy was a salesman and he didn't have a wife and kid with him."

"Right, right," Jacob agreed.

"Well, how about the drunk and the drunker?" Jacob wanted to know.

"Nah," he said as Jacob's suggestion was waved off with Esau's shaking right hand. "That one was about two men, but it was funny. Want to hear it, Father?" he asked.

R. C. didn't think that he did. He asked them to think if they could remember any stories about a man, his wife, and a baby. Then Esau's eyes began to sparkle and he said, "I do."

"Our father's first name was Isaac, Father Baxter, and his father's name, quite naturally, was Abraham. One of our favorite stories that our father told us was the story of the Ten-Dollar Tip. That's what we called it and why I didn't think about who was in it. It happened to his father, Abraham, on a run from Philadelphia to Chicago."

R.C. didn't think the Ten-Dollar Tip story was worth anything, at first. He often had tipped ten dollars or more and thought nothing of it. Then he realized that ten dollars to Abraham Walters back in the 1860s might be worth listening to.

"What do you remember, Esau, about that story?" R.C. wanted to know.

"Help me out, Jake," Esau pleaded. "If I leave anything out, you know?" he said. "Here goes. A ten-dollar tip in those days was as much as a month's salary, Father," Esau began. "Our grandfather, Abraham, a Civil War veteran and former slave, I might add, had never received a tip so large. Usually a penny or two was all he and our father, Isaac, ever received for helpin' out with a bag or a package. But, as the story goes, a young couple with a baby arrived in Philadelphia and was heading west. Philadelphia was the station where the Boston crew changed and the Philadelphia crew took over, you know," Esau added. "Anyway, the man was tall and had real red hair, just like you have, Father. And so did his wife. Their baby had red hair, too. And he was cranky. Seems his mother's milk production wasn't keeping up with his hunger 'cause the train didn't have the kinds of things on board she needed. When the train got to Pittsburgh, Pennsylvania, it had a twenty-minute stop. Grandfather Abraham, so the story goes, left the train, ran into the town, and bought fresh tomatoes and apples and pears with his own money."

"Don't forget the two steaks, Esau," Jake urged.

"Right, and two small steaks which he had the butcher sear 'cause he had only twenty minutes to buy everything and get back to the train," Esau added. "He also found some cloth for diapers and some more so the lady could take care of her, you know, period. Don't know how he knew, but it seems he did. Grandfather Abraham, so our daddy told us, just made it back to the train as it was pulling out of the Pittsburgh station heading for Chicago. He found the young father, told him what he'd done, and asked if he wanted the goods? The bill was two dollars and change. The young man repaid Grandfather in coins. And then the tip came. I'll never forget the smile our father got on his face when he told this story because it was so dramatic. He said the young man reached into his pocket and pulled out a silver eagle money clip. From what looked like a small fortune, a ten-dollar bill was removed and handed to Grandfather Abraham."

R.C., who was standing, found the floor beside Esau and sat on it quickly. It looked to Jake as though he had been struck from behind. Barely able to form his words because his mouth had suddenly gone dry, R.C. whispered, "A silver eagle money clip?"

"That's what he said," Esau replied. "Does it mean anything to you, Father Baxter?" Esau wanted to know.

R.C. had given away the answer by his strong reaction to the money clip. Rather than cover it, he admitted that, indeed, it meant a great deal to him. He wanted Esau and Jacob to know that he was about to be more generous to Abraham's descendents than his ancestor was to Abraham. Both brothers began to protest that that wasn't necessary, but R.C. wouldn't hear another word. He had to get back to San Francisco to talk with his father. But, before he left, he wrote out a check for $10,000 to each brother and told them how much he appreciated their help. The old Walters' family story of the ten-dollar tip placed R.C.'s family on the train coming into Philadelphia. R.C. wanted to know if either brother could remember any of the names. They could not. R.C. gave Jacob his card and asked them to call him if he and Esau could remember anything, anything at all, in addition to what they already had told him.

He shook the brothers' hands and thanked them for their help. R.C. instructed the limo driver to take him back to the hotel. He asked him to return to the retirement home at the end of the day to pick up Jacob so that he could visit longer with Esau.

CHAPTER THIRTEEN: Bones

The Bishop insisted that R.C. add his recent activities and discoveries to the family narratives. What were the chances of the Frankie Wilson silver eagle money clip being the same one that train robbers took from their dead ancestor more than a hundred years ago? Fairly high, they reasoned, if Mr. Wang's description of the man who supplied it to him was correct. The Bishop reminded R.C. of the off-handed remark Mr. Wang had made to RCB, the First. Someone who Mr. Wang thought looked almost like Ren bought Tommy Moran's vase. That person mentioned that he came from Boston.

"That's it, I'll bet," R.C. jumped to a conclusion. "Boston has got to be our city. It's got to be," R.C. nearly shouted.

"What if it's New York?" the Bishop asked.

But R.C. would have none of it. Again, he reasoned, what were the chances of a Rennie look-alike coming from New York when one had appeared in the flesh in San Francisco – and said that he was from Boston? The Bishop had to agree, but asked him not to ignore New York. There was a large Irish population in that fair city, too. The phone rang in the library. When R.C. answered it, he was connected with Jacob Walters who was calling from Philadelphia. He said that he hoped that he wasn't interrupting anything, but after R.C. had left, Esau remembered something that he thought was quite amusing. He said that when the young couple finished eating their nearly raw steaks, they chewed on the bones like dogs.

"We were poor, Father Baxter, but even we didn't chew on the bones," Jacob offered.

The phone call went on for a few minutes of questions and answers. When R.C. thought that it was almost over, Jacob Walters said that Esau thought that the baby's name was Patrick, but he wasn't sure. It had been a long time since he had heard the story and it might have been the father's name, but, either way, he felt sure that the name of Patrick was right.

CHAPTER FOURTEEN:
Millicent the Magnificent

R.C. wanted to drop everything and head for Boston, but the Bishop reminded him that he had obligations. He was emphatic that he wasn't about to cover for him so he could chase the ghosts of their past. Reluctantly, R.C. agreed and returned to what he did best, which was to preach.

After one of his speaking engagements in Sacramento at St. John's Episcopal, a young woman, who was about his own age and almost as tall as he, propositioned him. Cupping his ear with her hand so that no one else could hear what she said, she whispered, "I want to fuck your brains out." She had long blond hair that she platted in the back into a French braid. R.C. stammered because the proposition was proffered exactly the way his father had predicted.

Knowing that he needed to be rescued, the beauty smiled and said, "Then, coffee?" in full voice. "Surely you drink coffee, Father Baxter?"

"I do," he replied, knowing full well that he shouldn't. He accepted the beauty's offer of coffee anyway.

There was a shop two blocks from the church and the youngsters walked there. "I'm Millicent Garfield, Father. I'm an intern at Sacramento General Hospital," she introduced herself. "I'm a gynecologist or, at least, I plan to be one very soon," she added.

"And I'm horny as hell."

Pleasure bells were going off in R.C.'s head, but warning sirens also were sounding in his ears. She was a "big girl," he reasoned. Ding, ding, ding. And a gynecologist, he added in his mind. More dings. But I don't know her. Sirens wailing. She seems nice. Ding, ding, ding. And she was drop-dead gorgeous. Ding, ding, ding. He was hooked because, all of a sudden and without warning, he was thinking through his dick. He was a young man. He knew and so did Millicent the Magnificent (her nickname as she later told him) that he was going to be very late getting home that evening – or the next day.

They agreed to meet in Rancho Cordova, just two exits east of Sacramento on Interstate 80. There was a Holiday Inn at the interchange and R.C. booked a room for them. He paid cash.

Millicent had been sexually intimate with three other priests and each one had been a disappointment. Joking with her sister back in Los Angeles, she said their little pink thingies were pathetic. So what was there about this priest that made her take a chance a fourth time? She didn't know.

R.C. was famished following services and said so. Millicent had an empty tummy, too, and was ready for the huge buffet that the Holiday Inn spread on Sundays between ten and two o'clock. They ate and talked, ate and talked. R.C. found her hospital war stories hilarious. She was making him laugh as hard as he had made her laugh back in the church. Maybe this was just a good laugh, he reasoned. Ding, ding, ding.

Over coffee, R.C. told Millicent about his hidden cannon. Instead of being repelled, her eyes lit up and she said, "I hope you aren't kidding 'cause I need a really big one right now."

They hardly could wait until the door was closed and locked. They tore off their clothes and hopped onto the bed. It had been a long time since R.C. and Peipei had been together so he was ready. Millicent clapped her hands, applauding what she saw. She pushed back his foreskin and began to suck his cock. As she did, she started umming and aahing to make it grow to its greatest size.

She lay back, spread her legs, and said, "Give it all to me, baby." He did. She took it and gasped for more. What an extraordinary woman, R.C. thought.

About seven o'clock the next morning, Millicent's appetite for wild uncontrollable sex finally had been satisfied. R.C. thought that he was going to die and said so. She laughed. She informed him that breakfast would be ready in half an hour and that they should get ready for it. She was starving and had rounds later that day.

At breakfast, Millicent suggested that they stay in touch. She wanted no romantic involvement, especially with a high profile priest like himself, even though he had exactly what she wanted. That suited R.C. For years, Millicent would call R.C. when the hornies got the best of her. He would call her for the same reason. Sometimes it took a couple of days for the heat to burn itself out. Over the years, they looked forward to their three or four meetings in a year for nothing but sex and more sex.

In 1986, R.C. was thirty years old and still living at home with his seventy-one-year-old father. Neither man saw anything wrong with the arrangement and each was perfectly content with his life. At breakfast one morning, the Bishop asked R.C. if he had any plans to marry again. R.C. said that he might if he found the right person.

"I'd like to know that I had a grandchild before I kick off, R.C. Who knows how many more years are left for this old boy," the Bishop joked.

R.C. saw his point. When Dean McGinnis retired because of poor health in 1984, R.C. was appointed as the dean in his place. Although he delegated most of his responsibilities to competent priests, R.C. still had considerable parish work to handle on his own. He traveled less, which allowed him to write more. He had several papers published in The Journal of Theology and was working on an exegetical book dealing with Biblical names. As he had learned long ago, when you translate the name, generally speaking, you get the job description. It was a way for the Biblical storytellers to remember the stories, long before they were committed, or reduced as R.C. thought, to writing.

Every once in awhile, R.C. would take out the old family narratives to see if he could add another line or two. He couldn't. There was nothing to add. He had to go to Boston. He just had to.

CHAPTER FIFTEEN:
P.R.?????

One of the newer priests on staff was Father Arnold West. He had come to the cathedral to provide pastoral counseling for those in need. He was R.C.'s age, married, and had four children. It was obvious to all that he was a happy man. R.C. and the Bishop were leaving after services one morning and Father West, surrounded by his children, was several yards ahead of them. They were laughing and poking, as children do, and R.C.'s heart began to ache. So did the Bishop's and he said so.

"Would you like me to call our lawyers and direct them to find you a wife, like I did for myself over thirty years ago?" he asked.

"Maybe that's not such a bad idea," R.C. responded. "I'm told that arranged marriages can sometimes work out. I know the one I arranged didn't go so well," he lamented.

Neither man was joking, but it was R.C. who made the first move. He asked Father West if he had time to see him and, of course, he did. R.C. took him to the club, where they had lunch in the alcove. R.C. began by saying that he and his father were quite jealous of the West family brood. They had watched them leave services the day before and it tugged on their hearts.

Father West asked directly why it was that R.C. wasn't married. He told the story of Peipei, which still brought tears to his eyes. Arnold West knew that he was looking at a man who had not resolved his grief yet – and this was guilt about the death of his beloved wife that had occurred about a decade ago.

"Have you dated or been with other women?" he asked.

R.C. told him there were a few women since Peipei, but nothing serious.

"Why is that, R.C.?" he pushed.

"Who knows, Father?" he shrugged. "I was hoping you'd tell me over lunch and I could get on with my life."

"Doesn't quite work that way, R.C., and you know it," he responded. "I'm good at what I do, but not with members of the same staff I serve. Conflict of interest, you know. But I am going to recommend that you see a friend of mine in private practice. She's a psychiatrist here in San Francisco. She's excellent. She's probably your father's age, but don't let that fool you. Like your father, she's still the tigress she was forty years ago."

"What? You think I need a shrink?" R.C. asked defensively.

"I'm the one you held up as the model, R.C. When you did the comparisons, you invited me to lunch, remember? All I know is that if I were a healthy young man, single, wanting a family for a decade or more, I'd see something wrong with this particular picture," he ended.

"Right," R.C. replied. "Set it up," he ordered.

"No can do," Father West replied. He asked the waiter for a sheet of paper. When the waiter returned, Arnold West wrote down the name of Dr. Frances Brooks along with her address and phone number. He pushed the paper in front of R.C. and said, "Call her yourself." Then he left. R.C. thought, "Well, that went well," signed the tab, and walked out.

Instead of returning to his office, he decided to stroll through Chinatown one more time. But he didn't make it that far. For whatever reason, he needed to see and to feel the silver eagle money clip – and he needed to do it right then. Before he went into the bank, he stopped at a hardware store and purchased several rags and some silver polish. The last time that he saw the piece, it had tarnished. He wanted to restore it to its former glory. He went into the bank and opened safe deposit box number 152.

He took his box into one of the newly built, private rooms set aside for such purposes. He carefully opened the old box. He left the vase inside and removed the eagle clip. Using the rags and polish that he had brought with him, R.C. followed the cleaning instructions on the bottle. Soon the old clip sparkled. Turning it over and over while looking for anything that might give him some clue, he noticed what he thought were the letters P and R on the back of the eagle's right talon. "Patrick R," he said aloud. "Who were you, Patrick R? Tell me, damn you, tell me! You're driving me crazy and, as Arnold West will tell you, I don't have far to go to get there." Then he laughed at himself. He wrapped the newly polished treasure in one of the special rags that he had purchased and placed it back in its coffin. He returned it to its proper place and locked the door to his box.

At dinner that evening, R.C. recounted his day to his father and mentioned the initials that he had seen on the money clip. The Bishop had news of his own. "I know Frances Brooks," his father began. "I consulted with her just before your mother and I married. She was of tremendous help to me and I think she will be to you, too. Call her, R.C. Don't put it off," he counseled. Then he said "PR" in a contemplative tone of voice. "Patrick R. what?" He jumped to his feet as though he had been goosed. "R.C., in one of Rennie's old books, there was one I just glanced through. It was on early craftsmen of New England. Do you remember it?" the Bishop asked.

"Not really," R.C. replied. "I was more interested in the railroad books and the theology books that he'd collected."

"Same here," the Bishop agreed.

They headed to the library and removed the old volume. They thought that their eagle money clip would be pictured in all its glory. But it was not there. Few examples of actual pieces were pictured. However, a beautifully crafted silver tea service was pictured. The narrative praised its design and execution by one Paul Revere. Further, it showed the bottom of the teapot with a close-up of his identifying mark, the letters P and R stamped on the edge of its underbelly. Even though R.C. was not an expert, he told his father that the letters on the eagle talon and the letters on the bottom of the pictured teapot were identical.

Now the game heated up. The Bishop agreed to use his contacts to see if a list of objects made by Revere existed. If it didn't, he would pay to have one made. A week went by. Then another. Soon a month passed and a second. Feeling like he was being ignored, the Bishop called his contact and asked about the delay. He was told that these things took time because books and libraries had to be combed. His contact asked if he could send more money since the retainer already had been used in the search. "Of course," was his reply.

At dinner, he told R.C. about the pace of the Revere search. He also asked how the therapy was going. R.C. said that his last session was scheduled for the next day and that Dr. Brooks was very helpful to him.

"What about my arranged marriage, Father?" he asked.

"Are you serious, R.C.?" the Bishop wanted to know. "Surely you can find someone on your own," he added.

"Did your lawyer matchmakers fail you, Father?" he asked.

"No, they didn't, but that was a long time ago, R.C., and I was just joking when I made that offer," the Bishop answered.

"I thought that if you were willing to pay good money to find out about a silver eagle, you might spend a little more to narrow the field of possible brides for me," he said in all earnest. "You, of all people, know what I require," he ended.

"I'll look into it if that's what you want, R.C.," he offered.

"I do," R.C. confirmed. "Don't throw out a drag net so that word gets out that I'm looking," he began, but his father cut him off.

"R.C., I know what I'm doing. I'm an old fart, I agree, and a dinosaur. But never forget, son, the size of a dinosaur's teeth and his bad disposition." And they both laughed while remembering the time in the club when their disagreement began a new and satisfying chapter in their lives.

R.C.'s last session with Dr. Brooks was scheduled for the next afternoon. He was her last patient for the day. She never liked to set an appointment for anyone's final therapy session in the morning. Because the exiting patient deserved her full attention, she always scheduled this important consultation after all of her other patients had been seen. Due to her extraordinary skills, Dr. Frances Brooks had become the most successful doctor in the city. Her achievement was even more outstanding because she was the only woman – and the only Negro – practicing in her profession in the vicinity.

The doctor reviewed the patient's progress. "I asked my father to search out possible brides for me last night. When I did, he told me he'd consulted with you prior to his marriage. You never told me," R.C. said.

"I don't talk about my patients, R.C. You know that," she replied.

"Well, I thought ..." he began, but Dr. Brooks interrupted him and repeated her ethical standards.

"It was when he told me about you that I decided to ask him to help me find my bride," R.C. offered. "Whatever it was you told him has served him quite well ever since," he added. "And I now think that I'm the beneficiary of your services twice," he ended.

With that, they rose, shook hands, and R.C. left the Hewes Building. That old building stood as a reminder to R.C. and to the Bishop of the length and breadth of his family's reach in San Francisco.

The Bishop's Secret

CHAPTER SIXTEEN:
Lost and Found

Bishop Baxter was beginning to show his age. He would be 72 years old on his next birthday. It bothered him. Reynolds Carter Baxter, the First, died when he was 72 and the Bishop wondered if lightning would strike twice. So he threw himself into the two projects that he had remaining on his plate: Find a wife for R.C. and find out about the silver eagle money clip. His duties at the cathedral were of no interest to him anymore and he gave them to R.C. Everyone knew that R.C. was the acting bishop and it was accepted as both right and proper. The Bishop's signature was all that mattered and he still was able to sign documents.

Daily, the Bishop called his private investigator, Rolland Pierce, and asked if he had any news. To his credit, Mr. Pierce took the Bishop's call and reported no significant progress. However, his staff was getting close and he felt that he would have something for the Bishop in a week or two. The search had become centered in Boston. An estate historian was searching old papers that might prove valuable. He would call if anything developed. Hours after he hung up the phone, Rolland Pierce called the Bishop and reported that his investigators had uncovered the most remarkable bit of information regarding an estate sale in 1869. One Mary Noble purchased two Paul Revere silver eagle money clips for five dollars each. "Further, we've learned that a small pocket of Noble family members still live in Boston." His investigators were chasing them down. He promised to call again when he had something to report.

When the Bishop told R.C. about the development, R.C. knew that his family history was about to be revealed. It pleased him more than he could say. Immediately, he and his father went into the library and added all of the information to the family history, now nearly 55 pages in length. The following day, Rolland Pierce called to report that the mystery was solved. He had found the owner of the matching silver eagle. His name was Patrick John Collins, Jr., attorney-at-law, Boston, Massachusetts. He faxed a factual history dug up from newspaper stories and library accounts of the day. But he added the following narrative from stories shared by various Noble family members that he, himself, interviewed.

CHAPTER SEVENTEEN:
So, It Was Boston?

In Boston in 1869, Mary Noble finally gave up her hope of ever seeing her California-destined family again. Her heart broke. She moped about the house and fell ill. She took to her bed and stayed there for the next three years. Nothing anyone said or did could get her to return to life. Her weight dropped. Her leg muscles atrophied. On the coldest night of the winter of 1873, while wearing only her bedclothes, she pulled herself over to her window, opened it, and crawled out on the slightly pitched roof. The cold made her sleep and, the next morning, Timothy found her frozen to death. He was twenty-one years old.

Megan and Molly were both beauties and Timothy felt like he could no longer beat off suitors. So he asked them what they wanted him to do. "Let us marry, Tim, and raise our own families," they answered.

"Do you want help in finding a proper husband," he wanted to know. They said both yes and no. They would consider his choices, but they reserved the right to say no or to find someone to their own liking. It didn't take long for either youngster to have Timothy walk her down the isle. Molly, being the older, went first. She married her brother-in-law, Kenneth Collins, a successful attorney, who looked so much like his older sister, Kathleen, that he could have been her twin. Megan married Tim's newest apprentice, Twilliger MacTavish, a big Scot, just off the boat two years ago. They called him Mac.

For the first year, Molly and Kenneth Collins lived in the Collins' family home. Her in-laws were anxious for her to produce a grandchild because they still missed Patrick so very much. She and Kenneth complied almost instantly. In nine months and one week, they had a girl who was stillborn. The family was racked with pain. How could it have happened? Everything seemed to go just fine through the entire pregnancy? But the baby suffered a breech birth and the cord had wrapped around her beautiful neck. She died before she ever sucked one breath of air. They buried their unnamed baby beside her maternal grandmother and grandfather, Patrick and Mary Noble, originally from County Sligo, Ireland. Eleven months later, they produced a healthy boy who they promptly named Liam Kenneth Collins. Thirteen months later, they had another boy and named him Patrick John Collins.

Megan was just as prolific. She and Mac continued to live in the family home over the shop. In rapid-fire succession, Megan popped out Twilliger, Jr., Timothy John, and John Patrick MacTavish.

Timothy Noble remained unmarried and worked fourteen to sixteen hours a day. Harry Sarver's widow, Lilly, was a diminutive dark-haired lady who was Timothy's senior by three years. She had taken over her husband's saw-sharpening business, but struggled mightily to find anyone who could do the demanding and accurate work that was needed. When she found such a craftsman, he usually stayed just long enough to make enough money to open his own shop. Lilly made the deliveries and collected the accounts. On one particularly bright and sunny summer day when Lilly was returning the Noble's saws, Timothy realized that he was by himself and so was Lilly. She and Harry had been married only a few months when Harry was killed in the timber accident. Timothy decided to speak to her to see if she would accept his attentions. She would. Six months later, Lilly Sarver and Timothy Noble were married. They moved the Sarver business into new quarters that Timothy had built for that very purpose. Mac took to the craft eagerly and displayed a great talent for the work.

Neither the bride nor the groom had ever been out of Boston, but Tim always had wanted to go to San Francisco to look for his older brother. What if he had not been killed on that train? Molly and Megan were dead set against the trip. They didn't think that they could stand losing another brother, especially to that damn train. But Lilly thought that it was a good idea. They were about to buy their tickets when Lilly said that she felt ill. Timothy called for a physician who confirmed that she was a few weeks pregnant, but she was not reacting well to the changes going on inside her. If Lilly was to carry the baby to full term, her doctor advised, she must have complete bed rest. Her sister-in-law and fellow house sharer, Molly MacTavish, was her nurse. Lilly bore a ten-pound, six-ounce boy who they named Timothy, Junior. The brute tore Lilly unmercifully and the doctor struggled to save her life. But save it, he did. However, Lilly would have no other children as a result.

A dozen years slipped by before Timothy and Lilly were able to make their honeymoon trip to San Francisco. Tim, Junior, a dark-haired, fat, and mentally slow boy, stayed at home with his MacTavish cousins.

Neither Timothy nor Lilly were prepared for the vastness of the country. When they passed Denver and were going through the Humbold Mountains, Timothy asked the conductor if he knew anything about a train robbery back in 1869. Indeed, he did. Trains always slowed down at the very spot where it happened and the conductors in each car told the story of the robbery to the passengers. Timothy Noble said that he had lost a brother, sister-in-law, and baby nephew on that train. He asked if the train could stop long enough for him to walk to their graves. The conductor didn't think that it would be allowed, but he was willing to ask the engineer. To his surprise, the engineer said that it was the least he could do for the family. So when the train reached that spot, it stopped. Timothy and Lilly Noble were taken to what was believed to be the spot where the 63 were buried. It was close, but the actual gravesite was another seventy-five feet beyond. Lilly sensed the mistake, but elected to say nothing for the moment. Only after they got back on the train, did she tell her husband what she sensed. The distance wasn't important to Tim. It was over, as far as he was concerned. He had been to his brother's grave and closure now was possible for him.

In San Francisco, they stayed at the finest hotel, located in the heart of the city. It was called The Nicholas and it stood seven stories! In three days, Timothy had seen everything and had done everything that they had planned. Unfortunately for them, they were unable to find any traces of his older brother, John. They were anxious to go home and they had a long ride ahead of them. Lilly wanted to venture into Chinatown so that she could say that she had been there. Timothy was hesitant. He didn't feel safe, he said. But Lilly begged, so he relented. The two of them walked into several quaint shops. In one, she bought a small ring for Molly. In another, she bought trinkets for the children. In the last one, her eye caught sight of a pair of maroon vases with a white crane on each one. Could she buy just one? Yes, she was told. How much? Only six dollars. The owner tried to sell her both of the vases for $11.50, but Lilly wanted only one. When she remarked that she would be the only woman in Boston who had such a vase, the storeowner smiled. And, for some strange reason, he kept staring at Timothy as though he knew him. When asked, the man apologized for his bad behavior by saying that it wasn't often that he saw anyone with such red hair. And then he laughed.

Lilly treasured her vase and willed it to her nephew, Patrick John Collins. Patrick John bore a striking resemblance to one Reynolds Carter Baxter of San Francisco – who was never born, as such. He was the only one of the children who ever admired it and who requested it "when the time came." Timothy hated the damned thing. It seemed as though it mocked him every time he laid eyes on it. He was glad that Tim, Junior, hated it, too.

Tim, Junior, had his eye on his father's silver eagle money clip, which he always carried. When his uncle, John, left for California, long before Junior was born, his grandmother had given the matching money clips to her two sons. She bought them from an estate sale just before her elder son left with his wife and baby. They weren't expensive and she thought that they made handsome gifts. Their owner's widow had inherited them from someone back in his family tree. Besides, five dollars for each was a good price for tarnished silver.

But Tim, Junior, was not his father's son in any way. His hands didn't work right and he was as dumb as Adam's off ox when it came to solving math problems. His one saving grace was his ability to sing. His parents thought that he had a lovely tenor voice that was worthy of training. When he was eighteen years old, they sent him to New York to study at the newly formed College of Music. In time, Timothy Noble, Junior, became one of the world's best operatic tenors and he toured Europe and America. He never married and died suddenly at the age of forty-two of a massive heart attack. He was on stage at the Metropolitan in New York. The high C in La Boehm did him in. His uncle, Attorney Kenneth Collins, was the executor of his estate. Timothy, Junior, willed the silver eagle money clip to his cousin, Patrick John Collins.

Patrick John's son, Patrick John Collins, Jr., was now in possession of the vase and the money clip. He had followed his grandfather and his father into the legal profession. He was as anxious to meet the Bishop and R.C. as they were to meet him.

CHAPTER EIGHTEEN:
The Shoes of a Titan

The Bishop cleared both of their schedules and arranged for a private jet to fly them to Boston the following Monday. Both men were in high spirits. The trip to the airport was filled with anticipation and excitement. R.C. had retrieved both the silver eagle money clip and the vase from their crypt and had them packaged properly for travel. As the limo neared the gate, the Bishop lurched forward, grabbed his chest, leaned to his left, and was dead before his head hit the seat. R.C. was looking out of the window and hadn't noticed his father. When he turned back to say something, he looked down and knew that his father was dead. He instructed their driver to cancel their flight and to take him to the cathedral immediately.

R.C. lifted his father's slumped body and cradled him as though he were a child. Tears ran down his handsome but sad face and began to soak his collar and shirt. He made no sounds. When the limo arrived at the cathedral, R.C. instructed the driver to find the Assistant Dean and to bring him to the car. When Dean Cramer arrived, he found R.C. still holding his father and unable to speak. Instantly, he realized why R.C. had come to the cathedral. He told R.C. that he would call the mortuary and someone would come quickly. R.C. sat motionless, more like a stone than a man. He barely breathed. When Milo George, founder and senior member of the George Funeral Home, arrived, he found R.C. and the Bishop in the same position reported to him by the Assistant Dean. For the next ten minutes, he sat beside R.C. and said nothing. When a hearse arrived, Milo touched R.C.'s arm and said, "It's time, R.C. We have to take him. We'll have him back before you know it."

"Okay," was all that R.C. could manage. His huge frame unwrapped its hold on his father. Milo George's staff lovingly and tenderly lifted the Bishop out of the car, onto the gurney, and into the hearse in one continuous motion. The Assistant Dean entered the limo and sat where the Bishop had sat just moments before. Milo George sat on the other side of R.C. Neither man spoke. Each took one of R.C's enormous hands and held it between their own. Finally, R.C. asked his assistant if he would handle everything because he didn't think that he could. Then R.C. asked the limo driver to take him home. Both men asked if he wanted or needed company, but R.C. declined their kind offers. He had several phone calls that he needed to make, as did they, and he believed that he had only limited energy to make them.

R.C's first call was to his long-term lover, Millicent the Magnificent. He needed to be held. Could she drop everything and come to the mansion? Unfortunately, she could not. She had met and married a cardiologist two months ago. R.C. wished her all the best and did not tell her of his father's passing. Next he called The San Francisco Chronicle. He asked to speak to its editor, Aarne Durst, an old friend of the family. When Aarne picked up his phone, R.C. informed him of his father's death. "The funeral will be a circus, Aarne, and father would have liked that. You know how much he liked a good party. Give it as much play as you think the public can stand. He'll be laid out in the nave of St. Martin's, probably by tonight. Invite the faithful and the public. I'll let him stay there for a few days before I bring him home for burial. Just say that the burial will be private. Thanks, Aarne," and he hung up the phone.

Then it hit him. Father Reynolds Carter Baxter, IV, was completely alone. No real friends. No lovers. Nobody. Just associates at the cathedral. He called his old psychiatrist, Dr. Frances Brooks, but she was with a patient. He left a message that his father had died and asked her to call him back. Moments later, R.C.'s phone rang and it was Dr. Brooks. She wanted to know how she could help. "Do you make house calls?" he asked.

"Never," came her reply, "But I'll make an exception, R.C. Will you send a car for me? I don't know how to get to your home and I have one more patient to see."

"I'll send our limo. James will be outside your office by the time you reach the front door. Thank you, Doctor," and he hung up the phone.

When Dr. Brooks arrived, James took her into the library where R.C. had planted himself. He stood to greet her. She ignored his extended hand and held him close to her. It was only then that the emotional dam broke and R.C. sobbed uncontrollably. He had to sit down before he fell, crushing the good doctor and injuring himself in the process. His grief engulfed him for the next fifteen minutes. All the while, Dr. Brooks sat quietly beside him and rested her small brown hand on his shoulder. When he was spent, R.C. turned to her and said, "Thank you. Can I get you something?"

"A brandy for me and another one for my patient," she replied. R.C. rose from the couch and nearly stumbled while making his way to the liquor cabinet. His hands shook and he was unable to pour a drink for them. He acknowledged his condition to the doctor, so she was pressed into yet another service. Her steady hand poured a stiff one for each of them. Then raising her glass, she said, "To Bishop Baxter." It was exactly the medicine that R.C. needed. He responded, "To the Bishop." And they both knocked back the slug of peach brandy.

"I loved him, you know, Doctor," R.C. began. "Yes," she replied. "We all loved him. I will miss him more than you'll ever know." They talked for about an hour. Both enjoyed reminiscing and telling their most favorite stories about R.C.'s father. "R.C.," Dr. Brooks began, "your father hated sports of any kind. Your mother was a wiz at tennis and that made him uneasy. She endlessly niggled him to pick up a racket. On a fine summer's day, when you were about five or six, he came to see me after being humiliated by her on the court. He couldn't figure out how she played so effortlessly. It exhausted him just watching, let alone being on the court with her. When she had a tennis racket in her hand, Kathleen took on a different persona. She looked like a warhorse ready to ride into battle. Oh, R.C., I wish you could have seen her with her eyes bulging, her breathing increasing, and her muscles rippling in anticipation of that first wack of the ball. Because of his inability to return a single serve, your father left the court. He was humiliated. Kathleen didn't mean to hurt him. She simply was unable to soften her approach to the game, which was 'take no prisoners.' It took several sessions for me to restore his self-image and his self-confidence to what it was prior to that tennis match. He never picked up a racket again."

R.C. replied that he had only a vague memory of that event. He could remember only one time that his parents did not talk to each other at the dinner table for several weeks. Now he knew why. "Thanks for that, Dr. Brooks. Weaving together pieces from my past has become a passion with me. We were on our way to meet relatives in Boston when Dad died. Only recently had we learned that they existed. They know more information about our shared ancestry. I'll always feel like he was cheated even though we both know he lived a privileged life."

"Can I pour you another drink, Doctor?"

"No, thank you, R.C., I really must be going. I have a dinner engagement with an old friend at the club. Your father made it possible for me to become a member shortly after he was married. Do you know what courage it took to recommend a woman for membership in that exclusive club, especially a woman of color? I have always eaten in the family alcove. You'll soon be getting the bill for my dinner. Your father was so generous to me and to everyone else. I know you are exactly like him in every way, save one," she smiled with a twinkle in her eye. Then she reached up to his face, pulled it down, and kissed him lightly on the cheek. James drove her to the club and returned to the mansion.

Dr. Brooks' kindness made it possible for R.C. to sleep peacefully that first night. A wholeness washed over him and he slept the deep sleep of knowing that all was right with the world and that he was going to be okay in spite of his loss.

Telegrams poured in from all over the world. The Archbishop of Canterbury offered to conduct Bishop Baxter's funeral and R.C. accepted his offer. His predecessor conducted the Bishop's investiture and R.C. saw the present holder of the high office as the logical celebrant. He called his assistant, Dean Cramer, and told him of the arrangement. R.C. also arranged for a Lear jet to transport the Archbishop to San Francisco.

The clergy poured into the city for days. R.C. kept the cathedral open 24 hours a day to accommodate the mourners. It was as though royalty had died, so great were the crowds. Finally, on Saturday, the great funeral mass for Bishop Reynolds Carter Baxter, III, was held. Only the music of J.S. Bach was heard during the actual service, but, for an hour before, the chancel choir sang Mozart's magnificent Coronation Mass in C. R.C. sat mesmerized as the voice of God spoke to him through the notes and words of Mozart.

The Archbishop rose to eulogize Bishop Baxter. He slowly climbed the twelve steps leading up to the hooded pulpit. He said: "The king is dead. Long live the king. If ever a man should have held the high office of Archbishop of Canterbury, it should have been Reynolds Carter Baxter, the Third. He was born to the silk and to the throne. It was in his blood. His father was a priest and his son, who follows him, is a priest. Three generations of priests. Their progenitor was not a priest. Rather, he was a successful businessman whose generosity is legendary. It is more than fitting that all of the music today is from the pen of J.S. Bach. I'm told that it has had the effect of calming the wild beast that surges through the veins of four generations of Baxters.

"That the Bishop was rich is well known. His generosity is equally well known, not because he publicized it, but because so many have been the recipients of it. His courage was beyond words. I'm told that he could confront a hungry growling lion on one of his good days. His arthritic right hand was the reminder of one such battle, I'm told." Laughter rippled through the cathedral. "Ah, I see some of you know that story. If you don't, I suggest you talk to Father Baxter, the younger." More laughter resounded.

"His skills as an exegete, Biblical Hebrew scholar, master preacher, superb administrator, and negotiator are well known. A catalogue of those attributes would have us here until next Sabbath. So I want to focus our attention on his private life." R.C. began to squirm since he wasn't quite certain where His Grace was going. "On several visits to San Francisco, the Bishop and his lovely wife, Kathleen, entertained me in the most lavish style possible. It almost was embarrassing. But not quite." Again laughter arose. "Because I was a widower, Kathleen was my dance partner and she was, by far, the best dancer I ever knew. She somehow avoided my huge feet and I've always been amazed at that skill. No other woman was so gifted – or lucky." More laughter. "But when she and the Bishop graced the dance floor, they were the most beautiful couple in the room. Other dancers simply stopped and moved to the sides in order for them to have the floor to themselves. They made having fun look like the easiest thing in the world to do. Their banter sparkled. Their teasing sizzled. When Kathleen died, Bishop Baxter called to tell me of her death. He cried between sentences and I knew that his heart of hearts was broken, never to be repaired.

"But, luckily, Bishop Baxter and Kathleen had a son who pleased them in every way imaginable. While dancing, Kathleen would tell me R.C. stories. I knew, for example, R.C., that you cannot read a note of music, yet you can sit down and play Bach or Mozart or any of the others like a concert pianist. I also knew, R.C., that as a youngster you were less than impressed with the parading and the pomp of the clergy. Kathleen especially enjoyed that aspect of your development. You were her final thought when her life ended tragically so many years ago. She loved and was devoted to you and your father. He treated her like a goddess. She was his principal advisor and consultant. Once he told me that Kathleen was the best theologian he'd ever known. As far as 'administrivia' was concerned, Kathleen was as tough as the Bishop when she represented St. Martin's on boards and in organizations.

"The image that comforts me today is that a grand reunion has taken place in the heavens. Maybe, just once, Kathleen will let the Bishop win one game of tennis. But I doubt it. She's been there longer than he. She's probably been appointed to more boards and serves on more committees, so she's way ahead of him. But I'd like to think of them as being at rest and dancing when they feel like it, or sipping an extra-dry martini. Whatever the realities are that they currently enjoy, I'm sure that they are sweeter because they are enjoying them together.

"God bless you, Dean Reynolds Carter Baxter, the Fourth. And God bless the good folk of this cathedral and this city. Amen."

It took several hours to empty the cathedral. The Archbishop stood beside R.C. and received those members of the congregation who wanted to speak an encouraging or appreciative word to them both. The list of political personalities in attendance was as long as the list of ecclesiastical heavyweights. When the last mourner left, R.C. and the Archbishop were exhausted both physically and emotionally. R.C. invited the Archbishop to stay as long as he wished before he returned to Canterbury, but he was anxious to get back. R.C. understood completely and arranged for him to be flown home in the morning.

The Bishop's coffin was removed from its catafalque and driven to the mansion where a single grave had been dug beside Kathleen's resting place. The men placed the coffin over the grave and waited several hours until R.C. and Dean Cramer arrived to conduct the interment. They were the only two people in attendance and it took only a few minutes to read a line or two of scripture, say a simple prayer, and pronounce the benediction. R.C. shook his assistant's hand and indicated that he would like to be left alone with his father. He complied and was driven back to the cathedral. The gravediggers asked R.C. if they could lower his father's coffin into the grave and R.C. nodded yes. It only took a minute to complete that task and another minute to remove the lowering straps. The small Bobcat roared into action and picked up the heavy cement lid of the cement vault that received the coffin. R.C. sat motionless and watched as though he were watching a television show. The Bobcat operator shifted gears and began to fill the grave with the dirt that had been thrown off to the side when he had dug the grave earlier that day. As soon as he had finished, he drove his machine over to a flat bed truck, loaded it, and drove away. Neither man said a word to the other. R.C. walked back to the mansion and wept quietly for the next hour.

Cook asked if he wanted something to eat. He asked for a rare steak, a baked potato, apple pie with Colby cheese, and coffee. After he had eaten his meal, he walked into the library and wept again until exhaustion overtook him. He climbed up the stairs and fell across his bed. At three o'clock in the morning, he awoke due to his need to urinate. At first, he was disoriented. He wondered why he still was dressed. Then he remembered. Tears filled his eyes again, but they did not prevent him from falling to sleep. His house staff was also in deep grief. They were solicitous of R.C.'s needs and gave him all the space and time that he needed to work through his loss. For the next four days, R.C. spent most of his time in the library. He didn't shave or bathe or dress. He was a disheveled lout when Dr. Brooks called to check on him.

So surprised was he to see her small frame entering the library that he immediately was embarrassed by his appearance and his demeanor. He began to make excuses, but she waved them aside. "R.C., in two days a delegation from the Diocese will be here to inform you that you've been elected to fill your father's office of Bishop. I, for one, would like you to be presentable when they arrive."

Her words bounced off his ears as though he had a thick coat of Teflon over them. She repeated herself, knowing that R.C. had not recognized any of the words that she had spoken. She knew that she was speaking in English, but R.C. was hearing her in Ding Bat or Estonian or Swahili. The haze began to lift and R.C. rubbed his eyes as if he were Rip Van Winkle emerging from his 20-year sleep.

"That's very funny, Doctor. And, by the way, hello," R.C. responded.

"You may think that it's funny, young man," she continued, "but its reality will be here before you know it. So I suggest you get ready. Surely it can't be much of a surprise to you. Who out there could ever fill your father's shoes? He doesn't exist, except for you, of course. And hello back. Sorry if I forgot my manners, but I'm being paid to deliver this news to you in case the shock sends you into fits of depression or mania or psychosis."

CHAPTER NINETEEN:
A Second Boston Tea Party

The Bishop of Washington, D.C., the Bishop of New York City, and the Bishop of Rhode Island made up the delegation commissioned to approach R.C. and to announce the results of his election. It was a good thing that Dr. Brooks rousted him back into the present because, without her intervention, R.C. probably would have been sitting in the library in his unwashed state. Instead, he was dressed in his finest hand-tailored suit and, on the appointed day when The Three Wise Men from the East arrived, they congratulated themselves many times over on the rightness of their only choice. They talked for half an hour and left as promptly as they arrived. R.C's investiture was to take place in a month and he had much to do to get ready for it.

He decided that his investiture would be as simple as possible. Those clergy who still were living and who had attended his father's gala affair noted the marked contrast between the two ceremonies. R.C. did not spend lavishly on his elevation to high office. Nor did he fly in the entire College of Bishops for the service, as had his father. Those who wanted to attend did so on their own nickel or on the nickel of their diocese. Immediately, some of the older bishops resented R.C. and thought him stingy for not footing the entire bill for everyone. Sitting on a pile of money was sinful, they said. R.C. began to see what a burden his father contended with year after year. But he was not his father. If his "brothers of the cloth" didn't like it, they could go suck sour grapes or lemons or eggs or whatever it was that petty men suck.

Although R.C. had never liked the parading that clergy did, he was, nevertheless, tolerant of it most of the time. In spite of his request for simplicity, great pomp and parading prevailed at his investiture. R.C. decided to ride the wave that was carrying him into high office and to keep his mouth shut. His only comment was, "The more traditional, the better." So, tradition carried the day and the night. In St. Martin's during Sunday Mass, Reynolds Carter Baxter, the Fourth, became the seventeenth bishop of the Episcopal Dioceses of California. He was 31 years old.

From early childhood, he had observed his father for many years. He knew the ins and outs of the office, but it was not until he assumed control of the office that he truly began to appreciate his father's genius. Nor did it hurt that he had functioned in the role of Bishop during the last few years of his father's life. But that was different. The Bishop was always there for advice, consent, and signature. Now, R.C. was on his own. He began to see the value of prayer. Until then, prayer was a ritual to be performed in services. Now it was as essential as the air he breathed. Over the years, he had acquired certain lines and phrases, but the one that kept him going was: "O God, who art closer to us than hands and feet and even the air that we breathe."

R.C. still preached at least once a quarter at St. Martin's. He limited his outside preaching to one sermon a month elsewhere. The seminary asked if he would fill his father's teaching obligations and he said yes. It was clear to everyone who knew the present Bishop Baxter that he was definitely his father's son – and more.

Two years into his appointment, R.C. suffered a mild heart attack while preaching in St. Martin's. His head suffered more damage when he fell forward in the pulpit than his heart did by the arrhythmia detected later by the cardiogram. Something had to change. All agreed that it was the Bishop's grueling schedule, but he would have none of it. He attacked his physical therapy with the same wildness that he attacked any other problem on his plate. He was a man possessed and he was going to get better faster than anyone else who suffered from the same problem. The Dean of St. Martin's, his former assistant, took over for R.C. until he returned to work, which was just four weeks later. R.C. took one look around and saw that the joint was running without him. He told his secretary that he was taking a much needed vacation and not to expect him to return for at least a month, if then.

He still had the silver eagle money clip and the vase at the mansion. When his father died, he had boxed them both for the trip to Boston to meet his distant relative, Patrick John Collins, attorney-at-law. He called Attorney Collins and chatted again for a few moments. He confirmed that he intended to fly to Boston to meet him and all of his other relatives who wanted to participate in the small family reunion. Logan Airport was crowded when R.C.'s private plane landed. Travelers were everywhere. They rushed thither and yon while trying to find this gate and that gate in order to catch their flight or to meet people arriving for business or personal purposes. Nearly two dozen people were bunched up with a big sign that read, "Welcome, Cousin R.C." As he approached the group, he saw a man who was almost his exact mirror image. That man was his long-lost "cousin," Patrick John Collins, Jr. R.C. was mobbed. It took nearly an hour for everyone to get his or her piece of him. He was an only child of only children. He silently sent up a prayer of thanksgiving for his good fortune in finding so many of his relatives.

For the next week, R.C. listened to stories of his Boston family. Although he was a rich man monetarily, he realized that he was impoverished familiarly. But no more. It took another week for them to hear all about what had happened to the Boston baby named Reynolds Carter Baxter of San Francisco, who never was born, as such. Before he left San Francisco, R.C. hired a professional photographer to take pictures of all of Lian's water-color portraits of their common ancestor, Reynolds, or, more accurately, Patrick. He had them enlarged to 12 by 18 inches and had two dozen copies made as gifts for his Boston family. Remarkably, the Boston family also had photographs and paintings of their own. The family resemblances were unquestionable. Most of all, it was the saga of the Boston baby's progeny that fascinated everyone and R.C. did not edit anything, except his own commission of the crime of murder. He unwrapped the vase and the silver eagle money clip and placed both items on the dining room table for all to see and handle. Before he left, he gave his matching vase to his cousin, Patrick, who was overwhelmed by R.C.'s generosity.

So much information taxed even the hardiest of the family and, after a week, R.C. realized that it was time to leave. He thought about Paris or Hawaii or Australia, but nothing appealed. He wanted to go home. Boston was nice, but San Francisco was home. Besides, he had to get ready for the annual meeting of bishops that was only six weeks away. He had never been to New Orleans and he was looking forward to the trip.

CHAPTER TWENTY:
Family Secrets Revealed

The question of ordaining avowed, practicing homosexuals was near the top of the list for discussion and possible action. The presiding bishop was Alexander Newman from Tallahassee, Florida. He was known for his great tolerance of ideas, theology, practices, and interpretation. He was slow to anger and plenteous in mercy. It took much to piss him off, as the saying went, but R.C. managed to do that handily. R.C. had been invited by the bishops to address the question before the body. Bishop Newman and R.C.'s father had been great admirers of each other and they agreed on most subjects, with the exception of homosexuality. Newman was dead set against having anything to do with anyone who was a homosexual or had those tendencies. Never once did he ever suspect Hewes of being gay. After all, the man was married and had produced a fine son. So it was with great shock and then anger that the presiding bishop, Alexander Newman, heard R.C. rise as an advocate for the ordination of homosexuals. He began his remarks quite casually.

"My late father, Bishop Reynolds Carter Baxter, the Third, was an undeclared, but practicing homosexual until the day my mother died. From that day forward, he remained celibate, but he was still a homosexual."

The room exploded! "No!" was shouted from every corner of the room. Bishop Newman felt as though he had been sandbagged. He was really angry – mostly with himself for having befriended a man who had lied to him during his entire adult life. Disbelief was easier to deal with than the direct testimony of the man's only son.

When order finally was restored, R.C. continued.

"Bishop Baxter married when he was 40 and then only because a former house servant accused my father of homosexuality and the story came out in the newspaper. My mother was undeclared, also, but was a practicing lesbian to the day she died."

The room exploded for the second time. It probably wouldn't survive a third blast. Bishop Newman suddenly felt ill and asked his parliamentarian to take over the chair. Bishop Charles W. Whitesides pounded the gavel for order, which the beautifully mannered gentlemen grudgingly restored. Shouts of "Get him out of here," and "How could you say such a thing?" were heard from various parts of the hall.

R.C. had expected the outbursts and, when order finally was restored, he played the moment for every ounce of emotion that he could wring from it. He drew himself up to his full six-foot, four-inch height and looked everyone in the eye before he continued. "My parents both wanted a child and were willing to humiliate themselves once in order for me to happen."

Delegates lost all decorum and began to shout, "Boo, boo, boo." Bishop Baxter was, after all, a well-known and well-loved personage in the church. He had many friends in the gallery who simply couldn't believe their ears. Again, R.C. waited patiently for the house to settle. Then he continued.

"The master bedroom in our home was only for show. My parents slept there only when company required them to do so. They were the very best of friends. I know, in their own way, they loved each other like brother and sister. In public, they were a handsome couple. They were always the best dressed and the best dancers on any floor. But when they were at home, they had long-time lovers of the same sex who shared their respective beds in their respective bedrooms on opposite sides of the master bedroom. When my mother died, my father paid his lovers a handsome severance fee and set them up with annuities that would care for them for life. He did the same for my mother's long-term lover. The only thing he ever demanded from them was complete silence. Perhaps some of you will recall that, at one time during my father's tenure, he was accused of being a homosexual. The story ran in the San Francisco papers. A month or two after that, my father married. I was born nine months later.

"So, what have we? A homosexual bishop who was probably the most revered among his colleagues. This fact about his life never interfered with his abilities as a bishop, a scholar, or a human being. His inherited wealth has been given generously for the benefit of thousands over the years. I dare say some of you can remember the year he hosted this august body in San Francisco. He spent three million dollars of his own money to make sure you had the best accommodations and the finest robes when you left. Because you thought he was straight, he was permitted to function as an ordained clergy. What a loss it would have been to the church had he been denied access based on his sexuality!

"I'm sure you are wondering whether I'm gay or straight or a switch hitter. You're also wondering what it must have been like growing up in a house where you had two homosexuals for parents. I am what you see and I have not been damaged as a result of my parents or their choices.

"I've prepared a position paper for your consideration and, after you've had time to read it, I'll come back in two days and answer any questions you may have."

The paper read: "Clearly, homosexuality is alive and well and living side by side with us, whether or not we like it or acknowledge it. Levels of discomfort and comfort vary and the degree of each is predictable by a careful examination of one's psychological profile, geographical surroundings, and theological background. The group that is the most uncomfortable in dealing with homosexuality is the "Born-Againers." They're against everything that's different from them. We've all known people who fit that profile and we, ourselves, may fall into it. It would take courage on our parts to look critically at ourselves, wouldn't it?

"One subject that used to spark this same level of feelings was racial integration and we all know integration is quickly becoming a non-issue. Other topics that some good folk oppose or support include abortion, environmental issues, and saving the whales. For whatever reason, we have become a society that likes to fight about anything and everything. Apparently our church has been sucked into that same fighting mode. Homosexuality seems to have drawn the most hardened battle lines. I wish it weren't so, but, until we get to the point where we see homosexuality as just another non-issue, we will expend money better spent elsewhere and destroy friendships better served by realizing we have more in common than we have in difference. Until we get to the place in our lives where we realize that this is none of our business, we will continue to have an unhealthy curiosity about where he sticks it and with whom.

"Battle lines find Bible-thumping warriors hurling one-liners that support their position and destroy their opponents. For whatever reason, they've turned the Bible into a ball bat and they beat each other with the couple of passages that deal with the subject to prove why they're right and the other side is wrong. So much for friendships! So much for good exegesis! If Alexander the Great's homosexuality did not interfere with his military genius, personal courage, or ability to conquer, his exclusion from the military based solely on his homosexuality would have resulted in the loss of a genius, whose battles still are studied in our own military academies. If my own father's homosexuality did not interfere with his duties as Bishop of the Episcopal Church of California, his exclusion from the church based solely on his homosexuality would have resulted in the loss of a theological genius, whose indelible mark on the church still is recognized everywhere. I'll not bore you with hundreds of other examples.

I'm sure you get the point.

"So, what do we do? Fight? Call names? Fight some more? That's probably what we'll do. Somehow we can't seem to get beyond our psychological and theological constraints. When homosexuality is mentioned, it becomes our internal puppeteer who jerks us this way and that, as though we were mindless rag dolls. Are we not intelligent? Can we not reason together?

"So, what will it be? Thump the faggots and lesbos? Bar the gates? Hide the children? If ordination is to be denied to homosexuals, let it be denied on some basis other than the Bible. And, lastly, think about this. Not one of the Ten Commandments is broken or ignored by persons who love homosexually. Yet we continue to ordain liars, adulterers, thieves, parent-haters, murderers, and coveters. Why do we do that? Is an adulterer somehow less than? Is a liar somehow more acceptable than? Are thieves and murderers somehow preferred?

"My father and my mother were the two most generous, capable, and loving people that any of us will ever know. There are more of their 'kind' out there. The Church will be the poorer if we judge them as unworthy of our high calling and office simply because they are what they are. Stop the rock throwing. Stop the side choosing. Stop the verbal violence. If this is an 'over-our-dead-bodies' issue, what fools you are. Stop it. The Church deserves better from you.

"The sexual orientation of any candidate for the priesthood is none of your business. Homosexuality, gay or lesbian, isn't a communicable disease. Our children can't catch it by being associated with 'them.' Homosexuals are the least likely to commit crimes. They have the fewest number of representatives in the prison population in any jail in America. They obey society's rules better than any other group. They pay their taxes on time. For the most part, they are model citizens. Yet, in spite of it all, that little bit of skin that they rub somehow rubs some of you the wrong way and, because of that, you would deny them this high office. They deserve better and, frankly, so does the Church. If you can't find it in you to get beyond this issue, then resign. Stand aside. We'll be better off without you and your kind. 'Your kind!' A brand. A label. A smack in the teeth. Hurts, doesn't it? Well, get used to it because it isn't going to stop. All your huffing and puffing and testosterone demonstrations will not prevail. Remember the line that Gandhi, as played by Ben Kingsley, delivered to the British. Gandhi was asked if he thought that the British should just walk away. He said that, in the end, that is just what the British would do. Walk away. It is the same with you and your opposition to the ordination of homosexuals. One day, it will not be an issue. Why don't you just walk away, today, and save us all time and heartache?

"I'll leave you with one last thought. In order for a word to be considered an important word in the Bible, it must appear at least 200 times. There is no word for homosexuality in the entire Bible. And the five or six entries that might contain it by inference are hardly enough to bring an indictment today. The words 'peas and beans' have as many entries in the Bible as the non-existent but inferred word 'homosexual.' One can easily say that the Bible is only as interested in that subject as it is in peas and beans. It is a non-issue! I urge you to vote yes on the question so that we can ordain other qualified candidates like my late father, Bishop Reynolds Carter Baxter, the Third – who, whether you like it or not, was a homosexual until the day he died."

For two days, the House of Bishops debated the question of ordaining avowed practicing homosexuals. By three votes, the question passed and the Episcopal Church, once again, led the way for all other denominations to follow.

CHAPTER TWENTY-ONE:
Gravestone for the Ages

When R.C. returned home from New Orleans, he was exhausted. His office staff would have to handle whatever was on his plate for a few more days. He had an important project that he had to start and complete in the course of a few days. He looked through the yellow pages for the names of tombstone establishments and settled on Boyle's. The reason that he chose Boyle's over the other thirty-seven listed was the owner's first and middle names. Molly Megan Boyle, proprietor. That's all it said, plus the phone number and address. R.C. called Molly Megan Boyle and asked if she made house calls.

"Rarely," was her answer. She needed details about why she had to travel to the client rather than the client coming to her shop where her wares were on display. R.C. introduced himself and said that he would send the limo for her if she would visit the mansion and look at an old grave with him.

How could a girl resist an offer like that? The next morning, Molly stepped out of the limo at 10:30. She was tall and lean. Her face was very pretty, but her hands were as rough as a man's that were familiar with hard work. She wore jeans and a sweatshirt with the name Boyle's Engraving silk-screened on the front and back. Her feet were shod with steel-toed clodhoppers that were laced up to her ankles. Her hair was auburn and R.C. was smitten. When they shook hands, he forgot to let hers go. There they stood, two strangers hand-in-hand.

"Thank you for coming, Ms. Boyle," he began awkwardly as he released his gentle grip.

"No problem," she replied. "After all, it isn't every day that a girl like me gets to ride in the Bishop's private limo. By the way, I've been a member of St. Martin's all my life and I've been to every service you've ever conducted."

"Really?" R.C. floundered. "Why have we never met before?" he asked.

"I usually slip in the back after things get going and I leave just before they end. A girl dressed like this would stand out in St. Martin's, don't you think?" she replied. "Take my shoes for example," she said as she held one up for him to see. He did see, but, somehow on her, they looked perfectly normal.

"Tell me," he continued, "just how did a girl like you take up working in such a difficult trade? I mean, surely you could have done anything you set your mind to, I imagine," he added.

"Boyle's is the oldest stone engraving business in San Francisco," she continued. "I was an only child, like you, and I sort of grew up knowing one day the business would be mine. My father was pleased that I wanted to continue it. He was happy to pass it to me before he died, about the same time your mother died," she answered.

R.C. didn't want this magical person to escape. So he asked James, the limo driver, to tell Cook that a second person would be joining them for lunch. Then he asked Molly Megan Boyle to walk with him to a sacred spot on the grounds. On the way, he regaled her with his family's history and how Griffin Hewes had built the mansion in the last century. He explained that all of his ancestors were buried near a 350-year-old oak tree. The only gravestone that he wanted changed at this time was that of Reynolds Carter Baxter. He said that he wanted a full slab of granite four feet wide by seven feet long by six inches thick. He wanted these words engraved on it:

Here Lies the Body of

Patrick John Noble

of Boston, Massachusetts

Born on March 6, 1869

Orphaned in the

Great Train Robbery in Utah

in June of 1869

Died under the name of

Reynolds Carter Baxter

late of San Francisco

on January 4, 1941

Businessman Extraordinaire
Life-Long Benefactor of St. Martin's Cathedral

Progenitor of
Father Reynolds Carter Baxter, II
Bishop Reynolds Carter Baxter, III
Bishop Reynolds Carter Baxter, IV

Molly said that she could accommodate the Bishop within the next two weeks and that she required half of the money before she could begin. Her down-and-dirty estimate would be nearly $10,000 for everything, including setting the great stone in its proper place. R.C. tenderly took her hand in his and walked her to the mansion's kitchen. Cook had prepared a scrumptious lunch of chicken salad, made with slivered almonds, sweet green grapes that were sliced in half. This delicious salad was mounded high in the center of the plate with slices of cantaloupe ringed around it. Potato chips were everywhere and the Coca-Cola was served slightly frozen. Molly began to feel a strange magic weaving its pattern on her when R.C. announced that he was 35 years old and didn't want to turn 36 without discovering if a future was possible with Molly Megan Boyle. With that, he left the kitchen and Molly. He went to the library where he quickly locked the door, opened the safe, and withdrew $25,000 in hard cold cash. When he returned to the kitchen, Molly still was seated where he had left her. The look in her eye told him that she was considering his idea. But, when he put the money in front of her, she did not know what to do. She had given R.C. a preliminary figure of how much the stone would cost. The final figure would have to wait until she returned to her shop where she could do the math properly. Or so she thought. She had heard that he was very rich, but this was too much.

"Are you trying to buy me, Bishop?" she asked with an edge to her voice.

"Only if I have to," he replied with a lovely smile. "Please call me R.C.," he requested.

"Well, R.C., I'm not for sale," she remonstrated. "But I am reasonable," she laughed.

Then he began to tell her about Lian Sheng and all the others from his family's past.

Two weeks to the day, as promised, Molly delivered and set Patrick John Noble's new head stone. She also gave the Bishop a refund of $15,000 – cash.

Chapter Twenty-One: Gravestone for the Ages

Three months later, Bishop Reynolds Carter Baxter, IV, and Molly Megan Boyle were married in St. Martin's with all of his Boston relatives in attendance.

About the Author

The author and his wife, Kate Fairley

T.C. Fairley is a multi-talented man with an unusual background. He spent thirty years as an ordained minister of the Presbyterian Church and became a scholar of Biblical Hebrew. He has been the Chaplain of the Allegheny County jail, a designer and maker of hardwood furniture, and a real estate searcher — while continuously being a storyteller deluxe.

Since the author has such a superior gift of telling stories, he decided to begin writing fiction after his honorable retirement from the Presbyterian Church. In 1999, he published his first novel, *Absolute Responsibility, Strict Accountability*, a tale of greed-run-amok.

He and his wife, Kate, live in North Topsail Beach, North Carolina, where he is finishing his third and fourth novels.

For single copies or bulk purchases of
this and other books by
T.C. Fairley,
send check or money order to:
American Legacy Books
PO Box 1393
Washington, DC 20013

For MasterCard or VISA credit/debit card orders:
call toll free: 1-888-331-BOOK
or call **202-737-7827**
Monday through Friday, 9:00 - 5:00 Eastern Time
or order online:
www.AmericanLegacyBookstore.com

One book: $14.95
+ postage and handling: $4.95
= $19.90

This book sells for $14.95. If you are ordering by mail within the United States, please add the postage and handling charge of $4.95 for one book and $1.00 for each additional book ordered at the same time. Call for bulk discounts.

Please allow four weeks for delivery.

MasterCard and VISA credit/debit cards are accepted when you call the telephone number above. For payment by check or money order, please mail to the address above.

Please call to learn if the price or postage has changed.